"My mommy never kissed anyone before," little Jeremy said, blinking hard as if he still couldn't believe his eyes

The way Luke looked at her then made Meg flush to the roots of her hair. With as much dignity as possible, she extricated herself from Luke's arms. "Jeremy, for heaven's sake. That is not the kind of information Luke needs to know!" Meg reprimanded him firmly.

Jeremy shrugged and happily continued to broadcast what he knew. "Well, it's true," he blurted out. "I've never seen you kiss a guy before." He propped his hands on his hips, perplexed. "How come you're kissing him?"

* * * * *

Don't forget to look for a very special single title from Cathy Gillen Thacker...

TEXAS VOWS:
A McCabe Family Saga

Available March 2001

And this will be followed in April by the final installment in

THE LOCKHARTS OF TEXAS

Dear Reader,

It's February—the month of love. And what better way to celebrate Valentine's Day than with a Harlequin American Romance novel.

This month's selection begins with the latest installment in the RETURN TO TYLER series. *Prescription for Seduction* is what Darlene Scalera offers when sparks fly between a lovely virgin and a steadfast bachelor doctor. *The Bride Said, "Surprise!"* is another of Cathy Gillen Thacker's THE LOCKHARTS OF TEXAS, and is a tender tale about a secret child who brings together two long-ago lovers. (Watch for Cathy's single title, *Texas Vows: A McCabe Family Saga*, next month from Harlequin Books.)

In Millie Criswell's charming new romance, *The Pregnant Ms. Potter* is rescued from a blizzard by a protective rancher who takes her into his home—and into his heart. And in *Longwalker's Child* by Debra Webb, a proud Native American hero is determined to claim the child he never knew existed, but first he has to turn the little girl's beautiful guardian from his sworn enemy into his loving ally.

So this February, treat yourself to all four of our wonderful Harlequin American Romance titles. And in March, look for Judy Christenberry's *Rent a Millionaire Groom*, the first book in Harlequin American Romance's new promotion, 2001 WAYS TO WED.

Wishing you happy reading,

Melissa Jeglinski
Associate Senior Editor
Harlequin American Romance

THE BRIDE SAID, "SURPRISE!"
Cathy Gillen Thacker

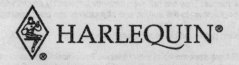

TORONTO • NEW YORK • LONDON
AMSTERDAM • PARIS • SYDNEY • HAMBURG
STOCKHOLM • ATHENS • TOKYO • MILAN • MADRID
PRAGUE • WARSAW • BUDAPEST • AUCKLAND

ISBN 0-373-16862-4

THE BRIDE SAID, "SURPRISE!"

Copyright © 2001 by Cathy Gillen Thacker.

This edition published by arrangement with Harlequin Books S.A.

® and TM are trademarks of the publisher. Trademarks indicated with
® are registered in the United States Patent and Trademark Office, the
Canadian Trade Marks Office and in other countries.

Visit us at www.eHarlequin.com

Printed in U.S.A.

ABOUT THE AUTHOR

Cathy Gillen Thacker is a full-time wife/mother/author who began typing stories for her own amusement during "nap time" when her children were toddlers. Twenty years and more than fifty published novels later, Cathy is almost as well-known for her witty romantic comedies and warm family stories as she is for her ability to get grass stains and red clay out of almost anything, her triple layer brownies and her knack for knowing what her three grown and nearly grown children are up to almost before they do! Her books have made numerous appearances on bestseller lists and are now published in seventeen languages and thirty-five countries around the world.

Books by Cathy Gillen Thacker

HARLEQUIN AMERICAN ROMANCE

*The McCabes of Texas
†The Lockharts of Texas

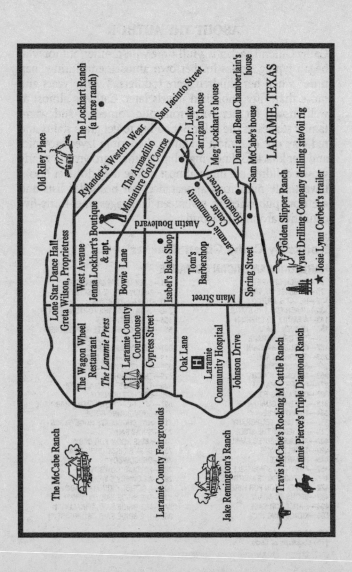

LARAMIE, TEXAS

Chapter One

"How much longer do you think you can keep avoiding me?" Luke Carrigan demanded early Thursday morning.

Meg Lockhart was so startled to see the attractive young family physician striding into her backyard, she nearly dropped her sanding block. Determined not to let his unexpected presence or the deceptively easy-going, all-male way he moved get to her, Meg rocked back on her heels and looked over at him. It was only seven in the morning, but, freshly showered and shaved, Dr. Luke Carrigan looked more than ready to take on the day and any challenge—including her—that came his way.

Privately wishing he weren't so smart, sexy and intuitive as all get out where she was concerned, Meg ignored the sudden pounding of her heart and looked into his golden-brown eyes with all the directness she could muster. "I've spoken to you," Meg said stiffly, wondering how Luke had known she had the day off and was planning to use it to refinish an old wooden park bench for her backyard, then deciding she didn't want to know if there was matchmaking going on.

"Only at the hospital," Luke corrected her grimly, moving closer yet. "And only when absolutely necessary. And then only about hospital business."

Meg refused to feel guilty for avoiding Luke and his
three adorable little girls at her sister's wedding the day
before. She had only been doing what she had to do,
which was keep Luke and her five-year-old son, Jeremy,
well apart. "So?" Meg kept her eyes trained on his rug-
gedly handsome face. She did not want to think about
how sexy Luke looked in faded jeans that clung to his
lean hips and muscular thighs and a sage-green polo shirt
that showed off his broad shoulders, flat stomach and trim
waist. Any more than she wanted to fall prey to his charming smile.

"So we were *friends,* Meg," Luke reminded her gently.
He shoved a hand through his neatly cut sandy-blond hair
and, still regarding her patiently, hunkered down next to
her, his muscular, jean-clad knee nudging her bare thigh.
"At least until…"

Meg took a deep, bracing breath and resumed sanding
the old wooden slats with a vengeance, rubbing away the
splinters the way she wished she could erase the problems
of the past. "I don't want to talk about this," she said
firmly, breathing in his woodsy aftershave. She moved
back slightly, so their bodies were no longer touching.
"Jeremy could wake up and overhear."

"And realize we were once the very best of friends?"
Luke stayed right where he was and continued to regard
her in that approachable, guy-friend way that had gotten
to her the way no Casanova moves ever could have. "At
least—" Luke's voice dropped another notch "—until we
slept together."

Memories of the two of them, their bodies intimately
entwined, cascaded over her like a waterfall on a hot summer day. Her heart and mind filled with the passion they
had shared, Meg cast a glance over her shoulder at the
cottage behind her. She turned back to him, her eyes rov-

ing over his tall, solidly built frame and broad, powerful shoulders before coming to rest once again on the arrestingly handsome contours of his face. "I had hoped we would never have to discuss this." As she had hoped— by her silence—that he would have gotten the message.

Luke took her wrist in hand and tugged her to her feet. "And all I've ever wanted to do is talk about it," he countered softly, meaningfully, reluctantly letting go of her wrist, "and tell you how very sorry I am I let things get out of control that way."

Meg sighed. "I am as much to blame for what happened that night as you are, Luke." Hindsight and maturity had combined to show her that.

"I don't think so," Luke replied in a clipped tone, heavy with self-reproach.

Meg had to tilt her head back to see his face. Both his height—at six-five he had a good eight inches on her— and his closeness were disconcerting to her. As was her potent reaction to his sheer physical attractiveness. Every time she was near him, her heart beat a little faster, her senses got a little sharper and the loneliness she'd felt since their friendship abruptly ended became more acute. And yet, how could she regret the mistake that had ended their friendship, knowing how that night had changed her life for all eternity?

"You didn't know what you were doing, you were so upset," Luke continued.

Meg shook her head. "It's still no excuse. I might have already broken up with Kip Brewster, but I also knew you were about to ask Gwyneth to marry you." The fact she had always felt Gwyneth was all wrong for Luke was of no consequence. He'd still been Gwyneth's steady, and Meg had ignored that fact when she'd let a comforting hug take on an entirely different meaning.

"You had just lost your parents in that deadly tornado and become head of the family. You needed someone to hold on to, while you waited for morning and a flight home. I just happened to be there."

He hadn't just been her friend—he had been her lifeline that night. "Even so, I should never have kissed you, Luke," Meg said around the unaccustomed dryness of her throat. "Especially not that way." A way that said he was the only man there would ever be for her.

Luke shrugged matter-of-factly, looking not nearly as regret-filled as she would have expected. "I kissed you back."

How well Meg remembered that. Through high school, college and into grad school, she had dated a lot of different guys. Many of those dates had ended with goodnight kisses. But none had ever been like that. Meg suspected, there might never be again. But that was just chemistry, and the chemistry between them had ruined their friendship and nearly wrecked both their lives. Would have, if Meg had allowed Luke's guilt over their lovemaking to break up his relationship with Gwyneth. But she had done what she had to do then, just as she would do what she had to do now. "It was a long time ago," Meg said wearily. She dropped the sanding block onto the bench.

"I agree." Luke stood, arms folded in front of him, legs braced apart. "What I don't understand is why you're still acting as if it just happened yesterday. Why, years later, are you avoiding me like the plague?"

Meg wiped her hands on the rag she'd stuck in the waistband of her shorts. She turned away. Doing her best to quell the growing heat in her cheeks, she studied the quarter acre of tidy green lawn that separated her two-bedroom "guest cottage" from the much bigger "main house" next door. Once all part of the same residence, the two properties had been split up years before and sold to different owners, then sold again. "Because I am ashamed and humiliated by the way I behaved," Meg said.

Luke lifted a brow. "Because you're human? Because you're a woman? Because you were reeling with grief and acted impulsively?" As Meg turned back to face him, he studied her implacably. "Or is it something more that has made you keep me at arm's length?" he continued, giving her the slow once-over. "Like Jeremy."

Meg swallowed around the sudden knot of emotion in her throat and tried to still the sudden trembling of her heart. "My son has nothing to do with my feelings about that night," Meg replied firmly. "Or you."

"Where is he?" Luke asked, his voice taking on a protective, parental quality Meg didn't like one bit.

Her confidence at being able to handle this situation, simply by steering clear of Luke as much as possible, wavered. "He's still asleep."

"And his father?" Luke grilled Meg deliberately. "Where is he?"

Meg knew what Luke was driving at. She put up a hand to prevent Luke from asking any more questions. He ignored her and pushed on anyway.

"When exactly was Jeremy born, Meg?"

That, she could answer. "Eight months after my parents died, on December first."

Silence fell between them. Disappointment flashed across Luke's face. "Meaning his father is that guy you almost married—Kip Brewster," he said, almost sadly. Anguish glimmered in his golden-brown eyes. "And not me."

Meg's shoulders stiffened as she stared at the light dusting of sandy-brown hair on Luke's arms. Guilt and confusion filled her heart. She was tempted to confess all, to lean on Luke's broad shoulders and inherently gallant and romantic nature once again. But even as she was tempted, she knew Luke and knew she couldn't do it. Luke was the kind of selfless-to-a-fault man who took his obligations seriously. He was quick to help anyone and everyone else out. The fallout came later when the good intentions in his head did not match the feelings in his heart. How quickly—and irrevocably—she had learned that.

She had decided what was right years ago. Amid much attempted interference from family and friends, she had taken responsibility for her actions and stuck to her guns in protecting her son from the kind of hurt and rejection she had suffered. She wasn't going to change direction now. Reminding herself that she was protecting everyone with her silence, Meg lifted her head indignantly. "Haven't you heard? I don't discuss Jeremy's father with anyone. I never have and never will." Life was so much simpler that way. She and Jeremy weren't a burden to anyone.

Still studying her bluntly, he took another step closer. "Surely your sisters know the truth."

They all certainly *wanted* to know, Meg thought, as feelings of guilt and remorse hit her anew. "If my sisters knew the identity of Jeremy's father they would be on that man's doorstep in a red-hot Texas second, demanding he step up to the gate and do right by us whether he wanted to or not." And that Meg couldn't allow. Especially after all this time had passed.

Luke's brow furrowed. "What's wrong with that?"

"What's wrong with it is that I know what it's like to be suddenly shouldered with the care and responsibility of another human being," she said curtly.

Luke's glance softened. "Which is what happened when you became the legal guardian to your sisters," he noted compassionately.

Despite herself, Meg warmed to the understanding in Luke's low, sensual tone. The goodness in him was what had made them such fast friends in the beginning and kept her from hurting him and his family later. Taking the cloth rag from her belt, she wiped down the bench, checked for splinters, found none. "I love my sisters and I was glad to do it," she admitted with gut-wrenching honesty, "but I'd be lying if I said there weren't times when I resented having such enormous responsibility thrust on me that way."

"Did you feel that way about Jeremy, too?"

Meg sank down on the bench, grappling with her feelings all the while. She wasn't sure why. She just knew she wanted Luke to realize how confused and distraught she'd been back then. "From the first moment I realized I was pregnant, I was happy about having a baby," she admitted slowly, overcome with an onslaught of feeling. "But I was also dismayed," she continued softly. Shaking her head, she stood, slid her hands into the deep pockets of her khaki walking shorts and began to pace away from Luke. "The timing was all wrong. I wasn't married. I wasn't ready for a baby." She whirled back toward Luke. "I had to sell the family ranch and settle the debts and deal with my sisters and help them get over their grief, and all the while try to manage my own sadness, which was darn near completely overwhelming." Meg paused and lifted her eyes to Luke's. "I just...I couldn't take on any more back then." If she'd had to deal with the immensely complicated situation regarding Jeremy's father, she wouldn't have made it, that she knew.

Luke trod closer. "Jeremy's father could have helped you cope," he said quietly.

As always, when this subject was introduced, Meg felt her defenses come up. "He also could have sued me for custody. Or gone overboard to help and then later resented me and Jeremy for the disruption we caused in his life." Neither option had been wanted. Meg hadn't been able to bear the idea of Jeremy's presence hurting anyone, for fear Jeremy'd realize he wasn't wanted the way he deserved to be wanted by absolutely everyone.

Luke studied her. "You think Jeremy's father would have done that?"

Meg shrugged, abruptly feeling as confused and helpless as she had back then. "That's the point. I didn't know what his reaction might be under the circumstances." Never mind his wife's. "And I didn't want to find out the hard way, especially if it meant Jeremy—and others— would be hurt in the process. I had all I could do to take care of my parents' estate, my sisters, my baby and myself. There was no room in my life for a man who was never meant to be with me and who didn't want or plan this child, either."

Luke frowned. He massaged the muscles on the back of his neck. "I think you're not giving Kip Brewster enough credit. I know the two of you parted badly, but you must have liked something about him—you two dated for months and even talked about getting married—and, from what I remember, he seemed like a decent guy."

On the surface, that was true, Meg knew. Kip was from a wealthy Texas family. Bright and articulate, he had always behaved like a perfect gentleman and treated Meg with care. It was what Kip was capable of behind the scenes that had led to their breakup. But again, that wasn't the kind of personal angst and drama Meg shared with anyone. It was bad enough she knew what a complete fool Kip had made of her, without letting everyone else know how deeply she had been humiliated. And that especially included Luke. For some reason Meg couldn't quite put her finger on, she didn't want Luke knowing how truly clueless she had been back then. And because Kip had been in the university law school, Meg and Luke in the medical and nursing schools, there was no reason Luke should ever know, no reason Kip's and Luke's paths should ever cross again. Especially since Kip had never even been to Laramie. And he and Meg hadn't had contact since she left Chicago.

"I never said Jeremy's father was Kip," Meg said, piqued.

"Are you saying he isn't then?" Luke probed.

Warmth climbed from Meg's neck into her face. "I'm not saying anything other than that Kip Brewster has no business in this matter, period," Meg insisted stubbornly, and saw the hollows beneath Luke's cheekbones grow more pronounced. Clearly, he disapproved of the way she had handled this situation from the start. Which was something else Meg didn't need—Luke's condemnation.

Luke stared at Meg as if he no longer had the slightest clue who she was. "I gather this means your son has no idea who his father is, either," he said grimly.

Meg's feelings on that were firm. "Why fill his head with stories of someone who will never be able to be a father to him? It would only make him want something he could never have." Having secretly been in love with the same man for most of her adult life, Meg knew what that was like. It wasn't fun.

Silence fell as Luke continued to study her without a hint of apology. "I can see you're trying to help," Meg said finally, a little in awe of his tenacity.

"I never stopped caring what happened to you, Meg."

Nor had she ever stopped caring what happened to Luke, Meg thought. But that changed nothing. Every time she was near him, every time she looked at him, she couldn't help but recall what it had been like to pour out her heart to him and make love to him like there was no tomorrow. Only to see his regret and realize—when the new day dawned, emotions subsided and common sense returned—that he did not feel the same way about her. She had never been so devastated. She couldn't—wouldn't—let the same thing happen to her son.

"Look, we can be neighbors and co-workers. But we can't pretend what happened did not occur because it did." And consequently her life had never been—would never be—the same.

Luke's gaze narrowed in silent challenge. "That stand-offish attitude of yours is going to make our lives mighty difficult," he drawled with easy familiarity.

Every muscle in her body was stiff with tension. "And why would that be?"

Luke gave her a goading smile. Desire, pure and simple, was in his eyes. "Because in about half an hour my three little girls and I are moving in next door."

FINALLY, LUKE NOTED, he had Meg's full attention. It sure hadn't been easy getting it. She had been treating him like an outcast from the moment he arrived in Laramie a week ago, ducking whenever she saw him, only smiling or absently greeting him when she simply could not get around it.

Given the way they'd parted, her refusal to talk to him since, he couldn't say he'd expected her to greet him with open arms. He'd known the moment they'd actually come face-to-face again that she was no less stubborn or self-reliant. She said she forgave him for giving in to her grief, confusion and need, but she didn't act as if she'd forgiven him. She acted as if she resented him more than ever.

The part of him that said he didn't need this—feeling unwanted and unnecessary—was tempted to turn away and let her and the son he'd thought, hoped for one brief incredibly happy moment was his be, just as they had been. The other part of him, the stronger, more noble side, wanted to hang in there, find a way to get past Meg's hurt and wariness, forget the night that had ended their friendship and find their way back to each other again. Meg needed a confidante and companion as much as he did. Maybe more.

He had hoped, of course, that Meg already would have reached the same conclusion by the time he actually arrived in Laramie. He had hoped enough time would have passed for her to simply meet him halfway. Unfortunately, it hadn't happened. So he'd been left to take matters into his own hands and seek her out at a time when they were both away from the hospital and could say whatever needed to be said privately and be done with it.

Once again he'd been surprised. Not just by her continued resistance to get close again, but also by her impact on him in a physical sense. He'd met a lot of women in his life, dated more than a few of them, and he'd never wanted any of them the way he wanted Meg Lockhart. To his amazement, during the half dozen years they had been apart, that feeling had only increased. And not just because Meg still had the same easy good looks, inherent gentleness and unconscious spunk and sexiness that had turned his life upside down from the get-go. Yes, she was still as drop-dead gorgeous as ever—even in demure shorts, blouse and white tennis shoes. Her dark-auburn hair was as thick and glossy as ever, and she still liked to wear the thick loose waves swept up in a loose, tousled knot on the back of her head. But his attraction to her went far beyond her mesmerizing aqua-blue eyes, full, soft lips and enticing curves that had been made even lusher and more womanly with the birth of her first and only child. He was attracted to her for the way she made him feel. He had only to look into her eyes to know how special was the immediate emotional connection that once allowed them to become friends. And one day soon, Luke promised himself silently, Meg would realize their attraction needed to be explored. One day soon they'd start over and get to know each other the way they should have the first time. Not just as friends, but as friends and lovers.

"What about your wife?" Meg asked.

Luke tensed as the talk turned to his marriage and that unhappy time of his life. Meg wasn't the only one who had a romantic life full of regrets she'd rather not dwell on—he had made his share of mistakes in that arena, too, that could not be undone. Like Meg, Luke thought, all he could do was move on. "Gwyneth died two years ago, in a car crash," he said quietly.

"I'm sorry." Shock filling her eyes, Meg laid a slender hand across her breasts and sucked in a breath. "Was anyone else hurt in the accident?"

Luke grimaced, working hard to keep his emotions at bay. This was one area of his life he didn't want to talk about, even with Meg. "She was alone when it happened," he said tersely.

"It must have been very tough for you all," Meg said compassionately.

Luke nodded. That was the understatement of the century. In many ways he was still grappling with the circumstances surrounding Gwyneth's death.

"Where are your three little girls now?" Meg asked,

abruptly looking and acting very much like the nurse/natural healer she was professionally.

"With John and Lilah McCabe," Luke explained as Meg knelt next to the freshly sanded park bench. "We've been staying at their ranch the past couple of days, while I closed on the house, got acquainted with the hospital and had the utilities turned on here."

Meg opened a can of primer and began applying it to the wooden slats with slow, even brush strokes. Looking relieved to talk about something other than herself and her son, Meg glanced over at Luke. "How old are they?"

Appreciating the genuine interest and understanding in Meg's eyes, Luke dropped to the grass beside Meg and got comfortable. He knew he should feel relieved Jeremy wasn't his son after all—he had his hands full just trying to bring up his three daughters—but he found himself wishing he were Jeremy's father. He wanted that link to Meg. He wanted an irrefutable reason for them to start over and forge a relationship again.

"Susie is five. She's all sunshine and storms. Everything is either truly wonderful or a complete disaster. Becca is four. She's the negotiator of the family and is always trying to strike a deal or make things better for everyone. Amy is three, and she has a very mellow personality. Cooperation is her motto."

Meg slanted him a glance, beginning to relax even more as the talk stayed on what were, for her, safer subjects. "Sounds like you have your hands full," she said admiringly.

Luke breathed in the familiar fragrance of Meg's cinnamon perfume as it mingled with the soap-and-water freshness of her skin. "I do."

"Do you have help?"

Luke watched the capable movements of her slender

hands, unable to help but recall how those same hands had felt sliding over his skin. "In California I had a housekeeper and a retired nurse, who worked as their nanny."

"Neither came with you?" Finished with the seat, Meg stood and began working on the rest of the bench.

Loathing the deliberate way she held him at arm's length, Luke shook his head. "Both have family there and didn't want to move." As much as he hated to lose them, he understood. He hadn't just taken the job in Laramie because he'd learned about Jeremy and thought—hoped— he and Meg had a child together that she'd been too afraid to tell him about. He'd come back to Texas for good, this time, because he needed to be closer to his Texas roots. And even though he'd grown up in Houston, next to the oil refinery where his dad had worked, Laramie was such a warm and friendly town it already felt like home.

Meg lifted a brow. "Are you going to hire a nanny here?"

Aware she was gauging his reply carefully, Luke shook his head, his glance tracking the swell of her breasts, pushing against her blouse, and the graceful shape of her bare arms. "I'm planning to put them in the employee day care center over at the hospital," he replied. "That way I can check on them several times a day and go down and have lunch with them. If they ever need me, I'll be right there on the premises. When Susie starts kindergarten in the fall, she'll remain in the center's before-and-after-school program."

Blissfully unaware of the effect her close proximity was having on him, Meg swiveled around to look at him with a mixture of empathy and approval. "Jeremy is enrolled there, too," she said, regarding him, one concerned parent to another. "He really likes it."

Trying hard not to notice the snug way her shorts stretched over the delectable curves, Luke stood and shifted in a way to ease the growing pressure at the front of his jeans. "Looks like our kids will really be getting to know each other," he said, glad to know she cared about her son as much as he cared about his daughters. Even if she wasn't yet doing right by her son's father, whoever he was.

"I guess so." Meg smiled at him helpfully, comfortable now that she'd finally decided on a role for them to play, that of emotionally uninvolved neighbors. "Is there anything I can do for you? Maybe make some lunch for you and the girls and bring it over later?"

Luke nodded. He knew what Meg was doing. Falling back into the familiar role of gracious Texas lady while keeping him at arm's length. She might not know it yet, but this was only a starting place. Although where it would end up, given Meg's wariness where he was concerned, was yet to be seen. "That would be great," he said, smiling, too.

Finished, Meg put aside her brush and slapped the lid back on the can of primer. She smiled at him like the "good neighbor and no more" she intended to be. Luke felt his hopes for a quickly resumed friendship fading fast. "Do they like macaroni and cheese?" she asked with a politeness that grated.

Luke nodded, aware this was not working out anywhere near as well as he had hoped. Meg wouldn't use their kids as an excuse to get close again. She'd use them like a perpetual shield, to keep them apart.

"Mac 'n' cheese is their favorite," Luke said. The moving truck drove up and parked in front of the big house next door. "I'd better go," Luke said reluctantly.

Meg nodded. "I'll see you later."

As MEG EXPECTED, her five-and-a-half-year-old son, Jeremy, was deliriously excited by the sight of such a big truck. She was glad to see it, too, relieved to end her time alone with Luke. She had known he would catch up with her eventually. She had even guessed he would ask about Jeremy's paternity the first chance he got.

What she hadn't imagined was how hard it would be for her to be evasive.

Even now, knowing there was no way they could go back and right the wrongs and rewrite the past, she wanted to tell him everything that had happened. And why. If she knew for certain he would understand why she'd done what she had, maybe there'd be a chance for them to be close again. At the very least, caring friends. But life came with no such guarantees.

And that being the case, Meg decided, she couldn't risk her son being hurt by any mistakes she made. Jeremy had struggled enough, growing up without a father in his life, and didn't need his life turned upside down now. Maybe she hadn't been able to give Jeremy a father, but she'd given him everything else—a home, family, security and lots of love. She wasn't going to risk that being taken away from him.

"Can I go out and watch the movers unload the van?" Jeremy asked as he finished his favorite breakfast of cereal, milk and fruit.

Feeling steadier now that she'd reassured herself her decisions had been the right ones, Meg shot an affectionate look at her son. With his auburn hair, a shade darker than Meg's, fair freckled skin and chocolate-brown eyes, he was definitely a Lockhart. Already tall for his age, he'd added another inch to his sturdy little body over the summer. "Just make sure you stay in our yard," Meg cautioned as she helped him tie his sneakers. She shot a look at Luke next door and felt her stomach tighten. "I don't want you getting in the way of the movers."

"Okay," Jeremy said agreeably, going back to the table to quaff the last of his juice. "Do they have any kids?"

Happy about the additional children in the neighborhood, Meg told him about Luke's three girls.

Jeremy grinned as he ran to get one of his toy trucks. "Now I'll have someone my age to play with all the time." Dashing back, he stopped just short of Meg and asked, "Can Alexandra come over and watch the movers unload the van, too?"

Alexandra Remington was Meg's sister's new stepdaughter, also five. Upon meeting, Jeremy and Alex had quickly become friends. "Sure," Meg smiled. "If Clara says it's okay."

"How come she has to ask Clara instead of Jake and Aunt Jenna?"

"Because Jake and Aunt Jenna just got married yesterday afternoon, honey, and they went to spend their wedding night at a country inn." Alex had stayed home with her housekeeper-nanny, Clara.

Jeremy wrinkled his nose, perplexed. "How come they wanted to do that?"

"Because they just got married and they wanted to be alone for a while," Meg said.

Jeremy frowned. "Are they gonna take a honeymoon, like Aunt Dani and Uncle Beau did when they got married?"

"Yes, but not until later this fall, when things are more settled."

"How come you aren't getting married, too?" Jeremy demanded, running his truck back and forth over the tabletop.

Out of the mouths of babes, Meg thought. "Because

I'm not in love with someone yet," Meg explained. And the way things are going, she thought dispiritedly, might never be, especially with Luke underfoot, distracting her and reminding her what was and wouldn't be again.

"But you had me," Jeremy continued.

"Yes, I did," Meg smiled, knowing that was the one thing—the only thing—she would never regret. "And I love you very much." Meg knelt so they were face-to-face, wrapped her arms around Jeremy and hugged him tight. Loving the peace and happiness he brought to her life, she breathed in the baby shampoo scent of his hair and then drew back. Grinning at the excitement dancing in his eyes, she asked, "Now, do you want to call Alex?"

"And Trevor and Teddy and Tyler, too?" Jeremy insisted.

Meg smiled as she thought of the triplet sons of Annie and Travis McCabe. "Okay. Ask them to stay to lunch." That would keep her and Luke from being alone. It would keep her from realizing all over again just how very attracted she was to him.

UNFORTUNATELY, her sisters, Kelsey and Dani, who dropped by midmorning, were every bit as curious about Meg's new neighbors as her son, Jeremy, had been.

"I can't believe Luke Carrington actually bought that house and is moving into it, as is," Dani murmured, keeping a watchful eye on the five kids now congregated in the side yard, watching the unloading, while Meg, taking solace in the abundance of company, busied herself by rushing around the kitchen, intent on making enough kid-pleasing macaroni and cheese to feed an army.

"It's a very big house, structurally sound and was sold at a pleasing price. With three girls, Luke Carrington needs a lot of space," Meg murmured, casting a glance out the window at the large turn-of-the-century Cape Cod next door.

"The lavender exterior paint and the deep-purple trim aren't exactly guy colors. Not to mention the clashing dark-green shutters and snowy-white door," Kelsey began critically, watching as Dani's husband, Beau, and Kelsey's business partner, Brady Anderson, went over to introduce themselves and lend a hand to Luke and the moving crew.

"That house has the most garish interior paint I have ever seen. I know, because I saw it before I bought my place," Dani said as she sliced ham for sandwiches.

"So Luke Carrington has his work cut out for him. I'm sure he can manage. To get inspired, all he has to do is look at my place," Meg said as Kelsey began to help with the salad making. Maybe the redecorating would take up all his spare time and energy.

"Or you," Dani teased.

Meg rolled her eyes at Dani. Luke had desired her once, but that didn't mean it would ever happen again. "Just because you and Jenna are happily married and head-over-heels-in-love with your husbands does not mean I have romance on my mind."

"Maybe you should," Dani said, covering the filled platter with plastic wrap and sliding it back into the refrigerator. "After all, Luke's a doctor. You're a nurse. You both work at Laramie Community Hospital. You both are single and both have kids."

"You know what I find interesting?" Kelsey interrupted as she washed the lettuce. "That the new doctor in town would have the same name as that buddy of yours from your grad school days in Chicago. Remember how much you used to talk about that guy on the phone to us? It was always Luke this and Luke that."

Leave it to baby sister Kelsey, the most fickle of all the Lockhart women, to remember a detail like that, Meg thought. And then bring it up at the worst possible time. When she was still feeling vulnerable from Luke's visit.

Dani's amber eyes brightened. "That is a coincidence."

Meg knew she might as well be honest—her sisters would find out soon enough that Luke and she had known each other before. If not from John and Lilah McCabe, who were responsible for bringing Luke to Laramie, then from Luke himself. "It's the same guy."

"How did he end up in Laramie?" Kelsey asked as she put the washed lettuce into the salad spinner and gave it a whirl.

Wary of divulging her emotions, Meg gave more than usual concentration to the cheese sauce she was making. "Lilah told me he met John at a family medicine conference on rural medicine in New Mexico last spring," she replied in the most casual voice she could manage. "John knew he was going to retire this summer, and he encouraged Luke, who was looking for a way to come back to the state where he grew up, to apply for the position at the hospital here."

Looking every bit the native Texas cowgirl she was, in jeans, chambray shirt and boots, Kelsey leaned against the kitchen counter and munched on a carrot. "You never did tell us why you had that falling out with Luke after Mom and Dad died."

Meg did her best to curtail a blush as she drained the cooked macaroni through the colander in the sink. "It wasn't a falling out."

"Seemed like one to me," Dani noted as she began slicing red cabbage into thin strips. "You wouldn't take his calls or read his letters."

Meg put the drained macaroni into the buttered casserole and poured the cheese sauce over that. "I was just upset that summer, that's all."

"Meaning it was all your fault and not Luke's?" Dani asked, suddenly acting more counselor to the hopelessly romantic and perennially unattached than the film critic she was. "Or simply that you still don't want to talk about it?"

Leave it to Dani, a person who knew a good story when she found one, to zero in on the problem. Her shoulders stiff with building tension, Meg sprinkled the dish with bread crumbs and slid the casserole into the oven to bake. "I am not going to discuss this with you two."

Dani and Kelsey exchanged mischievous looks. "The question is, did you discuss it with Luke?" Kelsey pressed.

"Discuss what with Luke?" Jenna asked curiously, coming in the door and glowing like the very recent bride she was.

Kelsey quickly brought their other sister up to speed on what was happening. "Meg has just informed us that the new doctor at the hospital—who just happens to have also bought the house next door—is the same Luke she knew in Chicago years ago."

Looking lovely in a fashionable dress of her own design, Jenna quirked a red-gold brow. "Interesting."

"Isn't it?" Dani agreed as she put the finishing touches on the salad.

Knowing she had to nip this meddling in the bud before it got any worse, Meg made eye contact with each and every one of her three sisters. "Okay, ladies. Lay off."

Kelsey grinned and took a long swig of the bottled water she'd brought in with her. "Ohh. Me thinks that man has gotten under her skin again."

Meg did her best to contain a telltale flush. "Luke has

done nothing of the sort," she said firmly, looking around in vain for something else to do to prepare for the welcome-to-the-neighborhood luncheon she was having for her new neighbors. "If anyone has gotten under my skin, it is you all."

"You sure?" Kelsey continued to tease playfully.

"What went on between us was a long time ago," Meg said firmly, as she began counting out napkins.

"And yet, looking at the expression on your face just now," Jenna interrupted, setting out the old-fashioned Texas sheet cake she'd brought from Isabelle's bakery, "I'd swear it feels like it happened to you today."

Meg counted out silverware. "Luke Carrington and I are going to be working together. We've got kids the same age. We are living next door to each other."

"So?" All three of her sisters asked in unison, studying her.

"So I can't change the reasons for the tension between us years ago," Meg said, her exasperation growing by leaps and bounds with every new question.

"Meaning what?" Kelsey's eyes narrowed. "That you forgive him for whatever he did?"

Meg drew a deep, bolstering breath. Forgiveness had nothing to do with it. It was self-preservation, maintaining the serenity of their lives, that was key. "Meaning I am going to let bygones be just that and treat Luke just like any other neighbor of mine. No better, no worse." And certainly not any more intimately, Meg promised herself determinedly. Because this time she and Luke had not just themselves to think of, but also all four of their children.

SOON AFTER, John and Lilah McCabe arrived with Luke Carrington's three little girls in tow. Like stairsteps, they were the image of their mother, Gwyneth, with blond hair, golden-brown eyes and pretty, delicate features. All three had the same haircut—silky, chin-length bobs with bangs—and were dressed in pastel shorts and matching sleeveless tops, tennis shoes and socks. As John and Lilah brought them over to Meg's to introduce them to the children gathered on the lawn, watching the unloading of the moving van, Meg went out to join them.

"And this is Jeremy's mom, Meg Lockhart," Lilah said, concluding the introductions.

"Hello," Susie, the oldest, said shyly.

"Can Jeremy and the other kids play with us sometimes at our house?" Becca asked.

"Absolutely," Meg smiled, finding it impossible not to warm to the three adorable little girls. "And you can come over here, too, as often as you'd like."

Amy, the youngest, smiled at Meg and the other kids, then tugged on Lilah's hand. "Where's my daddy?"

At the mention of the word, Jeremy frowned.

"Right there." Lilah pointed and lifted her hand in a wave, motioning Luke over.

Jeremy gave Meg a petulant look, abruptly taking up the dispute they'd been having off and on all summer. He propped his hands on his sturdy little hips and scowled at Meg. "How come everybody else gets to know who their dad is, even if he isn't hardly ever there no more, like with Teddy, Tyler and Trevor, and I don't?"

Tyler, Teddy and Trevor looked at Meg, waited expectantly for her reply. As did everyone else, including Lilah McCabe, all three of Meg's sisters and all three of Luke Carrington's little girls. "Honey," Meg felt herself beginning to blush self-consciously despite her desire to stay cool, calm and collected under fire, "I think we should discuss this later."

"Why?" Jeremy shot back belligerently, his patience

with Meg clearly at an end. "You always say the same thing." He turned to Luke and the other men who had just joined the group. "Do you know who my daddy is?" Jeremy asked Luke. Ignoring the collective gasp of all the adults present, Jeremy pressed him contentiously, "Because I don't think my mommy knows."

Meg blushed all the more.

"Of course she does," Luke said firmly. Then looked at Meg with all the intimacy of a once-dear friend, letting her know with a single glance that he agreed with everyone else and thought she wasn't being fair to anyone, by keeping Jeremy's paternity a secret.

Unfortunately, Meg knew it wasn't that simple. Jeremy didn't just want to find out who his father was. He wanted a daddy in his life and Meg's. He wanted the kind of two-parent family other kids had. And while there was always a slim chance that might happen in a sort of marriage-of-convenience way, were Meg to try to get Jeremy's father to take responsibility for their son at this point. There was also the equally strong possibility that Jeremy's father would—once the first flush of excitement wore off—be interested in a much less taxing arrangement than what Jeremy had in mind.

Meg had seen it happen plenty of times in her years as a nurse. Fathers who were thrilled and attentive one year, too busy or just plain not interested the next and practically estranged the following year. When the romance of it all wore off, it was always the kids who suffered, who felt somehow they were to blame for the father walking away from the child they'd never planned on and the woman they had never really loved in the first place.

Meg would rather have her son do without than have his hopes raised and then crushed, his heart broken, as hers had been. She didn't want him to think he had magically found the love he had been looking for all his life, only to see it slip away the next. As it was, Jeremy had her to rely on. She would never make him feel he was a burden or be too busy for him, never lose interest as time went on and walk away from him.

"Let's not discuss this now, please," Meg said.

The three sisters exchanged glances. Lilah and John McCabe looked worried, too. The kids all appeared confused. "I'm going to put the finishing touches on lunch," Meg said, hardening her heart and letting everyone know the subject of Jeremy's paternity was closed, just as it had always been.

THANKS TO LILAH AND JOHN MCCABE and their insistence in drafting everyone who stopped in to help Luke unpack and get his house in order, by bedtime the work was finished. There were towels in the linen closet, sheets on the beds and plenty of food and beverages stocking his pantry and fridge. The only thing that hadn't gone quite according to plan were the sleeping arrangements. Although there were bedrooms for all, his three little girls wanted to share one room. Knowing how hard the move had been for them, Luke had put their bureaus, clothes and bookshelves in one bedroom, all their toys in another and their beds in the third so that they could sleep together in the bedroom across the hall from his. It made for a rather strange arrangement of furniture and belongings upstairs, but he figured that as time passed and they grew more comfortable in their new house, they would go back to each having her own room again. Meantime, he had three very tired little girls on his hands, Luke noted, as he tucked them into their beds. Weary as they might be, however, they still had a lot on their minds.

"You have to help Jeremy, Daddy," Susie said.

Becca nodded. "We told him you were real good at finding things."

Amy added, "Jeremy's real sad because he can't find his daddy."

His girls looked increasingly worried as Susie explained, "He can't find him because he doesn't know where he is."

Or even who *he is,* Luke thought, once again wishing that he were Jeremy's father so he could quickly put everything to right for Meg and the boy.

"I am sure Jeremy and his mommy are talking about this very thing right now," Luke said gently, doing his best to reassure his daughters the way he wished he could comfort Meg's son. "And I'm also sure they will work everything out." If only because Jeremy was not about to let the subject rest until they did so. "Now you girls go to sleep," Luke said, tucking them in one by one.

"Okay, Daddy." There were kisses and hugs all around. Then, minutes later, deep, even breathing.

With a sigh Luke headed back downstairs. He wished he could fix things for Jeremy and Meg, but the truth was, since he wasn't Jeremy's father after all, it wasn't any of his business. Luke looked out the window, blinked at what he saw, then paused and blinked one more time.

Then again, maybe it was his business, Luke decided as he walked outside and confronted the person marching down the sidewalk, dragging his loaded red wagon behind him. A backpack that looked crammed to the gills, a stuffed animal, a sailboat and a toy dump truck were inside it. "Hello, Jeremy."

Jeremy looked at Luke and, chin set stubbornly, kept right on going, pulling his little red wagon behind him.

Unable to help but admire his gumption, even if his mother clearly had no idea what he was up to, Luke fell into step beside Jeremy. "Just where do you think you're going?"

Chapter Two

Jeremy tried to use his judiciously suddenly took his ten older than his were... as running away from home.

Things were obviously more serious than Meg, however, Luke thought, he noticed in Meg's cottage. The lights were still on outside. But the downfield was dark, which probably meant Meg was either in bed or getting ready for bed. Resisting the only way to keep Jeremy from running away again was to beat him out and convince him this was absolutely not the way to solve his problem.

"How about we have a man-to-man talk before you go, then," Luke said, "I'm..."

"What do you think?" he asked.

"Luke..." he said...

Linda Goodnight

Unable to help, but admire his gumption, even stub-
bornness, Luke stood no to reveal he was on his. Luke fell
into step beside Jeremy. "Just where do you think you're
going?"

Chapter Two

Jeremy turned to face Luke contentiously, suddenly looking far older than his years. "I'm running away from
home."

Things were obviously more serious than Meg knew
here, Luke thought. He glanced at Meg's cottage. The
lights were still on upstairs, but the downstairs was dark,
which probably meant Meg was either in bed or getting
ready for bed. Figuring the only way to keep Jeremy from
running away again was to hear him out and convince
him this was absolutely not the way to solve his problems
with his mom, Luke suggested calmly, "How about we
have a man-to-man talk before you go, then? I make a
pretty mean chocolate milkshake. What do you think? Got
time to stop in and have one with me?"

Clearly not wanting to be kept from his quest, Jeremy
hesitated. "Will Susie, Becca and Amy be there?" he
asked.

Luke shook his head matter-of-factly. "No, they're
asleep. It'll be just the two of us. A guys only sort of
thing."

Again Jeremy had to think about it. Eventually his thirst
for a chocolate milkshake won out over his need to hurry.

"Okay," he said finally. He looked at Luke seriously. "But then I really gotta go."

"I understand completely." Hand on his shoulder, Luke guided the five-year-old up the sidewalk. "I think you can leave your wagon parked beside the porch. It'll be okay." And would also serve as a red flag to Meg if she noticed Jeremy was missing before Luke had a chance to call her.

He and Jeremy stepped inside and made their way quietly to the kitchen. Luke seated Jeremy at the kitchen counter and got out his blender. "So, how'd you get this idea?"

Jeremy propped his elbows on the counter and his chin on his hands. Oblivious to the fact his dark-auburn hair was standing on end, he watched Luke bring out ice cream, milk and chocolate syrup. "My teacher at the day care center at the hospital read us this book. It was about a little bear cub who lost his mama, and couldn't find her anywhere. So he went off through the forest and asked all the other animals if they knew where his mama was. The chipmunk didn't know. And the blackbird said he didn't know, either. Anyway, the little bear just kept going until he finally found someone who knew where his mama was."

"And where was she?" Luke asked, as he scooped ice cream into the blender.

"In the forest, down by the river, looking for her baby bear." Jeremy's brows knit together as he shifted closer. Still watching Luke inquisitively, he continued his recitation in all earnestness. "She was crying, too, because she couldn't find her baby bear cub." Briefly Jeremy's eyes clouded up as he recounted wistfully, "They were real happy when they found each other. So I'm going to do the same thing." Jeremy swallowed hard, then continued in a voice laced with heartfelt determination, "I'm going to ask everybody if they know who my father is until I find him. And then we'll both be happy, too."

"It could work," Luke agreed slowly, irked that no one else seemed to realize how desperately Jeremy wanted and needed his father in his life. What had Meg been thinking to deprive Jeremy and his father of each other's love? Maybe she hadn't meant to be cruel, but she had been. And the situation was going to get worse.

Luke poured milk and chocolate syrup over the ice cream, put the lid on tight and set the glass pitcher on the base. "But first don't you think you should get a good night's sleep?"

"I can't go home," Jeremy said emphatically as color swept into his fair, freckled face. He regarded Luke defiantly. "I already left."

And if Luke took him back now, before talking some sense into Meg, Jeremy would turn right around and leave again. Perhaps to disastrous results, Luke thought, knowing what kind of things could happen to unattended children. No one was taking this kid seriously, Luke thought furiously. Especially Meg. "I can see your dilemma." Luke blended the shake, then poured Jeremy a glass and one for himself. He found straws for both of them and then sat down at the counter next to Jeremy. "How about putting a bedroll on my sofa just for tonight, then. You'll go farther if you get a good night's sleep."

"I am kinda tired." Jeremy finished his shake, then rubbed his eyes.

Luke got Jeremy settled on his sofa. He was asleep as soon as his head hit the pillow. Luke picked up the phone and dialed. Meg answered on the first ring. Luke identified himself, then said, "I think you'd better come over here. Now."

"I couldn't even if I wanted to," Meg responded, piqued. "Jeremy's asleep."

"He sure is," Luke agreed grimly.

There was a pause on the other end. Suspiciously Meg asked, "How do you know that?"

"Because your son is sacked out on my sofa."

A scant minute later Meg was at Luke's door. She was dressed in a pair of pink cotton pajamas that buttoned up the front, and her auburn hair was damp. She smelled like soap and perfumed bath salts. "How did he get over here?" she demanded in shock and dismay as Luke ushered her in.

"He ran away from home," Luke said.

Color rushed into Meg's cheeks, highlighting the delicate curves of her cheekbones in her oval face. As she glanced past him at the living room sofa, where her son was curled up sound asleep, she was vulnerable in a way he hadn't seen her since the night, the only night, they had ever made love. It was all Luke could do not to take her in his arms and hold her close.

But, knowing that was not what she—or Jeremy—needed now, Luke escorted her in to check on her son. As soon as she saw for herself he was indeed all right, Luke led her out to the kitchen, where they could talk without fear of waking any of the children. Trying not to notice how lovely she looked, Luke got out a couple of glasses and a pitcher of ice water and explained Jeremy's thinking.

Meg felt her way into a chair. "He's been peppering me with questions for weeks now." She shook her head, her lower lip trembling slightly, her aqua eyes full of regret. "I had no idea he was this determined."

Luke tore his eyes away from the soft curve of her lips and took in the enticing swell of her breasts. Returning his glance to Meg's face, he warned her bluntly, "You're going to have to do something."

"I will." Meg nodded, enthusiastically. "I'll talk to him first thing tomorrow morning," she promised.

"And tell him the truth?" Luke asked.

Meg nodded firmly. "That he and I are it, as far as family goes. Plenty of kids grow up in single-parent homes these days. I admit it's a lot more common in Dallas, where we were living, than here in Laramie, but it happens just the same, and the families do just fine." Meg shrugged her slender shoulders, the movement jiggling her breasts just enough to remind him she wasn't wearing a bra under her pajama top.

"It's not as if he doesn't have any men in his life," Meg continued defensively. "Now that Dani and Jenna are married, he will have uncles around to do guy stuff with him."

Luke sat back in his chair. He stretched his long legs out in front of him, bumped Meg's under the table, then shifted them to the side. "That's probably true as far as Jake Remington goes, since he's an independent businessman who owns a ranch. But Beau Chamberlain is a movie star. He'll be off making movies a lot."

"That's true." Meg also sat back in her chair, oblivious to the way the curve of one breast was revealed in the gape of her pale-pink pajama top. Meg kept her eyes on Luke's as she continued defending her game plan. "Beau *will* have to go off on location. But he is also building a sound stage near here so he can work a lot of the time in Laramie. He's already said Jeremy can come over and watch filming whenever he wants. The same goes for Jake. He said Jeremy is welcome out at the J&R ranch to play with his daughter, Alexandra, anytime."

Luke shook his head. "What you are offering Jeremy is not the same as having a father, Meg."

Meg gave him what he considered to be an outrageously self-righteous smile. "It's the best I can do," she said icily, slaying him with a glance. "And I would appreciate it if you would back me up on this."

How could he, Luke wondered, when Jeremy was suffering so, and Meg was clearly in the wrong?

Meg leaned forward earnestly. "Please, Luke." She took both his hands in hers. "Help me make Jeremy see it is okay for me to be both mother and father to him. Obviously, he'll listen to you in a way he won't listen to me."

Maybe because I listen to everything your little boy has to say, Luke thought, *not just what I want to hear him say.* Luxuriating in the feel of her soft, slender hands warmly gripping the backs of his, Luke said, "Have you asked Kip to be a father to him?"

"Luke, I've told you." Meg dropped her grip on him and sat back abruptly once again. "Jeremy isn't Kip's responsibility. He's mine." She pushed away from the table and began to pace. "You need to get that through your head, and so does Jeremy."

"Meaning what?" Luke watched the sway of her hips beneath the loose-fitting pajama bottoms. "You haven't told him? Or you told him and his reaction wasn't favorable."

Meg shoved both hands through the tousled strands of her damp auburn hair. "Meaning I was a wreck after Kip and I broke up and my parents died."

"What are you trying to tell me, Meg?" Luke asked gruffly, aware she was hurting him whether she meant to or not by shutting him out, pushing him away.

Meg's fair skin turned red, white, then red again. She

had trouble meeting his eyes. "I'm trying to tell you that sleeping with you wasn't the only foolish thing I did. There were other things I regret doing, too, both before and after you and I—" Meg stopped, unable to continue, and looked away. She took a deep breath, then turned back to him. Her hands knotted in front of her, she continued emotionally, "The truth is I made a series of mistakes. I'd give anything if I could go back and do it all over...do it differently. But I can't." She released a ragged sigh, pushed on. "And because I can't change things, including the less-than-desirable circumstances under which Jeremy was conceived, I think it's best that I leave those mistakes in the past, where they belong. And not hurt Jeremy or anyone else with the disclosure of the facts."

Luke knew what she was trying to say, that there had been a third or even a fourth person in her life and in her bed. But he didn't believe it. Meg had been so innocent and untutored the night they'd been together. And later, so upset at the passionate, uninhibited way she had behaved. He couldn't believe she'd jumped into bed with anyone else either before or after they'd made love, no matter how upset she'd been over her parents' deaths and her breakup with Kip. That was the kind of unplanned, unthinking thing that happened to a highly self-sufficient woman like Meg only once. On the other hand, he never would have believed she would summarily end their friendship, either, just because they'd foolishly and recklessly made love in a moment of crisis. "Then who is Jeremy's father if it's not me and it's not Kip?" Luke asked bluntly, wanting her to look him in the eyes and tell him everything. Here. Now.

Meg's jaw clenched as she spun away and haughtily resumed her pacing. "As I said, Luke, I am not discussing this with you or anyone else. What happened back then is over and done with," Meg continued firmly, "and it's no one else's business but mine."

Clearly, Meg had been hurt by whatever happened. It was obvious she felt very abandoned by whomever Jeremy's father was, though how anyone could turn away from a cute kid like Jeremy, he didn't know. Unless, Luke thought, Meg hadn't been exactly forthright about the depth of her dilemma back then, and Kip or whoever Jeremy's father was really didn't know he was a father. If it was Kip it would have been just like Meg, Luke realized, to go to Kip and see if they could get back together and, failing that, just not tell him about the baby. Meg was so independent, self-sufficient, and responsible. Always had been. The last thing she ever would have wanted was for someone to marry her only because of the baby she was carrying. The last thing she would have wanted was a loveless marriage borne out of responsibility and nothing more.

Luke forced himself to concentrate on the dilemma at hand—how to satisfy her son's growing curiosity about his male parentage. "But you will tell Jeremy about his father?" Clearly, Jeremy needed to be told *something*.

Meg nodded, reluctantly giving in just a little. "I'll tell him the basic facts, that his father was someone I knew a long time ago. For a lot of very complicated, grown-up reasons he's too young to understand, his father and I couldn't get married to each other. So I decided to be both mommy and daddy to Jeremy and raise him on my own."

Luke frowned. "I've talked to Jeremy, Meg. I don't think that's going to be enough to satisfy him." Or me.

"It's going to have to be," Meg retorted, looked every

bit as stubborn and determined as her son to have her way on this.

"And if it's not?" Watching Meg finish the rest of her ice water, Luke pushed back his chair and stood, too.

"It will be," Meg promised firmly. She looked him straight in the eye, and Luke felt the impact of their chemistry dragging him closer, like a rope around his middle, even as her defiant secrecy pushed him away. "Just as soon as Jeremy realizes I am not budging on this, either." Brushing past him, she headed for the living room. "Meanwhile, I want Jeremy in his own bed tonight."

As she started for her son, Luke put a hand on her arm. "Let me do this," he said quietly.

Meg shrugged off his concern and refused his help in a coolly determined way she never would have done six years ago, when they'd been the best of friends. "No, I'm used to carrying him. You stay with your girls." Holding her sleeping five-year-old son in her arms so his head was on her shoulder and his legs were wrapped around her waist, Meg slipped out the door and headed across the lawn.

Luke watched her enter her house.

He knew Meg thought he had given up trying to help. She was wrong.

Jeremy might not be his son; he still needed a man to look out for him. Whether Meg liked it or not—for the moment, anyway, until Jeremy's real father could be found and held accountable to both Meg and Jeremy— Luke was that man.

"THANKS FOR LETTING THE GIRLS play over here today," Luke told Patricia Weatherby the next day. Mother of five-year-old Molly Weatherby, Patricia was also a new resident to Laramie. Luke had met her at the chamber of commerce, where she now worked. Learning they had daughters the same age, Patricia had offered to have his three girls over for a play date as soon as it was convenient.

"Where are you going?" Patricia asked as Molly showed Luke's three girls where she kept all her toys.

Luke handed over his cell phone and pager numbers. "I've got some business in Austin to take care of. I hope to be back around four this afternoon at the very latest." He hadn't done enough for Meg when her parents died. Instead of helping her through her grief, he'd foolishly and recklessly made love to her, thereby adding to her distress. Had he known then that she was already pregnant with what was probably—despite her denials—her ex-boyfriend's child, he could have persuaded Kip Brewster to do right by Meg and their son. But he hadn't known then.

He did now.

And, having made half a dozen phone calls and found out where Kip was, it was time to act. Hopefully, Jeremy was Kip's son. If not, Luke decided, he would keep looking until he found the help Meg and her son needed.

THE DRIVE TO AUSTIN went swiftly. Two hours later Luke was being ushered into Kip Brewster's office at the prestigious law firm where he worked. As they shook hands, Luke noted Kip had changed very little since they'd gone to school in Chicago. He was still physically fit, handsome in that aristocratic, male model way, and very well mannered. "Thanks for taking the time to see me on such short notice," Luke said.

"No problem." Kip offered Luke a chair, then circled around to sit behind his desk. "You said there was some sort of personal emergency…?"

"It concerns Meg Lockhart."

Kip's eyes lit up with interest, his reaction confirming, for Luke, the fact that Kip was not over Meg. Any more than he himself had ever gotten over Meg and the abrupt way their friendship had ended. "How is she?" Kip asked.

"Thriving, professionally." Luke was pleased to report.

"And personally?" Kip's interest sharpened as he waited for Luke's reply.

"Never married."

"Wish I could say the same," Kip said with a rueful shrug. "I'm divorced."

Luke nodded. He knew what it was like to have things work out in ways you never expected. "I'm widowed."

"Sorry."

Luke nodded. "Same to you."

Silence. Knowing there was no easy way to broach this, Luke forged on. "Meg has a son."

Kip did a double take, looking just as shocked as Luke had been initially. "Meg—a single mother?" Kip asked in a low, stunned voice.

Luke nodded. He waited, but to his frustration, Kip did not leap to the conclusion Luke would have expected him to make. Which meant he was going to have to spell it out for him. "Jeremy is five now," Luke said patiently. "His birthday is December first. He'll be six."

Kip's brow furrowed. "Did Meg adopt this son of hers?" he asked finally.

"No." Luke exhaled slowly. "Jeremy is her biological child."

Another pause. "I don't suppose she was artificially inseminated," Kip guessed reluctantly after a moment.

Luke shook his head. Again, silence fell between the two men. Wondering what it was going to take for Kip to own up to his responsibility, Luke pushed on with difficulty. "The thing is, Jeremy's a terrific kid. And he wants to know who his father is."

Kip continued to look baffled. "You want my law firm to find this guy?"

"I want you to take responsibility for him."

"Whoa." Kip lifted both hands and held them in front of him like a shield. "No can do."

Luke had been afraid he might be met with this type of reaction. If so, it explained a lot about what Meg had been going through. "This boy needs a father," Luke said firmly.

"I understand that," Kip said readily enough, leaning forward in his chair. "I even sympathize. And if he were mine, I wouldn't hesitate to do right by him. But he isn't mine, Luke."

So Meg hadn't told Kip she was pregnant with Jeremy, just as Luke had thought. "Going by the birth date, you were still dating Meg when Jeremy was conceived."

"Which makes it all the worse." Kip frowned.

Luke's glance narrowed. "What do you mean?"

"Do you know why Meg and I broke up?" Kip rubbed the back of his neck, looking increasingly uncomfortable.

Luke shrugged. "All she would ever say on the subject was you two wanted different things out of life."

"Sounds like Meg." Kip shifted in his chair and shook his head. "Discreet to the max."

Luke waited.

Finally Kip rubbed his jaw and continued, "It boiled down to a couple of things. One, I was jealous of her increasingly intimate friendship with you. And two, she wouldn't sleep with me. Wouldn't even come close, which in turn led to a whole host of other problems between us. So you see," Kip concluded heavily, "whoever Jeremy's father is, it sure as hell isn't me."

TWO HOURS LATER, Luke was back in Laramie and still reeling from what he had discovered. He called Patricia Weatherby on his cell phone—learned all was fine with the girls—and asked for a little more time.

He drove over to John and Lilah McCabe's ranch. He knew as soon as they ushered him in that he was interrupting something important. They had paperwork scattered across the kitchen table and a laptop computer plugged into the phone line. "I should have called first," Luke apologized.

"Nonsense. We're just doing the paperwork for our trip to Central America in a few weeks. We're doing medical relief there."

Luke hadn't known. "That's wonderful," he said as he pulled up a chair alongside them.

"What's up?" John asked, as ready to help as ever.

Luke drew a breath and worked to ease the tenseness of his muscles. "There's no way to broach this subject gracefully, so I'm just going to be blunt. I need to ask you a few questions in complete confidence, and they're really important, or believe me, I wouldn't be here right now, inquiring."

Lilah and John exchanged concerned glances. "Go ahead," John said as Lilah got up to pour them all some coffee.

"Was Meg Lockhart's son, Jeremy, born here in Laramie?"

"Yes." A quizzical expression on her face—clearly she didn't understand why Luke was asking—Lilah set a stoneware mug down in front of Luke and filled it to the brim. Then she topped off John's mug as well as her own.

"Was he born prematurely?" Luke forged on. "Say by about a month?"

Again Lilah and John exchanged looks that indicated they didn't want to be in the middle of this "situation" between Luke and Meg any more than Luke wanted them there. "I don't think that's a question you should be asking us," Lilah said finally, as she returned the glass carafe to the warmer and returned to her seat at the table. "Medical records are confidential."

"I know that. I also know I could get the answer easily enough by asking around town. And I don't want to do that. I figure enough eyebrows have been raised regarding Jeremy's paternity as it is."

Abruptly John McCabe looked as protective as any parent. "Have you asked Meg these questions?"

Luke nodded grimly. "I talked to her about Jeremy's paternity yesterday. She was evasive, to say the least."

John rubbed his jaw and continued to regard Luke thoughtfully. "And yet you still think this is your business?"

Luke took a sip of Lilah's hot, delicious coffee. "If Jeremy was born prematurely, it is."

John and Lilah exchanged troubled glances. "You're saying you two...that Jeremy might be...?"

Luke sighed and shoved a hand through his hair. "Meg and I got to be very good friends when she was doing graduate work in Chicago. It was a strictly platonic relationship because we were both romantically involved with other people—except for the night her parents were killed. That night pretty much ended our friendship, at least as far as Meg was concerned."

John and Lilah looked at each other again, sighed and linked hands. "This explains a lot," Lilah said eventually. "Like why Meg was so upset when she learned John had met you at a medical conference and recruited you to take over for him. And why she's been ducking you ever since.''

"I wouldn't be asking you this if it weren't very important to Jeremy, Meg and me." Luke went on to explain about Jeremy's running away the previous evening. "Despite Meg's denials to the contrary, I assumed by Jeremy's birth date that his father was Meg's former boyfriend, Kip Brewster. I know Kip. I know Kip can be a little arrogant or over-the-top at times when it comes to getting what he wants, but I also knew he would want to take responsibility for his son, if he knew about him. But I just got back from talking to Kip. He says it's not him—he never slept with her. If it wasn't him…'' He paused before stating, "I know Meg."

She was not, had never been, promiscuous. She wouldn't have slept with someone on the spur of the moment under normal circumstances. The only reason they had been together that way was that she had just found out her parents had died, and she was out of her mind with grief. Helpless to do anything about the circumstances that had robbed Meg and her sisters of their parents, helpless to get Meg back to Texas any sooner than the first flight out the following morning, Luke had been desperate to just get her through the night and comfort Meg in any way she wanted or needed. It had only been later, after they'd experienced such mind-blowing passion, that Luke had discovered that hot, ardent lovemaking hadn't been what Meg wanted or needed, at least not on any rational level. Rather than lessen her despair, he had added to it.

"I know she is the kind of person who gives help, not the kind of person who asks for it," Luke continued. He was determined to help Meg now in the gallant way he should have helped her before, even if it meant marrying her so Jeremy could have both a mother and a father. "If I am the father, she probably thought—back then—that because I was engaged to someone else, she was doing the right thing in not telling me. But she's not. Not anymore. Not when her son wants answers so badly he's resorted to asking anyone and everyone he thinks might know something. Whether Meg wants to admit it or not, the situation is only going to get worse until she levels with Jeremy and tells him who his father is."

"Have you come right out and asked Meg if you're Jeremy's father?" Lilah asked.

Luke thought back to what had actually been said initially. "I asked her what Jeremy's birth date was. She told me. And that seemed to eliminate me. Now I'm not so sure."

"So she never actually said you weren't Jeremy's father," John determined.

"No." Luke rubbed the tense muscles at the back of his neck. "I asked her point-blank who Jeremy's father was but she refused to answer the question directly. And instead, talked about making a series of mistakes that couldn't be undone."

"So she could still be talking about you," John theorized bluntly, quickly realizing what Luke was getting at.

"If Jeremy was born prematurely, yes, then Jeremy could very well be my son." Luke waited, hoping they would reveal what he needed to know. To his disappointment they didn't.

"I understand what you want us to tell you, but…you really should get this kind of information from Meg," Lilah said.

Luke had been afraid they'd have this reaction. "And if Meg still won't tell me?"

John shrugged and exchanged a long, thoughtful glance with his wife before advising, "Then you wait until she trusts you enough to do so."

Luke sighed unhappily. "That might never happen." Which left him with even fewer options—find out on his own by whatever means necessary if Jeremy had been born prematurely or hire an attorney and demand a paternity test. Neither option appealed to him. More important, neither option was something Meg was likely to condone. Feeling more frustrated and shut out than ever, Luke knotted his hands into fists and shoved them in his pockets.

"We understand how you feel," Lilah said gently. She reached over and patted his hand. "We've tried to get Meg to unburden herself to us. Or at least to do right by Jeremy's father and tell him about his son. For a while I thought we had succeeded, because a few weeks after she learned she was pregnant she went off, determined to tell him."

Luke's hopes mingled with the fear that he wasn't the only person Meg turned to in her grief and her need...fear that he might not be Jeremy's father after all. "And?"

Lilah sighed. "Meg never said what happened when she returned, but it was easy to see she was absolutely devastated by whatever had transpired while she'd been gone."

Luke's heart thudded heavily in his chest. "You think Jeremy's father abandoned her?"

"That was our guess. In any case Meg told us then that she was going to bring up Jeremy on her own. She didn't want to do it that way, but she had no choice. We told her we would always support her, and we have."

"Meg never came to talk to me," Luke said, sad to realize all over again that he might not be Jeremy's father after all. "If she had...you have to know I would have been there for her and for Jeremy.'' It wouldn't have taken a baby to get him to marry her, either. All Meg would have had to do was give him the slightest sign that they had a chance to be together, and he would have waited for her forever. As it was, seeing no reason to hurt Gwyneth with the truth, he'd broken off his engagement to Gwyneth without a decent explanation, hurting her unconscionably. And only following through on his promise and marrying her six months later because she was still so devastated and determined to wait for him, and he didn't want to be responsible for ruining Gwyneth's life, too. The bitter irony of it being, of course, that he had ended up more or less ruining Gwyneth's life anyway, despite his efforts to be the best husband and father to their children he could possibly be.

"I don't want to hurt Meg," Luke said, meaning it with all his heart.

"Then be there for her now," Lilah said gently.

John nodded. "Be her friend."

The problem was, Luke thought, he wanted so much more than that where Meg was concerned. He always had. Always would.

Chapter Three

Monday morning, unable to shake the suspicion that Jeremy was his son, that Meg just wasn't telling him, Luke sat in front of the hospital computer in his office staring at the screen. As a physician on staff, he could access all patient files with the push of a button. It would be as easy as that to find Meg's medical records and discover not just if Jeremy was born prematurely, but also the estimated date of Jeremy's conception. He could learn Jeremy's and Meg's blood types and match them up against his. With that knowledge he could swiftly either confirm his paternity or eliminate himself completely.

But it would be wrong to violate Meg's privacy that way, Luke thought as he went back to the new-patient files he was supposed to be reviewing. It would be a breach of the medical ethics Luke had sworn to uphold. And Luke could not do that. No matter how much he wanted to know the truth.

''You didn't go to Meg and ask her those questions we talked about, did you?'' John McCabe asked Luke as he walked in several minutes later for their scheduled meeting.

Luke looked at the man he would be replacing as chief of family medicine. John McCabe had come over to make sure the transfer of patient files was complete and discuss the particularly difficult cases so Luke could start seeing patients later in the week. Luke was glad for the help and any wisdom John could impart about the patients Luke would now be caring for in John's stead. He just wished John McCabe weren't so efficient at sizing up his mood.

"No, I didn't." Unable to completely hide his frustration, Luke closed the folder in front of him and sighed. "How did you know?"

Clad in a sport shirt, slacks and casual boots that fit his newly retired status, John sat down opposite Luke. He laid his Stetson across his knee. "Because I saw Meg a few minutes ago, down in the emergency room, and she looked fine. If you'd asked her what you asked Lilah and me and told her you'd been to see her ex-boyfriend, well, I figure she'd be looking as troubled as you do now."

Luke frowned and turned a brooding glance to John. "I meant to confront her. I wanted to."

John looked momentarily concerned. "Then why didn't you?"

Luke sat back in his swivel chair and braced both palms against the edge of his desk. Feeling more tense and frustrated than ever, he recounted the events of the weekend. "By the time I got home Friday evening all her sisters were there. There was zero chance to talk to Meg privately. As the evening wore on, I had my hands full with my girls. Meg and Jeremy were gone all day Saturday and Sunday—where I don't know." Which had left him cooling his heels all weekend, still hoping he was a father to the son he had always wanted—a son who needed him desperately—yet unable to do anything to confirm or refute it without Meg's help, which she was unlikely to give.

John settled back with a sigh. "Meg spoke at a nursing

conference in Dallas over the weekend. She took Jeremy with her, and they spent the rest of the weekend going to Six Flags and the big water parks there.''

Glad to have that mystery solved, Luke nodded thoughtfully, then woefully continued his recounting. ''By the time Meg and Jeremy got back last night, it was late, and I knew we both had to come into the hospital today, so...'' Luke spread his hands wide and let his voice trail off.

John's wise dark-brown eyes narrowed. ''You're having second thoughts about grilling her at all, aren't you?''

Luke shrugged, not sure what he wanted except maybe a life with Meg and his son. He'd already missed Meg's pregnancy and a good chunk of Jeremy's childhood. He didn't want to miss any more. And knowing what a delicate situation he was in if he was Jeremy's father—and he still hoped there was a chance he might be—he was afraid of screwing things up even more than they already were. Which was exactly what would happen if he pushed Meg too hard.

''The more I think about it, the more I think confronting her now with what I found out from Kip is a bad idea. She resents me enough as it is.'' *With good reason.* Guiltily Luke pushed on. ''I have to wait for the right time. I want her to get to know me again, wait until she trusts me and wait until the kids settle in, before I tell her I went to see Kip and I want her to confide in me.''

''Don't wait too long,'' John warned. ''Meg'll be angry if she finds out you've figured out for certain that Kip Brewster is not Jeremy's father and kept this from her.''

Luke scowled. He knew that was true. And it wasn't fair. ''How is this any different from her not telling me in the first place if I am Jeremy's father?'' he demanded irritably.

"It's not any different. A lie of omission is a lie just the same. But we don't know for certain that Jeremy is your child. Meg was very confused that summer. Upset. She made it clear to everyone that she made not just one but a whole series of mistakes."

I'd do anything if I could go back and do it all over...do it differently...but I can't. Meg had said. *And because I can't change things...I think it's best that I leave those mistakes in the past.* Had she been talking about their brief tryst? Luke wondered, upset. Or something...someone else? And would he ever know? If that really was the case, did he want to know?

All Luke knew for certain was that Meg was not only responsible to a fault, she was one of the most selfless people Luke knew. She was always the one giving help, whether it be as a nurse, a sister or a friend. She never asked for help for herself. But that didn't make what Meg had done right, either, in cutting not just Jeremy's father, whoever he was, out of her and Jeremy's lives, but Luke, as well. As a friend he could have helped her. Sure it would have been difficult if he wasn't Jeremy's father, but he had still loved her and wanted to be with her and they would have figured out a way to work everything out.

"In any case," John continued, oblivious to the direction of Luke's thoughts, "this situation is going to take very careful handling, Luke."

Wasn't that the case, Luke thought, as footsteps sounded in the adjacent waiting room. Seconds later, Kate Marten—the hospital's thirty-year-old grief-and-trauma counselor—rapped on the door to Luke's private office and popped her head in. Looking as pretty and capable as ever, she said, "John, one of your nephew's boys is down in the E.R. Apparently, Kevin—the six-year-old—fell off a porch roof into some bushes. His brothers rescued him and brought him in. They're all pretty shook up and they're asking for you."

"Where's Sam?" John asked, frowning. Both men rose simultaneously.

A baffled expression on her face, Kate lifted her hands and spread them wide. "According to Meg Lockhart, no one's been able to locate your nephew thus far. That's why they want you. They figure if anyone can track Sam down, you can. They want Luke, since he's now the family doc of record, to take a look at Kevin."

Together the three headed to the E.R. at a brisk clip.

"I don't know what we're going to do without you when you leave next fall," John McCabe told Kate affectionately.

"Where are you going?" Luke asked curiously.

John was quick to fill him in. "Kate's getting married to Major Craig Farrell. He's an air force pilot."

"Oh, yeah?" Luke held the elevator door for them. "When?"

Kate suddenly looked a little uneasy. She situated herself at the back of the elevator between John and Luke, while Luke pushed the button for the first floor. "We haven't set the wedding date yet." Kate smiled and turned her eyes to the closing doors. "But we will as soon as Craig knows when he can get leave."

"And after you marry?" Luke asked, seeming to recall someone telling him that Kate had spent her entire life—except college—right there in Laramie, first as a guidance counselor at the high school, where her dad still worked as the football coach, then as a crisis counselor at the hospital.

"Craig is career military," Kate elaborated as the elevator came to a stop. She continued casually as the doors opened and they headed out, "So he and I will go wherever he's stationed for the next twenty-five years. Then he's going to leave the service and work for a commercial airline—hopefully one based in Texas."

"Sounds like an adventure," Luke said as the trio continued making their way through the halls.

Kate smiled, a little less enthusiastically than Luke would have expected, and said nothing else. Clearly preferring not to talk any more about her personal life, Kate led the way around the corner, past a big sign advertising the hospital's annual chili cook-off, to the emergency room admitting area.

Four boys were gathered anxiously in the waiting room. The oldest looked like a senior in high school and was wearing running shoes and athletic clothes. The next tallest was dressed in neatly pressed khakis and a shirt— his hair was blow dried to perfection and he radiated expensive cologne. The third tallest was wearing trendy clothing and had an air of mischief about him. The youngest of the four standing out in the hall looked to be about twelve or so and wore glasses and clothes that could only be described as nerdy. All four boys rushed forward out into the hallway when they saw John McCabe. All spoke at once.

"You gotta do something, Uncle John! Kevin's bleeding!"

"I can't find Dad—I forget where he's supposed to be today."

"I know we were supposed to be baby-sitting him, but it wasn't our fault."

"No one told Kev he could go on the roof. Honest."

Immediately taking charge of the situation like the veteran doc and family man he was, John held up a hand. "I'll locate Sam. You see to Kevin," John told Luke.

"You four," John regarded his nephews sternly, "calm down, and don't go anywhere until I get back to you. Kate, maybe you'd like to stay out here with the boys?"

"Sure thing." Kate smiled.

Luke couldn't help but note Kate looked a lot more comfortable and enthusiastic about her professional duties than she had about her pending nuptials.

"C'mon boys." Kate herded them off to the waiting room sofas while Luke headed inside the examining room.

Meg was bending over Kevin, talking quietly, as she gently tended to lacerations on his face and arms. Although his face was streaked with tears, Kevin McCabe was no longer crying. Impressed by the tenderness Meg showed their young patient, Luke strode forward. "Hi, Kevin, I'm Dr. Luke. I heard you took a tumble this morning."

Kevin said nothing.

Noting the boy seemed alert and that his pupils were equal and responsive, Luke tried again to engage him in conversation. "Must have been something pretty important to get up on the roof. How'd you get up there, anyway?" Luke continued, noting Kevin's pulse and blood pressure were okay.

His face registering no emotion, Kevin turned his glance away. Luke looked at Meg. "Has he been talking since he arrived?"

"Not a word, but apparently that's not unusual." Meg's voice was calm but her expression radiated concern. "His brothers said he hasn't talked much since his mother, Ellie, died, six months ago."

Luke continued his examination. To his relief he found no evidence of any neurological, internal or permanent injuries. "Okay, Kevin," Luke smiled down at him, "you just take it easy. We're going to get you fixed right up."

To Meg he said, "I want to get his right wrist X-rayed. I think it's just a sprain but let's be sure. We're going to need some stitches here on his forehead. And he's got some pretty nasty abrasions on his arms and legs. Let's get some antibiotic ointment on them."

Meg nodded. She was already preparing the suture tray. "No problem. Stitches first?"

Luke put the immobilizer back around Kevin's wrist. "Yes."

Meg smiled down at Kevin, squeezed his uninjured left hand. "You just hold on to me. This will all be over before you know it."

With Luke and Meg both working to put their young patient at ease, Kevin weathered the procedures well.

Luke left Kevin with Meg and was looking at the X rays of Kevin's wrist when Sam McCabe finally arrived. The successful Texas businessman bore a striking physical resemblance to the rest of the McCabe men. But Luke thought he looked awfully young—he guessed mid-thirties—to be widowed and the father of five boys, a few of whom would soon graduate from high school. Luke knew how tough it had been on him and his three girls when Gwyneth died. Judging from the looks of things, for Sam McCabe and his five boys it had been even tougher.

Sam looked harried and upset as he stopped briefly at the admitting desk, then strode toward Luke. "How's Kevin?" Sam demanded, concern etched on his face.

Briefly Luke explained. "We had to put seven stitches in a cut on his forehead. He's probably going to have a little scar, but it's right at the scalp line so it won't show, unless someone is really looking for it. He's got a sprained left wrist and some nasty abrasions on his arms and legs that are going to require a bit of care for a few days. But other than that he's one lucky kid, considering the kind of injuries that could have occurred if his fall hadn't been broken by those shrubs.''

"Thank God for that," Sam McCabe sighed, the shadows of fatigue around his eyes becoming even more pronounced.

Luke led Sam down the hall toward the examining room. "Initially," Luke continued, casually filling Sam in, "we had a little trouble evaluating him, since none of us could get Kevin to say a word."

Looking all the more anxious and upset, Sam shrugged off Luke's concern with a tired sigh. "That's not unusual. Kev hasn't talked much to anyone since Ellie died."

"Has he seen anyone about that?" Luke asked, as they rounded the corner.

"He'll be fine," Sam replied curtly, looking irritated at Luke for even bringing it up. "Kev just needs some time. Can I see him now?"

"Sure." Luke led the way into the exam room. Despite the attention he was getting from Meg, as well as John and Lilah McCabe, Kevin looked very happy to see his dad. The two hugged. "You gave me quite a scare," Sam told his youngest son, still holding him close. "I'm glad you're okay."

Kevin clung to Sam. Tears trembled on his lashes, but again he didn't speak.

Luke gave them a moment more, then, interceding gently, said, "Kev. I need to borrow your dad for a minute. Maybe while we're talking, your uncle John and aunt Lilah can get a special 'patient' teddy bear for you to take home with you."

Sam hugged Kev again, reassuring him gently, then Sam and Luke stepped out into the corridor. Luke knew what he was going to say was not going to be welcome—

nevertheless it had to be said. "Part of my job, as your new family physician, is to treat the whole family."

"You're concerned about how the accident happened," Sam guessed.

Luke nodded.

"I am, too," Sam said grimly. "Do you know where the rest of my boys are?"

"In a conference room down the hall, with Kate Marten, the hospital counselor." Luke led the way. To his surprise he found the boys, sans counselor. "Where's Kate?"

"She had an emergency with one of the oncology patients or something," murmured the next-to-youngest boy. "She said she'd be back in a minute." Meanwhile, all four of Sam's boys' glances were directly on Sam, who didn't waste a second laying into the rest of his brood.

"Someone want to tell me what was Kevin doing on the roof this morning?" he demanded.

"Don't ask me," the oldest son said with an irritated scowl. He aimed a thumb at his three brothers. "They were supposed to be watching him. I was out running."

Sam turned to the younger three. They all spoke at once, pointing the finger at each other. "Brad was on the phone with both of his girlfriends, trying to keep them from finding out about each other."

"Lewis was on the computer, playing some dumb game as usual."

"Riley was practicing his trumpet, really loud."

"And what about Kevin?" Sam demanded impatiently. "Who was supposed to be watching him?"

A guilty silence fell.

"You're telling me that there were three of you home and not a one of you saw him go out on the roof?" Sam demanded incredulously.

They all looked at each other and shrugged, then shook their heads.

Sam's mouth thinned. "Well, so much for being able to do without a housekeeper for the rest of the summer," he said grimly.

"Dad..."

Sam held up a hand, silencing them all with a stern look. "I don't want to hear it. You boys had your chance and you blew it. You're not going to be left on your own again." Sam locked eyes with all his boys, then turned back to Luke. "Is Kevin ready to go home?"

"Yes, but I think Kate Marten would like to talk to you before you go." In fact, Luke had asked her to do so.

"Some other time," Sam countered brusquely, then went off to collect his son Kevin and the rest of his boys.

Luke went into the examining room, where Meg was cleaning up in preparation for the next patient. Maybe it was because they were in a medical setting, but she seemed a lot more approachable to him than she had the last time they'd talked, after her son had run away from home. Luke lounged against the wall and folded his arms in front of him. "Did Kevin say anything to you while I was talking to Sam?"

"No," Meg replied worriedly, as she put a fresh sheet on the gurney. "And he didn't speak to John and Lilah, either, although he smiled at them kind of wanly from time to time."

Luke watched her make the corners, hospital style. "I think that whether Sam wants to admit it or not, his family is in trouble."

Finished, Meg straightened. She was wearing loose-fitting blue scrub pants with an elastic waist and a snug-fitting white T-shirt. A multicolored nurse's smock over that. Her auburn hair was caught in a clip on the back of her head, and she looked pretty in a healthy, all-American-woman sort of way.

"I totally agree with you," she said.

Steeling himself against his inevitable reaction—he couldn't be close to her like this, alone with her like this, without wanting to make her his all over again—Luke lounged against the wall and tucked his thumbs in the belt loops on either side of his fly. "I'd like to get all of them in for counseling with Kate Marten as soon as possible."

Meg edged closer, inundating him with the scent of her alluring perfume. "Not much chance of that."

"Why not?" Luke asked, wishing he already knew the people in the community as well as Meg did.

Meg shrugged and tucked her hands in the pockets of her smock. A rueful slant to her lips, she tilted her head up to his. "Sam doesn't believe in counseling. He thinks a family should solve its own problems."

Knowing Meg felt that way, too—at least when it came to her and Jeremy—Luke searched Meg's aqua eyes. "Sam admits there are some problems, then?"

"Oh, yeah." Meg rolled her eyes, as if Luke had just made the understatement of the year. She leaned forward slightly and her voice dropped to a confiding murmur, "That's supposedly why Sam moved back to Laramie in the first place, because he was having trouble riding herd on his boys in Dallas. He decided it would be easier to keep track of them here. He and Ellie spent their childhoods here, and he had the big house where he grew up that he had inherited from his folks. And the kids had fond memories of the town—they used to spend part of their summers and all their holidays here when their mom was alive."

Appreciating being able to talk to Meg so openly and intimately, Luke took a moment to absorb all that. "What happened to Sam's wife?'' He regarded Meg steadily, aware that because she was a local girl Meg probably had been friends with her. "Do you know?"

Sadness filled Meg's eyes. "Cancer. She wasn't sick all that long—it hit her hard and fast. By the time it was discovered, there wasn't a whole lot the doctors could do."

Luke let out a breath slowly as he thought about how hard that must have been for Sam McCabe and his entire family. Seeing the sorrow on Meg's face, it was all he could do not to take her in his arms and hold her until the pain went away. He touched her wrist gently. "I'm sorry."

"Yeah." Meg nodded, commiserating wistfully. "Everyone who knows them was, too. Ellie was a wonderful woman. Sam had loved her since they were in their teens, and her boys adored her, too."

Luke empathized. He knew what it was like for him when his wife had died. "Even more reason for them to get into some sort of grief counseling," he said, as Meg replaced an unopened gauze pad back in the appropriate container.

Meg folded up the blood pressure cuff and put it in the holder on the wall. "You think they're acting up as a way of acting out their grief?"

Luke nodded, commiserating. "I don't know what I would have done after Gwyneth died if Becca and Susie hadn't been able to go to the grief group for preschoolers, back in California."

"It helped?"

Luke's mood turned pensive as he recalled that difficult time. "Becca and Susie were only three and four at the time, but just because they were young doesn't mean they didn't feel the loss of their mother intensely. They were so sad and angry. They acted out all the time. Everything was a battle or a crisis or cause for a giant-size temper tantrum. No one could handle them, least of all me. Amy was just one—and I could soothe her with a lot of extra cuddling. But as time went on it became clear that Susie and Becca needed more specific help. They needed to be around other kids who'd also lost a parent, and talk with someone trained to help them. Becca and Susie went every week for six months.''

Meg regarded him admiringly, the easy intimacy between them reminding Luke of a time when they'd been fast friends and he hadn't had to pry every last little bit of information from her. A time when she had come to him readily and volunteered with amazing frankness what was in her heart and on her mind most of the time. ''Did you go?'' Meg asked eventually, her eyes softening all the more.

''With them, when it was appropriate,'' Luke said.

''But not by yourself,'' Meg ascertained quietly, still looking as if she were struggling to comprehend all he and his girls had been through.

Luke shrugged, able to tell from the look in her eyes that Meg felt he should have gone to counseling, too. But he knew it hadn't been necessary. ''I had a handle on things,'' he said.

''Still,'' Meg persisted cautiously, searching his face and working for some greater, more-in-depth understanding of those years of his life, ''it must have been hard on you, losing Gwyneth so suddenly and tragically.''

''Yeah.'' Luke sighed, not ashamed to admit how much and how openly he had grieved. ''It was.''

''Do you miss being married?'' she asked, almost shyly.

His heart thudding at her nearness, Luke gave Meg another exceedingly straightforward look. "There's a lot to be said for having a partner, for having companionship, for not having to go through everything alone." He hoped Meg would realize that soon, too, with his help.

Meg's lips curved as she studied him skeptically. "That sounds as if you want to get married again."

"I do," Luke admitted readily. He watched as Meg finished putting the treatment room to rights. "I know my girls would be a lot happier, having a mom again. And the idea of spending the rest of my life alone doesn't appeal to me at all." Luke gave her a moment to think about that, then looked at Meg inquisitively. "What about you? Do you regret not marrying?"

For a moment Luke thought she was going to say she did. But, as always, the moment passed without Meg confiding in him completely. "I would never marry just to give Jeremy a father," she said firmly, turning her glance away. "The only reason two people should ever get married is because they're head-over-heels in love," Meg continued, clamping her arms together in front of her. "To marry for anything less and risk an eventual divorce and all the hurt that goes with that is irresponsible."

"I agree with you there," Luke said. He knew firsthand what happened when the two people involved didn't love each other the way they should. He knew how the adults and the kids could suffer when the trust and communication between a husband and wife was less than what it should be. "Love is very important." Luke looked at Meg steadily. "As is friendship and companionship."

"I'm not sure I'd like being married, anyway," Meg said cavalierly. Uncomfortable with the turn the conversation had taken, she paced the treatment room restlessly, checking to make sure everything was precisely as it should be. "I'm so used to handling everything on my own." Finding her work was done, she headed for the door.

Luke followed Meg out into the hall where, for the moment, everything was quiet. "Oh, I don't know, Meg," Luke teased, unable to resist. "You might be surprised. If you were to give it a try, you might find you like marriage more than you think."

Meg rolled her eyes as if to say, Yeah, right. "I'll think about it...one of these days. Meantime I've got to go to the day care center." Meg checked her watch. "I promised Jeremy I'd have lunch with him today."

"I'll go with you." Thinking how great it was going to be to see Meg and Jeremy frequently, both at home and on the job, Luke fell into step beside her. Meg might not know it yet, but given a few more one-on-ones like this and soon their friendship would be back on track and as intimate as ever. Once that happened, Luke decided, it would be easy to put the mistakes of the past behind them and woo her the way he had wanted to—should have—from the first. Once Meg understood how much Luke had always cared about her and always would, the rest—reclaiming Meg as his friend and lover—would be simple indeed. Meanwhile Luke was going to have to be patient and take it one step at a time. If he wanted Meg to be able to trust him enough to tell him the truth about her son, if he wanted Meg to be able to trust him enough to come to him with her problems, whatever they were, if he wanted to be there for Meg and her son in a way he never had before, he couldn't afford any mistakes.

"I promised to have lunch with the girls, too," he continued, slanting Meg an affable glance. "That's one of the perks of working here."

"I'll second that." Meg gave him a relaxed, confident grin. The role of doting mom was one she loved and knew

well. Together they headed for the day care center. By
the time they walked in, the children were already seated
at tables. Lunch bags were being passed out. Luke was
pleased to see that Jeremy was fine with his. Amy—his
youngest—also seemed quite content. But Luke's other
two daughters were very unhappy.

Chapter Four

"What's wrong?" Meg asked as she and Luke joined his three girls and her son, Jeremy, at their lunch table.

Susie scowled as she looked glumly at the contents of her lunch box. "We all have peanut butter sandwiches today."

Becca sent Luke a disgruntled look. Then, turning back to Meg, she explained, "Yeah, and me and Susie don't like peanut butter. Only Amy likes peanut butter sandwiches."

Which, Meg thought, explained why Amy looked so happy while her two sisters were glum as could be.

"Now, girls, we talked about this earlier," Luke chided gently, encompassing all three of his daughters with an affectionate glance. "We're going to take turns," he reminded them, all knees and elbows, as he tried to fit his tall, muscular frame into the child-size chair. "We're having cheese sandwiches, which are Becca's favorite, tomorrow, and ham sandwiches, which are Susie's favorite, the next day. Then we'll start all over with peanut butter and go through the same rotation."

Not the least bit appeased by Luke's promise, Susie propped her elbow on the table and draped her body sideways over her chair. She eyed Jeremy thoughtfully, then began to smile, slowly and winsomely. "What kind of sandwich do you have, Jeremy?"

Jeremy shrugged, already shoving his favorite lunch-time concoction toward his mouth. "The same kind I always get. Apple, raisin and peanut butter," Jeremy said.

Susie frowned. Apparently that wasn't on her list of acceptable items, either. Wanting to change the subject before a full-blown temper tantrum occurred, Meg smiled. "I've got turkey, swiss and lettuce with mustard," Meg said. She looked over at Luke and caught his grateful look, "What do you have?"

"Peanut butter," Luke said as if that were his first choice. Meg could tell it wasn't. He and the girls all had applesauce and miniature carrot sticks. Thermoses of milk for them. Bottled water for him.

Susie reluctantly took a bite of her sandwich, sighed loudly, then chewed it as if it were sawdust. Narrowing her eyes thoughtfully, she looked at Jeremy. "Do you always get to eat what you want for lunch?"

"Yeah."

Her lips puckered into a pout, Susie picked off the bread crust in peanut-butter-smeared pinches and dropped it onto the table in front of her. "How come you and your mom don't hafta eat the same thing?"

Jeremy looked at Susie like that was the craziest question he'd ever heard. "Because she makes what she wants for her and what I want for me the night before, that's why."

All three girls turned to look at Luke accusingly. Luke turned to Meg and gave her a droll, thanks-for-raising-the-bar look before addressing the entire group. "First of all, we're new at this. We never had to pack lunches in California—the girls ate at home with their sitter. Second, that sounds like an awful lot of extra work to me."

Typical man, Meg thought.

"Yeah, but, Daddy, we'd be so much happier," Susie said, batting her eyelashes at her daddy hopefully.

"We could even make our own sam-wiches," Becca explained seriously, eager to convince Luke it was in all their best interest to come to some sort of compromise. "It's not even that hard, Daddy, exceptin' you'd have to cut 'em."

Luke's broad shoulders tensed beneath the soft cotton fabric of his shirt. He looked tired and overwhelmed. Feelings Meg knew only too well. Being a single parent was not easy under the best of circumstances. Luke had a new house, a new job, no family to lean on or help out and three little girls to care for. As they all struggled to adjust to the move from California to Texas, he had to be feeling the heat. Knowing that, Meg's heart went out to all of them. Maybe it was because she was a nurse, or maybe she was a nurse because of it, but she never had been able to turn away from people in need.

"I'll take it under advisement," Luke promised finally.

Susie uttered a beleaguered sigh and turned to Meg with palpable sadness, "That's what he always says when we ask him to make chicken noodle casserole the way Mommy used to make."

"Which means," Becca chimed in informatively, looking just as forlorn as her older sister and just as eager for some commiseration from Meg, "it's prob-lee not goin' to hap'n, either."

Luke's highly exasperated expression said this was an old argument, one he was getting tired of having. "I've explained to you girls that I would be happy to make chicken noodle casserole if I knew how. I just don't know how to make it."

Meg wondered what the girls were talking about. Off-hand, she didn't know of any casseroles made with chicken noodle soup, though she supposed there were some. "You don't have a recipe?" she asked above the chatter of the other kids—and their parents—eating lunch together in the center.

Luke shook his head. "Gwyneth had two dozen cookbooks. I've been through every single one of them, and none of them have a chicken noodle casserole."

Telling herself to stop noticing how touchable and soft and clean his sandy-blond hair looked—never mind how good he smelled, like rain-drenched woods—Meg sat back in her chair and theorized helpfully. "Maybe it's not called that. Maybe it's chicken fettuccine or chicken tetrazzini, something like that."

Luke made a face and threw up his hands, looking just as lost as before. "How would I know?"

"By doing a little detective work," Meg replied as she reassured herself that his cluelessness in this matter was not simply a ploy to spend more time with her, or discover the secrets she had sworn she would keep until Jeremy was old enough and secure enough to handle them. Because whether Luke knew it or not, he had enough to handle just settling into his new job and helping his girls adjust to the move to Texas without taking on her problems as well.

Meg looked at Becca's and Susie's mostly uneaten sandwiches. "I'll make a deal with you girls. You eat your lunch today—sandwiches and all—and maybe you can come over to our house tonight, and we can do some detective work and try to figure out what was in the chicken noodle casserole." That was the least she could do for Luke, given the way he had helped her with Jeremy the other night.

Immediately all three girls' faces shone with hope and

relief. "Then will you make it for us?" Becca asked excitedly.

Meg had only expected to provide Luke with a recipe he could make himself. But now that the suggestion was out there, she found she wasn't opposed to the idea of all six of them having dinner together. In fact, it sounded like a good idea. She wanted Luke to think of them as friends and neighbors and nothing else.

She shot a tentative glance at Luke, who gave her permission with a nod. "Sure," Meg turned back to the girls with a relieved smile and a glimmer of excitement about the evening ahead. "But you have to do your part, too. You have to eat your sandwiches now. And then help me with the detective work later. Deal?" She held out a palm.

Amy, Becca and Susie slapped her hand in turn. "Deal."

"THANKS FOR HAVING US over to dinner," Luke said hours later as he and Meg cleaned up the dishes while the kids played outside on Jeremy's swing set. Looking more California surfer boy than native Texan and father of three, in a pair of loose-fitting khaki cargo shorts and an olive-green polo shirt, Luke carried a stack of plates over to the double sink. He opened the dishwasher and gave her an appreciative grin. "I haven't seen them eat this much at one sitting for a long time."

"What can I say?" Mocking his glib tone to a T, Meg smiled. "They really like chicken tetrazzini." Deciding she'd better keep her mind on the dishes, if she didn't want this to start feeling like a date, which it most certainly wasn't, Meg forced her eyes away from the rippling muscles and enticingly masculine swirls of golden hair on his arms and legs. Noticing that Luke was having a little trouble figuring out how to load the plates—always a problem with an unfamiliar dishwasher—Meg stepped in to lend a hand. She took the plate from him and slid it into the bottom rack, facing the middle. "How did it compare to Gwyneth's recipe?"

Luke stepped back, watching closely and noting where Meg slid the salad bowls. "I have no idea. I can't recall ever eating any she made."

"You're kidding." Meg paused to glance at Luke. "The girls said she made it all the time."

Luke shrugged. "She probably did. The problem was, I was rarely home to eat with Gwyneth and the girls. Early in my residency I had all those thirty-six-hour shifts at the hospital, and then later, when those shifts eased up, I was moonlighting as much as possible to help bring in money to support the family."

Meg could imagine how tough that had been—for all of them. "So you didn't just miss dinner, you were rarely home even to sleep."

Luke concentrated on gathering up all the cutlery and dropping it into the silverware basket. "Yeah."

Meg began loading the glasses. "How did Gwyneth feel about that?"

Luke's expression didn't change, but for a moment he tensed at Meg's question, and his eyes turned more brown than gold. The corners of his lips turning down slightly, Luke replied, "She wasn't one to complain. Maybe if she had..." His voice trailed off, his expression became one of unbearable regret and sorrow.

"What?" Meg asked softly, wondering what on earth a man like Luke could have to feel guilty about. It wasn't as if he had a choice about the hours—all residents worked terribly long hours. Following patients from their admission to the hospital through the first critical hours of diagnosis and treatment was how they learned. Gwyneth, whose mother had suffered a long, debilitating illness and many complications and hospital stays, would have understood that better than most. Gwyneth had made no secret of the fact that one of the things she'd loved most about Luke was that he was a doctor.

"Nothing." Luke shook off the mood and went to retrieve the empty casserole dish from the stove top. He plugged one half of the double sink and filled it with hot, soapy water. "Listen, I'm having the exterior of our house painted, and I wanted to talk to you about the color."

Meg had been hoping whoever bought the house next door would get it painted as soon as possible—having one unkempt house made the whole block look bad. "Are you keeping it the same color?"

Luke rolled his eyes. "Lavender with deep-purple trim and dark-green shutters? I don't think so." Luke grabbed a scrubber sponge and worked on the burned-on food around the edges of the casserole dish. "No, I want something that will be as stately as our turn-of-the-century Cape Cod deserves."

So far so good, Meg thought. "What'd you have in mind?" Edging in beside Luke, Meg dipped a cloth in the hot soapy water. Being careful not to touch him, she wrung the excess water out of the cloth, then began wiping up the table and countertops.

"That's what I need to talk to you about." Luke examined the glass casserole dish, found it still needed more work and submerged it in the hot sudsy water once again. "The girls really like what you've done with yours in terms of color. And they wanted to know if our house could be painted pale-yellow with evergreen trim, too. I wouldn't even suggest it, if the two homes weren't side by side and architecturally linked." Luke regarded her thoughtfully, clearly not wanting to offend. "We could easily go with white and dark-green trim."

"Except there are already five other large white homes out of the ten homes on our block."

"Right. And I wanted something more distinctive that also wouldn't clash with yours, colorwise. That could be tough, since our homes sit so close together."

"I remember what our places looked like when I was a kid—before it got broken up and sold as two different residences. I hate to say it but both houses did look a lot better when they were painted the same color."

"That's what I thought when the real estate agent showed me pictures, but I didn't know how you'd feel."

It wasn't as if he were trying to link their lives or even their properties, Meg thought. He was just trying to return his house to its former dignity in a move that would end up, ultimately, enhancing both their property values. How could she disagree with that? Meg smiled. "Go with the yellow paint and green trim then. It won't bother me."

"You're sure?" Luke rinsed the casserole dish and set it in the rack to drain. He reached for the salad bowl and washed that by hand, too. "Painting our homes, which are already side by side, the same color could cause a lot of talk." He slanted her a warning glance. "People might make more of it than me trying to please my girls."

Meg's spirits tumbled as she realized Luke really wasn't trying to join both their lives in either a symbolic or a pragmatic sense. Telling herself she should feel relieved, not disappointed to find his motive squared so well with hers, Meg forced a smile as she got out the broom and the dustpan and began sweeping up the crumbs on the floor. She had wanted them to be friends, nothing more. It sounded as if she had gotten her wish.

"And speaking of making the girls happy, I have a

suggestion for you about their lunches,'' Meg said as she finished sweeping up, then put the broom and dustpan away. ''Why not give them the sandwich of their choice every day?''

Luke glanced out the kitchen window to make sure the kids were still playing happily. Satisfied all was well, he turned back to her, and let his glance skim approvingly over her trim walking shorts and sleeveless blouse, before returning leisurely to her face. ''Because it's hard enough to make all their sandwiches in the morning, without trying to do several different kinds all at once.''

Meg lounged against the counter opposite him. Determined to make him see reason on this one issue, even if it meant he'd be annoyed with her for a little while, she folded her arms in front of her decisively. ''Then do what Jeremy and I do—make their lunches the evening before and have the girls help you. They are old enough to help out a little, and it'll make them a lot happier. And it'll probably mean their lunches will get eaten even if you're not there sitting with them and making them do it.''

''You think it's that important?'' he asked casually.

Meg nodded. Otherwise she wouldn't be bringing it up. ''Kids want to know their opinions are heard and that their individuality counts for something.''

Luke lifted his brow as he scanned her from head to toe. ''Speaking from experience?''

Aware she was becoming more conscious of Luke with every second that passed, Meg struggled to explain what her childhood had been like. ''My parents were big on streamlining our lives, too,'' she said gently. ''There were practical reasons for that, of course. There were four of us girls, and my dad was busy running the ranch, and my mom worked in town as a teacher. But I have to tell you, Luke, as silly as it may seem to you and me now, as a kid there were times when I really resented us all having to wear the same brand of shoes or the same style clothes. Or eat peanut butter sandwiches in our school lunches, just because it was easier. And when it came to lunches we always had the same thing—peanut butter—because it was cheap and my mom didn't have to worry about it spoiling in the Texas heat."

"You didn't make your own school lunches?"

Meg shook her head. "Mom preferred to do that for us."

"Because it was easier," Luke guessed.

"Yeah."

"And it left you feeling...?"

"Regimented and frustrated—because they always wanted to do everything the same for all four of us and wanted us to do everything the same, too. We all had to take piano lessons and learn to sew and cook and clean. We all had to help my dad on the ranch and Mom inside the house, even though Kelsey was the only one who enjoyed working with the cattle and the horses and I was the only one who really liked domestic stuff."

"And yet you and your sisters all turned out to be so different," Luke noted, bringing up the fact that Dani had grown up to be a film critic, Jenna a dress designer and Kelsey a lady rancher.

"Exactly the point," Meg said proudly. "My sisters and I all are unique. And so are your girls."

Luke grinned, getting the hint. "Meaning I should start letting them express their individuality a little more."

Meg shrugged, aware it wasn't up to her to tell him how to parent, only to make him aware—as one single parent to another—there was more than one way to do things. "It'd make for happier lunchtimes, among other things," she suggested.

"Okay." Luke sent her a winning smile and continued to regard her with a contemplative manner that did things it shouldn't have to her pulse. "I'll institute a new lunch policy, starting tonight."

Meg suddenly realized, as her heart took on a slow, thudding beat, there were other things he would like to start again tonight, as well. Deciding they had been in here alone, talking intimately, long enough, Meg smiled back at him and breezed past him on rubbery legs, heading for the door and the safety of the clamor in the backyard. Luke caught her hand as she passed him. Ignoring her swift intake of breath, without saying a word, he reeled her ever so deliberately back to his side. Before Meg could move out of range, Luke had taken her into his arms and shifted her, so her back was to the counter. Eyes locked with hers, he looked at her with a distinctly male, distinctly sensual interest.

Unwilling to go further, unable to hold back, Meg clutched at the soft fabric of his shirt and reclaimed her space with a tilt of her head. "Luke..."

"What...?" His lips forged a burning path across her cheek, down her neck, until it was all she could do to continue to resist.

Her knees weakening, her heart pounding like a jackhammer in her chest, Meg splayed her hands across the solid wall of his chest and met his warm, compelling gaze. Much more of this, she thought as he guided her closer by slow degrees, and her head really would begin to spin. "The kids..." she murmured helplessly, feeling the impact of their attraction all the way to her toes.

"...are outside playing," he said, his hands tracing the curves of her shoulders, caressing her bare arms.

"Even so..." Meg moaned, being cautious not to get

too close. She was breathless and couldn't keep her glance from falling to his lips.

"I know exactly what you're thinking," Luke murmured as he rubbed his thumb across her lower lip, then tunneled his hands through the silk of her hair and tilted her face up to his. His eyes darkened seductively. His voice became as soft and encouraging as his smile. "Why ruin the good friendship we're on our way to recapturing with something as volatile and unpredictable as romance?" He rubbed his thumbs across her cheek, tracing the delicate shape. "But darned if I don't find myself wanting to kiss you again, anyway," he confessed wistfully, shaking his head. "Just to see if it's as good as I remember."

His intention stated, he bent his head and kissed her, long and hard and deep, until desire flowed through her in waves. He kissed her until she clung to him and moaned softly and melted in his arms. And still it wasn't enough, Meg thought, as she wreathed her arms around his neck and met him more than halfway. It had been so long since she had felt like a woman, instead of just a mom. So long since she had been loved, touched, kissed, held. So long since she had wanted anything for just herself. But she wanted this, Meg thought, as she strained against him, engulfed by a wave of passion long held at bay. She wanted Luke. She wanted Luke to desire her. And that was something that might never change, Meg thought. Not that it mattered, given all the reasons they needed to stay apart, the least of which were the four children who stood to be very hurt if their effort to reignite their friendship did not work out.

"You see there?" Meg sputtered, struggling to hang on to her composure when at long last Luke let the lazy kiss come to a halt and they moved apart. "It was…"

"Even better." Grinning his contentment, Luke bent his head and kissed her again. And it was at that moment, when Meg was melting in his arms that the back door banged open, startling them both and bringing them to their senses.

"Are you two kissing?" Jeremy blurted out.

Luke kept Meg right where she was, trapped against the counter in his arms, as all four children skipped into the kitchen, one right after another. "As a matter of fact, we were," Luke said calmly.

"My mommy never kissed anyone before," Jeremy said, blinking hard as if he still couldn't believe his eyes.

The way Luke looked at her then made Meg flush to the roots of her hair. With as much dignity as possible she extricated herself from Luke's arms. "Jeremy, for heaven's sake. That is not the kind of information Luke needs to know!" Meg reprimanded firmly.

Jeremy shrugged and happily continued broadcasting what he knew. "Well, it's true," he blurted out. "I've never seen you kiss a guy before." He propped his hands on his hips, perplexed. "How come you're kissing him?"

MEG HAD NO ANSWER for Jeremy. So she used diversionary tactics, the way she always did when confronted with a sticky situation she couldn't handle. She did a very good job of distracting all four children, but she couldn't quite distract Luke or eliminate the newly romantic gleam in his golden-brown eyes. And then, after they left, she put off for tomorrow what she didn't want to handle today.

Her approach worked like a charm until the next day at work, when Lilah, who was there to organize the annual chili cook-off, stopped Meg in the hall. Lilah shifted the stack of flyers in her arms and said, "It's all over the hospital that you've been kissing Luke." Lilah beamed. "I just want you to know. John and I approve!"

Meg wasn't surprised. After the success they'd had marrying off all four of their sons, Lilah and John McCabe had been determined to get all four Lockhart sisters married off, as well. Whether by chance or as a result of the McCabes' efforts, two of Meg's sisters were now married. Only she and Kelsey remained single. And determined to stay that way.

"How do people know?" Meg demanded unhappily.

"Show-and-tell at the hospital day care center today. Susie told all about the chicken noodle casserole dinner you cooked for them and how you talked Luke into letting them each have whatever kind of sandwich they wanted every day."

Meg blushed as her hands tightened on the master work schedule for all the hospital nurses. "We didn't have that conversation in front of them!"

Lilah shrugged. "Luke credited you with the change in his policy. Becca told everyone about the kiss they walked in on. And Amy announced they were having their house painted the exact same color as yours."

Meg's shoulders tensed. "Anything else?"

"Not so far," Lilah teased with a speculative wink. "But it's still early."

Wondering how she was going to manage to keep a romance with Luke from developing, with this kind of matchmaking pressure going on, Meg nevertheless managed to avoid seeing Luke the rest of the day.

He caught up with her in her office at the hospital, just as she was preparing to get Jeremy and leave for home.

"I missed you at lunch today."

Pretending she didn't know what she knew, and hoping desperately Luke hadn't gotten wind of the latest on the hospital grapevine, Meg adopted a look of total innocence as she locked up her desk. "I had the morning juice break with the kids instead." Fortunately, that had been before she'd known about show-and-tell.

"So they said," Luke drawled, shutting the door behind him. "You wouldn't by chance be avoiding me?" Merriment twinkled in his eyes.

Irked he could find their situation humorous, Meg switched off her computer. Standing, she shrugged out of her multicolored uniform jacket with the name badge affixed to the shoulder and hung it in her coat closet. Ignoring his slow, I'm-available grin, she retorted, "Why would I be doing that?"

"Exactly what I'd like to know." Luke lifted his shoulders in a wry shrug. Still watching her thoughtfully, he sat on the edge of her desk and stretched his long legs out in front of him. His golden-brown eyes darkened sexily. "Unless it's because of the way I kissed you last night."

Meg rounded on him, infuriated to discover she was tingling all over at just the mention of the heated embrace. She stalked closer, working to keep her voice low, lest they be overheard by someone walking by in the hall outside her door. "Which, by the way, everyone at the hospital knows about," Meg huffed, then went on to explain in very hushed tones about the enthusiastic disclosure during show-and-tell.

Predictably, Luke wasn't the least bit upset or surprised to find out his pursuit of her was now public knowledge. He shrugged his broad shoulders and continued regarding her with a grin. "I don't care if the whole world knows we are friends."

Meg's internal thermostat rose another notch. It was bad enough he had pushed the envelope, without everyone else knowing about that, too. "Friends who kiss!" she spouted right back.

"Kissing's good." In no time flat, Luke grabbed her and tugged her onto his lap. "Kissing," he drawled companionably as he wrapped one arm about her waist and laced his other hand through the hair at her nape, "is very good."

Meg caught a whiff of his cologne as his lips hovered over hers. Heart pounding, she pressed both hands to his chest and tried not to think how handsome he looked in shirt and tie, a stethoscope around his neck. "Luke—for heaven's sake—we're at work!" Meg protested, more than a little annoyed by his brashness as well as at the intensity of her feelings for him. She hadn't expected to be falling for him all over again, but she was.

Luke shrugged again, letting her know he didn't care where they were or who came in. "You're finished for the day. And so am I." Which seemed, in his mind, to make him entitled to pursue her wherever, however he pleased.

Still off balance, Meg drew a ragged breath as yearning swept through her, hot and swift. "Even so…" she said, protesting weakly as she settled into his lap, her bottom nestled securely in the cradle of his thighs, and felt his lips lower inexorably, perfectly to hers.

Luke chuckled as she made a muffled protest, and then all was lost in the tempestuous meeting of their hearts and minds. She might not want to desire him, but she did. She might not want to get involved with him romantically, but like it or not, she seemed to be doing that. As he continued his gentle, seductive kiss, Meg found herself doing the unthinkable and kissing him back. Tentatively at first, then with greater intensity, until her heart beat in urgent rhythm with his. And it was then, when she'd melted against him, and they both wanted to take it further than circumstances allowed, that he slowly, reluctantly tunneled his hands through her hair and languidly ended the searing, provocative kiss.

Flushing as she realized this was not going to be a relationship conducted on her terms and her terms alone, Meg sputtered furiously, "You're incorrigible."

"Probably," Luke admitted, the look in his eyes dark, sensual and admiring. "But life is short." Again he brushed his lips softly, insistently against hers. "Starting now, I intend to enjoy every second I've got left."

"LOOK, MOMMY," Jeremy said excitedly as Meg pulled into the drive half an hour later, "they're painting Luke's house and it's the same color as ours!" Jeremy swiveled toward her, as much as his seat belt would allow. "I didn't know they were going to start painting today!"

"Neither did I," Meg murmured. But it shouldn't have surprised her, either. Luke didn't seem to waste any time in anything he did. But then he had always been that way—fast, efficient, determined. The difference was, back in Chicago he hadn't pursued her romantically the way he was now. Back then all he had wanted was to be her friend. Back then she hadn't been forced to keep any secrets from him, or worry that if and when he found out what it was she was hiding he would never forgive her for her silence.

"Can I go over and see the painters?" Jeremy asked as they climbed out of the car.

"No," Meg said firmly, with a glance at the sprayers the painters were using. "You'll have to watch them from our yard, just like you did the movers."

"Okay." Jeremy balanced on one foot, then the other, waving his arms enthusiastically all the while. "Maybe

Becca and Susie and Amy can come over and watch with me when they get home.''

By the time Luke and the girls got home, Meg had changed into shorts and a T-shirt. Jeremy waved the girls over. They came running, Luke ambling along right behind them. Meg stepped out onto the back patio while Jeremy enthusiastically asked Luke if the girls could hang out with him for a while. Luke looked at Meg inquisitively. ''Do you mind?''

Although she was still ticked off at him for the kiss at the hospital—the last thing she needed was his continued seduction of her—Meg also knew, one parent to another, that he was in a bind. The last thing Luke needed was to try to watch over his girls while a crew of painters were putting the finishing touches on the exterior of their house.

Knowing Luke wouldn't hesitate to do the same for her, Meg said, ''Of course it's okay.''

''Thanks,'' Luke said. He cast a harried look over his shoulder, surveying the results. ''I think they're nearly done with the exterior. Tomorrow they're going to start on the interior rooms.''

Meg thought about what it would be like to have all that activity going on during the workweek, with children underfoot. ''Too bad you couldn't have had this done before you moved in,'' she said, glad they had something pedestrian to converse about.

''Isn't that the truth. But at least they're here now—as busy as this company is, I was lucky to get them so quickly.'' Still admiring his house, Luke grinned and shot a look at Meg. ''Sure is good to get rid of all that purple.''

Meg couldn't help smiling back at him. ''Have to agree with you there.''

''I'll come back to get the girls as soon as I can,'' Luke promised. Meg didn't doubt that for a moment, if only so he could have a reason to spend more time pursuing her—this time in an arena that did not require nearly as much restraint—at least in Luke's view.

Still regarding her happily, Luke waggled his eyebrows at her and strode off.

A SHORT WHILE AFTER THAT, the painters packed up all their gear and drove off. Luke was out in the backyard, pulling parts out of a box and putting something together. Jeremy stuck his head through the kitchen doorway, where Meg was busy making a garden salad and a peach cobbler to have with their leftover chicken noodle casserole. "Can we go see Luke now?" he asked, looking happier than he had in a long, long time.

"Yes. And then come back—" for dinner, Meg was about to say. Too late. Jeremy was already gone. Five minutes later all four children were racing across the lawn again and bursting into the kitchen.

"Daddy's setting up the barbecue grill!"

"We're having hot dogs and chips and lemonade."

"Yeah, and you *and* Jeremy are invited to supper at our house tonight."

"Please, Mom, can we go?" Jeremy asked.

Looking at the eager expressions of the four children gathered around her, Meg didn't have the heart to tell Jeremy no. She had disappointed him so much lately. And if this made him happy...if it made him forget all his questions... "Yes, you can."

"We'll tell Daddy you're both coming!" The kids raced back out again.

That wasn't exactly what she'd said, but Meg also knew she was sort of stuck, at least for the evening—unless she wanted to be considered rude or have to answer an awful lot of pointed questions from the kids.

Meg finished her salad, then checked on the peach cobbler baking in the oven. The crust was golden-brown, the fruit bubbling. Deciding it was done, Meg removed it from the oven, set it in a wicker carrier made specifically to transport hot dishes, then headed off, along with the just-made salad, across the lawn. The grill was set up some distance from both the house and the children, who were playing in the sandbox on Luke's patio. Luke was nowhere in sight.

"Daddy's inside the house," Becca reported, as she sifted sand into a funnel, and watched it pour out the other end.

"He said we shouldn't go in there," Amy chimed in.

Susie stopped digging long enough to hold her nose. "Yeah, it's real stinky inside."

Stinky was right, Meg thought as she made her way into Luke's kitchen. He was standing in the middle of the room, frowning big-time, and it wasn't hard to figure out why. "You've got some major paint fumes going on here," Meg observed. More were coming in from the open windows and still-wet windowsills.

"Tell me about it." Luke grimaced and rubbed his forehead. "I'm getting a headache after breathing them for just fifteen minutes. I had no idea it was going to be this bad. But then," he admitted with yet another grimace, "I've never had a house painted, either—inside or out."

Meg moved closer, her heart going out to him, one parent to another. "What are you going to do?" she asked, aghast. "You can't sleep in here with it like this."

Luke loaded hot dogs onto a platter, put buns on another. "I'm going to take the girls back to my office at the hospital and let them sleep on the sofas in the waiting room."

"You can't get a room somewhere?" Meg asked,

checking on the kids, finding they were still exactly where they were supposed to be.

"I've already tried." Luke got ketchup, mustard and relish out of the refrigerator. "I just called every motel in the area. Due to a wedding tomorrow, everyone is already full up for the night—there are several places that can give me a room starting tomorrow, but no one has a room for tonight." Catching Meg's concerned look, Luke said, "We'll be all right at my office."

"There's no need for you to do that." Meg helped him carry the food to the picnic table out back. "The girls can sleep at our house," Meg finished, as soon as they were out of earshot of the children.

"Thanks," Luke adjusted the cooking rack to the right height, then began laying hot dogs above the coals. "But they've been through a lot of upheaval the past few weeks, and I'd rather keep them with me at night."

"You can stay, too," Meg found herself offering, before she could stop herself. Promising herself that nothing romantic could happen with that many chaperones around watching their every move, she continued, "I'll put Jeremy in the room with me, and you and the girls can have his room." The arrangement would be as safe—and platonic—as could be.

Luke tilted his head to the side. He watched her steadily, the barest of smiles curving his lips, then said softly, "You'd do this for...us?"

Meg nodded, her heart already beating double time at the prospect of spending another night under the same roof with Luke. "On one condition," she stipulated firmly.

One corner of Luke's lips lifted in a testing smile as he prodded, "And that is?"

"Absolutely," Meg specified bluntly, "no more kissing."

Chapter Five

Several hours later, exhausted from her day at work and her equally busy evening, Meg was relaxing on a chaise on her back patio, cradling a tall glass of raspberry iced tea in her hands. She was surrounded by citronella candles and big clay pots of blooming geraniums, and overhead the stars burned brightly in the clear Texas sky. She appreciated the silence and the inner peace that came from knowing Jeremy had gone to sleep feeling happy and secure once again.

The screen door slid open. Luke stepped out to join her. "Girls asleep?" Meg asked Luke as he sank down in a chaise opposite her. She saw he'd found the glass she'd left for him on the kitchen counter.

"Yes." Luke sighed his relief as he sipped his iced tea. "Jeremy?"

Meg grinned as she stretched her legs out in front of her. "He's out like a light, amazingly enough." She shook her head fondly, recollecting how very easy it had been to put him to bed in her room while Luke put the girls to bed in Jeremy's room—where all four of them would eventually bunk. "He's completely worn out," Meg continued. And so, in many ways, was she. Having to deal with all her feelings about Luke was exhausting.

"My girls are wiped out, too. It was fun, having dinner together again."

Meg looked over at Luke, taking in the appealing line of his mouth, his strong, sexy jaw and chiseled face, and wondered if he was truly as unaware of the impact of his allure as he seemed. "The kids really enjoyed themselves," Meg said, smiling as she thought about it.

Luke took a long drink, then set his glass aside. He stretched his arms overhead, lazily flexing the taut muscles in his shoulders, chest, abs and arms. "What about you?" he regarded her steadily, as he settled more comfortably in the deep cushions on the chaise. "Did you have fun?"

"Oh, yeah," Meg said. More fun, in fact, than she wanted to admit. Enough to bring about all sorts of fantasies, like what would have happened if she had told Luke she was pregnant and needed a father for her baby? Would he have come to her rescue and married her instead of Gwyneth? Would all these children be theirs instead of "his" and "hers"? Would they have been one big happy family all this time? Or would Luke have gone ahead and married Gwyneth and tried to help her and Jeremy out simultaneously, and spent the last years torn between his own family and hers? Gwyneth certainly would have objected to Luke's assistance, and rightly so, since Luke had already admitted to Meg he'd barely had time to be with his own family during his residency, he'd been so busy. It would have been wrong of Meg and Jeremy to add to his stress. Had they done so...had she allowed herself to call on him, even as just a friend, the overwhelming strain might have broken up his marriage. And Luke would not have deserved that.

"I wouldn't mind doing this all the time, pooling our resources," Luke continued lazily.

Neither would Meg, but she also knew it was dangerous to start thinking that way. Much more of this and she'd be feeling as if she was married to Luke. And she wasn't interested in marriage to anyone, Meg reminded herself sternly. After being head of her own household for so long, she liked her independent life just fine. More to the point, she didn't want Luke pursuing her just because they were still physically attracted to each other and had the potential to be good friends, or because he found being sole head of his own family too difficult to handle completely on his own.

"We have to be careful not to give the kids the wrong idea," Meg cautioned. *We have to be careful not to find ourselves falling into bed again.* Because to do so and then realize, once again, that it was all wrong would make it awfully hard for both of them, since they would still have to live next door to each other and work at the same hospital and their kids would still be friends.

Feeling suddenly unbearably restless, finding the starlit and candlelit patio much too romantic a setting, she stood and carried her glass inside to the kitchen, where the fluorescent bulbs cast a very bright and realistic light.

Looking a little irritated to have their intimate tête-à-tête interrupted, Luke sauntered in after her. "What 'wrong idea' would that be?" he asked casually.

Avoiding the assessment of his knowing eyes, Meg turned away from him and set her glass in the sink, her motions as slow and deliberate as her words. "That because we work together and live next door to each other and are single parents that we're going to be blending families in some sort of permanent everyday way."

Luke put his hands on her shoulders and gently turned her to face him. "Are you saying that your interest in me is fleeting?'' he asked, point-blank. ''Or that you think my interest in you is temporary?''

To her mounting chagrin, Meg knew nothing would ever erase the way she felt about Luke. Not time. Not distance. Not even the regrets she held deep in her heart.

Aware it was taking all her courage to continue this conversation, Meg swallowed and, ever so determinedly, lifted her chin. Defiantly, she looked him in the eye. ''I'm saying there may come a time in the future when you or I want to date someone else and maybe marry them,'' she said, forcing herself to be realistic for all their sakes. ''And if we begin acting like a couple, it's bound to make things a lot harder and messier when we do move on with our lives, as we most certainly will at some point.'' Just as they had been before. Only this time, Meg thought, she didn't want to be caught off guard by his pursuit of another woman as she had been when he started dating Gwyneth, shortly after they'd met. This time she wanted to be prepared to be nothing more than his friend.

But once again Luke did not agree with her. ''First of all,'' Luke said as he braced his hands on the counter on either side of her, effectively caging her, ''there's nothing platonic about my interest in you these days, Meg.'' He paused and looked deeply into her eyes. ''I thought I'd made that clear with my kisses.''

Meg backed up as much as she could—it wasn't much. ''I know you're lonely,'' she continued, holding her ground with effort. ''I know you're new in town and that you're temporarily without a woman friend in your life...''

Resentment clouded his eyes. ''Is it being a nurse that makes you view this so clinically?'' His voice dropped to a husky whisper. ''Or the same kind of fear that kept us apart before?''

"What are you talking about? I was never afraid when it came to you."

"Sure you were." Luke completed a thorough study of her face. "And so was I of you. And you know why?" He moved closer, until their thighs and torsos met. "Because we became friends so quickly." Regret tinged his voice even as his eyes remained very clear. "I knew there was an attraction there, but at the time I thought it was strictly one-sided. I knew that to pursue you romantically would risk ruining our friendship, and I didn't want to lose that. It was far too important for me. So I did what was, in retrospect, probably the dumbest thing in my life," he continued gruffly. "I divided my life and began dating Gwyneth—as a love interest—and reserved all the true, emotional intimacy for you, my friend. Thinking we could pretend the passion between us just wasn't there was a mistake, Meg. It was the kind of mistake that landed us in bed the first moment you really needed me."

Meg closed her eyes and shook her head, realizing how terrifyingly easy it would be to fall in love...into bed with Luke...all over again. "You felt sorry for me that night." Even now she didn't want to fool herself into thinking his tenderness had been motivated by anything else.

Luke swore. "Pity had nothing to do with it." He tucked a hand beneath her chin and forced her face up to his. "I was with you because I wanted you. In my bed. And by my side," he said softly as he looked into her eyes. "And I still do. And had I not been such a fool I would've made you understand that before you ever got on that plane back to Texas."

Meg wished she could believe that it was his heart, not his guilt, that was driving all this. But she knew Luke. He was a healer by profession and by instinct. He was the kind of man who couldn't bear to see anyone hurt and not do something about it. That was what he was doing here, even if he wasn't consciously aware of it. He was trying to right a past wrong by making a single ill-thought-out toss in the hay and a friendship into something it could never have been. He was trying to turn their previous error into a romantic entanglement they could live with. And what better way than by romanticizing all this, in hindsight.

Aware it would be all too easy for her to buy into this fantasy, Meg broke free of his arms and moved away from him. "You shouldn't be saying all of this." Her emotions under tight control, arms clamped tightly in front of her, she turned her back to him.

"Why not?" Once again, Luke grabbed her by the arms and swung her around to face him. "It's true." He held her tenderly, his hands gentle and soothing as they stroked hypnotically up and down her arms, from shoulder to elbow and back again. "I know how I feel now," he whispered softly, bringing her close enough to feel the solidness of his chest and the steady, urgent rhythm of his heart. "I have for a long time." He wrapped his arms about her waist and tightened them around her. "It's one of the reasons I moved to Laramie, because John McCabe told me you were here again and were still single after all these years. It's one of the reasons I bought the house next door to yours. Because I knew I blew my chance with you years ago, and I don't want to blow it again."

Meg felt the ache rise in her throat. How she wished they could go back. Start over. Start fresh. But they couldn't. Not when she knew that ultimately Luke had chosen someone else over her. Not when she'd made her own share of what were turning out to be haunting, life-altering mistakes, too. "You promised you wouldn't do this," she said in a low, strangled voice. She didn't want to believe she and Luke could be together the way she had always secretly wanted them to be, only to have it later taken away. She didn't like feeling as fragile and vulnerable as he made her feel.

"I said I wouldn't kiss you again tonight if you and Jeremy had dinner with me and the girls," Luke corrected. "I didn't promise I wouldn't tell you what was in my heart." Luke was silent a long moment as he searched her face. "Maybe it's time you started telling me what's in yours."

Meg swallowed and rubbed a chill from her arms. Was it her imagination or was there now a hint of impending rain in the cooling night air? "You don't ask for much, do you?" she returned glibly, worried if they got any closer she'd start disclosing all the mistakes she had made. Mistakes Luke might not forgive.

Worse than the thought of being only friends with him was the possibility he would hate her forever if he found out all she had done to protect her son. Luke was an upstanding man. Decent to his very soul. Sometimes too decent for his own good. Which was what worried Meg. She didn't want him going all noble and self-sacrificing on her, confusing wanting to help with wanting her and Jeremy in his life.

"I'm tired of hiding what I feel, not going after what I want," Luke said, clearly annoyed by her continued resistance. "I would think you would be, too."

Meg went over to the sliding doors that led to the patio and locked them for the night. "I've never been one to wear my heart on my sleeve," she said as she closed the drapes, more aware than ever of the things that were keeping them apart.

Luke lounged against the counter, arms folded in front of him. "Or divulge the contents at all," he added.

Meg put the last two glasses in the dishwasher, added soap and switched it on. She turned to regard Luke stubbornly, furious at his continued attempts to upset the hard-won tranquility of her life with her son. "I've got a good job, a nice home and a son I love more than anything in this world. I'm back in Laramie with all my sisters. I'm content with my life the way it is, Luke. I'm sorry if you're not, but I can't help that."

"Meaning you don't want to rock the boat by seeing me in a romantic sense," Luke observed unhappily as Meg continued shutting down the kitchen for the night.

"Exactly." Her spine stiff with tension, Meg walked out into the living room and began closing down that room, too.

"Even if it means you're only half living?" Stone-faced, Luke watched her lock the front door.

"My life is fine, just the way it is," Meg insisted, turning back to face him.

"No, Meg, it isn't," Luke said, his voice dropping to just above a whisper in deference to the sleeping children at the top of the stairs. "And one of these days," he warned grudgingly, "you're going to realize that."

LUKE'S WORDS were still ringing in Meg's ears as she headed off to bed. The truth was, she had always been secretly attracted to him. But as much as she had wanted to date him, she had needed and wanted his friendship and companionship more. So she'd dated someone else. For a while at least, it had been simpler than if they had tried to be everything to each other. So much less pressure. Until the night her parents died and they slept together.

Now nothing would ever be that simple again. Luke knew she desired him. Not just then, but now, thanks to the way he'd been kissing her recently and the way she had been kissing him back. The trouble was, Meg didn't know how to be close to him without telling him everything that was in her heart and on her mind. And until she did, she had to continue to keep him at arm's length—allowing friendship and nothing more.

She went to sleep thinking about Luke and woke around 2:00 a.m. to the sound of rain pelting against the roof. Knowing she had the central air conditioner on and no open windows to worry about, Meg snuggled down into the covers, next to her sleeping son, content to go back to sleep. Then awakened with a start.

Careful not to disturb Jeremy or the children sleeping across the hall, Meg eased out of bed and tiptoed down the stairs. To her relief Luke was already up and just ahead of her. By then rain was pouring down from the skies and, no doubt, into the open windows and freshly painted wooden windowsills of his house.

Not bothering with shoes, he dashed outside and ran barefoot across the lawn to his big Cape Cod. Knowing the job was too much for any one person to handle alone, Meg dashed after him. Together they ran from room to room, stepping over damp carpet and floors and furniture to close the newly painted windows. They were breathless when they finished, and also, Meg realized, drenched to the skin.

Not wanting to leave the kids alone, Meg headed out the door and back to her place. She was halfway across the lawn when Luke caught up with her, umbrella in hand. He wrapped an arm around her waist and pulled her beneath the umbrella's protection. "Some might say too little too late," he murmured as he jogged along beside her, "but what the hay. It's gotta offer some protection."

"Some is right," Meg said breathlessly, her voice dropping to a hushed whisper as she stepped from the patio into the darkness of her kitchen and dripped onto the floor. "We're both soaked."

Luke dropped the umbrella by the door and plucked a soft cotton dish towel from the stack on the counter and pressed it against her cheeks, chin, forehead, the tip of her nose. The next thing Meg knew she was all the way in his arms, her damp body pressed against his. His lips were on hers, and he was kissing her like there was no tomorrow, like they had never been apart. And, heaven help her, she was kissing him back with the same overwhelming need and intensity. Maybe it was best this way, she thought. Best not to think. Best only to feel.

Luke knew he was taking advantage of the situation, of her. For maybe the first time in his life he didn't care. Meg would never realize how much she wanted and needed him unless he showed her, Luke decided as he tangled his hands in her hair and kissed her long and hard and deep. She surged against him, moaning her pleasure. And then he was drowning in the taste of her and the feel of her warm, supple body pressed against his. Her arms locked around him. Her lips parted. Unable to stop himself, he claimed her the way he had been wanting to claim her all night. Backing her against the refrigerator, he fit his body to hers, hardness to softness, until she sighed. And still he kissed her, with the urgency of long-pent-up emotion, holding her close and stroking her tongue with his.

Her pulse pounding, her body trembling, Meg tore her mouth from his. Her arms still wreathed around his neck, she turned her head to the side and muttered furiously, "Luke! Darn you. You said you weren't going to do this."

Luke couldn't just walk away from this, even if she

could. Meg was all he had ever wanted, dreamed about, and if his instincts were right, he was all Meg had ever wanted, too. He just had to get her to accept that.

Leaning forward, he traced the slope of her throat with his tongue. Aware he hadn't begun to have his fill of her, or Meg of him, Luke corrected teasingly, "I promised I wouldn't do this last night. It's morning now." Continuing to trail kisses down her neck, he slipped his hands beneath her damp pajama top and moved them up until the soft, warm curves of her breasts filled his hands and her nipples beaded and pressed against his palms.

Meg sucked in a tremulous breath, melting helplessly against him. "It's the middle of the night," she protested.

"Even better," Luke murmured, knowing there was no better time for making love and no man on this earth who would care for Meg more than he would. Able to feel how much Meg wanted and needed him, no matter what she said, Luke took her lips again. He kissed her until she gave him back everything he had ever wanted, everything he had ever expected, until the pleasure was sharp, stunning, the blood pooling hotly, urgently in his lower half and Luke wanted her more than he had ever wanted a woman in his life. But even as he longed to make love to Meg then and there, he knew he couldn't, not with the kids right upstairs.

Reluctantly Luke ended the kiss and tore his lips from hers. "As much as I want you," he said gruffly, "this isn't the time or place." This time, when he made love to Meg, and he would, he didn't want it to feel like something that just happened on a whim. This time he wanted her to know it was right, that their joining was just the beginning—not the end—of their relationship.

"You've got that right," Meg said, letting him know

with a glance that once again he was pushing too hard, too fast.

"But the time will come," Luke promised, taking her hand in his, letting his touch telegraph the steadfastness of his attentions, that Meg could count on him—even if she wouldn't quite let herself believe that yet. "You'll see...."

MORNING BROUGHT A FLURRY of activity and very little time to reflect on what had gotten into her the night before, for which Meg was relieved.

She had never thought of herself as a particularly passionate person—never really enjoyed kissing all that much—and she'd certainly never let a situation get out of control. Except where Luke was concerned. There all bets were off. All he had to do was look at her, and she began to go all soft and vulnerable inside. All he had to do was touch her or kiss her, and she was filled with desire. Not the easily managed kind that could be turned off with just a thought, but the kind that kept her up all night long. The kind that made her toss and turn in bed and daydream about kissing him again in the middle of the day.

And Meg did not have time for that.

Meg had a job to go to, a little boy to care for, and a secret—that was weighing more on her heart every single minute—to keep.

Fortunately, because it was a workday in the middle of the week, there was little time for her and Luke to do more than exchange pleasantries and cursory glances as they got all the kids fed and ready to go, packed their lunches and drove off to their jobs in their separate vehicles.

With some careful timing and judicious movements around the hospital, Meg didn't take a single route where she thought she might run into Luke—and managed to go the whole morning without running into him. At lunchtime they did bump into each other at the day care center, but their attention was on the kids, and Luke got paged before the meal was up, leaving them no time alone. Meg's afternoon coffee break was spent with her sister Jenna, who'd dropped by the hospital specifically to see her and bring her the proofs of Jenna and Jake's wedding photos.

"Oh, these are so great," Meg said appreciatively with a sigh, aware for the first time she was just the tiniest bit envious of her younger sister. Not because Jenna had a clothing design business that was going great guns, not even because she was now married to a wealthy Texas businessman who was as handsome and nice as could be. But because Jenna was so darn happy and content. Because Jenna had put all the angst of her past with Jake— over their botched elopement and resultant hurt—to rest. They had moved on with their lives, building a future together that was bound to bring them oodles of happiness. Meg wished she could do that with Luke. Meg wished she could forget the past and trust in her relationship with Luke the way Jenna now trusted Jake.

Instead, she was caught in this terrible predicament. If she told Luke now that she wished she had gone to him— even as a friend—and had let him help her get through her pregnancy and be "the father" Jeremy needed, he would probably think it made sense for him to help her out that way now. Meg suspected Jeremy would also feel that way. The problem was, she did not want Luke in their lives just because he thought she and Jeremy needed him, or vice versa. Not when they both deserved so much more. A husband or wife who loved them the way they should be loved.

Maybe, Meg thought, sighing, the best thing to do was simply to stay away from Luke until she had figured out what the right thing to do was. Right now she didn't have a clue...which was probably why she should start concentrating on the pictures instead of her own throbbing conscience.

Oblivious to the depth of Meg's dilemma, Jenna continued spreading proofs over Meg's desk. "Pick out which ones you'd like to have, write the photo number down, and I'll have copies made for you. And in the meantime—" Jenna sat back cheerfully, opening the two iced mochas to go that she'd brought with her "—you can tell me how your own romance is going."

Meg blinked self-consciously. "What romance?"

"Please." Jenna waved a hand airily. "I did not just fall off the back of a turnip truck."

"Did I say you had?" Flushing, Meg continued sorting through photos: Jenna and Jake, cutting the cake with Meg and Jeremy behind them.

"Your houses match."

Meg stiffened. "My house was already that color."

"You're telling me he didn't have your okay to paint his house exactly the same as yours?" Jenna probed.

Meg threw up her hands. "Of course we talked about it."

Jenna arched a brow and continued to regard Meg skeptically. "I'm listening."

"Since my house was originally the guest cottage on the property, and his place the main house, and they are the same architecturally, and originally both places had been the same color, and really looked better that way. It just made sense. And that's all there is to it," Meg said firmly.

"Okay—" Jenna rolled her eyes "—so you two

weren't trying to blend your properties as easily as you seem to be blending your lives...."

"We are not doing that!" Meg interrupted in a huff. Since Jenna had become a stepmother to Jake's daughter, Alexandra, she seemed to be mothering everyone, including all three of her sisters. Mothering the sisters was Meg's job.

Jenna looked dubious. "Did you or did you not have supper together the past two nights and even have Luke and his girls sleep at your place last night?"

"That was because of the paint fumes." Meg blew out an aggravated breath, then paused. "And how did you know that, anyway?"

"Jeremy. Alexandra and I saw him a few minutes ago at the child care center. Alex is down there playing with him now. Which brings me to my next request. Alex and Jeremy want Jeremy to come and spend the night at the ranch with us on Friday, so he can help her take care of Buster and Miss Kitty. Jake and I said it was okay with us if it's okay with you."

Meg knew how much Jeremy liked playing with Alexandra and her new kitten and puppy. "It's fine."

"Great. We'll pick him up Friday evening around suppertime, and then maybe we could just meet you at the chili cook-off Saturday morning, and he can go home with you then?"

Meg pressed the heel of her hand to her forehead and moaned. "The chili cook-off is this weekend!"

"That's what it said on the signs all over town," Jenna said. "My goodness, you are besotted if you've forgotten the hospital's biggest fund-raiser of the year. Don't you have to cook something for it or work behind the scenes or something?"

"Both." Meg exhaled slowly and shook her head. "I'm

usually so responsible—I don't know what's gotten into me.''

"I do." Jenna grinned. "And his name is Luke."

MEG FINISHED THE DAY without running into Luke, who apparently already had a full schedule of patients waiting to see him. Then, deciding she had been seeing far too much of him, she and Jeremy went over to Dani and Beau's for dinner and a movie in their home screening room Wednesday evening. Thursday was equally busy for her as she did everything possible to avoid running into Luke, at the hospital and outside of it. She and Jeremy had dinner out with Kelsey, again not returning home until late. Friday Meg had her monthly staff meeting with all three shifts of nurses, one shift at a time. Then, finished for the week, she went home, packed a bag for Jeremy and said goodbye to him as he set off for his overnight with Jenna, Alexandra and Jake.

As soon as he was gone, Meg got out her cookbooks. While she was trying to decide what recipe to use for her chili cook-off contribution, she saw Luke and the girls come home from the hospital. The painters, who'd been working on the inside of the house for the past three days, began packing up once again. They said goodbye to Luke, who shook their hands and gave them a check. Minutes later Luke came back out of the house with his three girls, all of whom had child-size suitcases in hand. He loaded them into the car and drove off once again.

Meg figured they were going to a motel to spend the night for the third night in a row, since the paint fumes in the house had to be unbearable, even with all the windows in the house open for maximum ventilation. Briefly she felt guilty for not inviting them to spend the night at her place again, then pushed the unwanted emotion away.

Luke's problems were not always hers—even if he was her next-door neighbor.

She had problems of her own. Like how to stop tripping over Luke or noticing his comings and goings and wondering about them every time she turned around. Like how to stop recalling the way he had held her and kissed her. And how to get what she needed to get baked before the cook-off tomorrow afternoon when she didn't even have all the ingredients she needed in the house.

Sighing, Meg did some calculations and finished her shopping list, then went to get her purse and car keys. Minutes later, she was on her way to Dot's Market. She parked in the lot, grabbed a cart from just inside the front door and began making her way down the aisles. Pulling out her list and pen, she headed straight for the dairy aisle and put six pounds of butter in her cart, promptly marking them off her list. From there she headed to the nuts and plunked down big bags of walnuts, pecans and almonds. She'd just added two big boxes of premium cocoa to her cart and was reaching for the confectioner's sugar when she bumped into something warm and solid and undeniably male.

An apology on her lips, she turned, saw Luke.

"So this is what you do on the nights Jeremy is away," he drawled.

"What are you doing here?"

"Grocery shopping. Same as you." Propping his hands on his waist, he turned and pretended to study the spice display. "Just out of curiosity, do you have even the slightest idea what goes in chili?"

Meg tried not to notice how handsome he looked in navy cargo shorts and a narrowly striped navy, white and emerald-green knit shirt and running shoes. "You're entering the competition?"

"Have to." Luke shrugged his broad shoulders matter-of-factly. "I'm a physician, and all the physicians in the hospital make chili and compete for a special prize. Unfortunately, I've never made chili in my life, and they're expecting me to make—and sell, once the judging is done—a great big vat of it."

"Well, lotsa luck," Meg said dryly. Telling herself this was definitely not her problem, she started to move off.

"Thanks." He smiled at her as if her enthusiasm had been genuine and moved to block her way. "What are you entering?" he asked, standing arms folded in front of him, legs braced apart. "Chocolate chili?"

Meg rolled her eyes and refused to laugh at his joke, reaching around him for two big bags of flour. "Triple-fudge, triple-nut brownies," she replied, being careful not to bump into him, despite the fact he was standing directly in her path. "And I'm not entering them in anything, I'm making twelve dozen of them for the bake sale at the cook-off."

Luke grinned as she struggled slightly under the weight of the two ten-pound bags of flour. His golden-brown eyes glinting with amusement—he seemed to know she did not want his help—he reached over wordlessly and helped her put the bags in her cart. Trying not to notice how her fingers tingled warmly as their hands touched, Meg backed off slightly and asked, "Where are the girls?"

Luke's smile widened even more. "At Alexandra's, for an overnight."

Meg's heart turned a somersault in her chest as she realized she and Luke were—for all intents and purposes—both alone and fancy-free for the rest of the night, courtesy of her sister Jenna, her new husband and stepdaughter. Playing it cool, Meg said, "You know Jeremy's there, too."

Luke nodded. "That was one of the reasons the girls felt comfortable going. That, and they wanted to play with Alex's kitten and puppy. Meanwhile, I've got to have a trial run at this chili." He sighed and shoved his hands through the rumpled layers of his sandy-blond hair. "So, what do you think? Obviously, I need chili powder." Luke plunked a bottle of that into his cart, next to forty pounds of premium ground beef. "And salt and pepper. Maybe some garlic. And onion. But what else? Cumin? Oregano? Parsley? Paprika?"

"Beats me. I always use a chili mix with all the spices already in it."

"I can see I'm on my own for this one," Luke said gravely.

"You certainly are."

Meg finished her grocery shopping and headed home. She had just gotten out her stand mixer when Luke pulled in the drive and carried his own groceries inside his house.

Five minutes later he was at her door, an armful of cookbooks with him. "Do you have any cookbooks I could look at? It'll just take a minute. I want to compare recipes."

She couldn't really deny him that—his efforts were for a good cause, as all the proceeds from the cook-off would go to the hospital. "Have a seat." Meg ushered him to her kitchen table.

"Thanks." His expression determined, Luke opened all the cookbooks to the pages he had marked with tiny slips of paper and spread them out over the table. He took the ones Meg handed him, thumbed through them quickly and laid those out, too. "Well, I certainly see a pattern here of usual ingredients. But it's going to take something distinctive to win." Luke stroked his jaw thoughtfully. "Maybe I should add some beans..."

Meg edged closer. "You have lived away from Texas too long. Texans don't ever eat beans in their chili, remember?"

Luke's brows knit together quizzically. "What about jalepeños?"

"That would work." Meg caught a whiff of his woodsy cologne.

"Green chilis and or Tabasco sauce?" Luke continued running down the list of potential ingredients.

"Going for something in the 'fire-eaters' category?" Meg teased.

Luke's eyes took on a wicked gleam. "What's chili without a little antacid chaser?"

Meg blew out the breath she'd been holding and eased away. "If you say so."

Luke inclined his head to the side and studied her curiously. "You don't like it hot?"

That was the trouble—she did like it hot, whenever, wherever Luke was concerned. But not wanting him to know that, she turned her glance away from his. "I don't like being up all night with indigestion," Meg answered, noting the relaxed way he had stretched his legs out beneath her kitchen table. "But to each his own, I always say."

Luke pushed back her chair and stood. "You don't think I can do this, do you?" he growled, completely misreading the reason behind her unease. But now that he brought it up...

"I didn't say that," Meg said finally. Although he was right—she did think the night before the competition was a little late for anyone to be making a first-time effort on any recipe.

"I'll surprise you," Luke promised.

Meg watched him gather up his cookbooks and swagger

out. "I'm sure you will," she murmured as he took off for home.

He was gone for the next hour. No phone calls. No dropping by. No interruption of any kind. As Meg mixed up batch after batch of brownies, she told herself she wasn't disappointed. He had cooking to do. So did she. Yet she found herself looking out the window and watching for him to come across the side yard, anyway.

To her further indignation, she didn't catch him looking her way once. Not when he set up a kettle on top of his barbecue grill and browned the meat in the same manner he was going to have to do tomorrow at the cook-off, only on a larger scale. Not the whole time he was opening cans and throwing in spices or when the delicious aroma of spicy chili wafted across the yard.

Darkness fell.

Luke merely switched on the backyard lights. And continued to stir and taste and throw in a few more spices at a time.

Meg finished baking the third and fourth pans of brownies and put the last two in the oven. She did the dishes she'd dirtied, up to that point, decided to wait on making the frosting until all were finished and cool. And looked out the window again. Aware she had twenty-five minutes until her last batch was done, she decided to see how things were going.

She ambled across the yard.

Luke turned as she closed the distance between them. "Those brownies smell mighty good."

Meg edged close enough to get a look at his efforts. "So does that chili." Not only was it thick and rich, it had a wonderful aroma.

Luke looked her up and down in a smugly assessing way that made Meg wish she'd taken the time to run a comb through her loosely upswept hair or at the very least checked her reflection in the mirror. "Want to pool our resources?"

"What do you mean?" Meg wished she could think of something besides kissing Luke whenever they were this close.

"I haven't had dinner yet. I'm guessin', as busy as you've been, that you haven't either. We could throw together a salad and sample the chili and maybe top it off with a brownie and ice cream for dessert."

He did not know how good that sounded. Or how much she had been craving a bowl of his aromatic chili. "You're on." Meg smiled, belatedly realizing just how hungry she was. "But we'll have to do it at my house. I still have a batch of brownies in the oven."

"No problem. The paint fumes here would knock you dead in a Texas minute."

"They finally get it all done today?"

"Yep." Luke sighed his relief to have that big nuisance out of the way. "I'll show you later, if you want to see."

"Okay." Meg had to admit she was curious about what the interior of his Cape Cod looked like now. "See you in a few minutes."

Meg had a salad thrown together by the time he showed up at her back door, big soup tureen of chili tucked under one arm, a couple of chilled beers in his other. "Should I have my antacid before or after?" Meg teased as they settled in their seats at the kitchen table.

"Maybe both." Luke ladled them both a generous serving, then waited anxiously for her to try it.

"Wow," Meg said as the mixture of beef, tomatoes and spices melted on her tongue. "This is incredible, Luke."

"You really like it?" Luke asked as he crumbled a few crackers in his.

Meg nodded. It was really good. "You're sure you've never done this before?" she teased.

"Positive." Luke sighed and made an exasperated face. "If I had, I wouldn't have had to hover over it all evening, adding a little of this and a little of that. I just hope I can duplicate it tomorrow. I think I can. I kept pretty careful tabs on the amounts of everything I put in, and I had time to study the cookbooks while it was all simmering on the grill."

"You really put a lot into this," Meg said admiringly.

Luke shrugged as he dug into his salad. "If I do something, I do it all the way. No halfway measures for me."

"I remember."

Luke caught her eye. They grinned at each other. "So tell me about this cook-off tomorrow," he said. "Have you ever been to one?"

"Sure." Meg took a sip of the icy, delicious brew. "Every year when I was a kid. It's a pretty big deal around here. Everyone in town goes and because the event is widely publicized in the Dallas, San Antonio, Houston and Austin papers, we get a fair amount of tourists, too."

"It's held out at the Laramie County Fairgrounds?"

Meg nodded, thoroughly enjoying Luke's companionship as well as the rare peace and quiet of an adults-only evening. "In addition to the chili cook-off, they have all sorts of game booths, which are manned by the local civic and charity groups in town, carnival rides, music and dancing. People start arriving at 9:00 a.m., and the festivities end with fireworks at midnight. All proceeds go to the hospital. They make hundreds of thousands of dollars on it every year."

As they ate they talked some more, about the various

medical equipment the proceeds from the cook-off had bought over the years. Then the oven buzzed, signaling the last two batches of brownies were done. While Meg got them out of the oven, Luke carried their dishes over to the sink. He frowned as he noticed the paper on the bulletin board tacked up on her counter. "Late registration for kindergarten is Monday night?"

Meg took off her oven mitts and switched off the oven. "I take it that means you haven't enrolled Susie yet, either."

"No, but I need to. Want to go together?"

Meg knew all the reasons they shouldn't go together—it would just generate more talk than they'd already managed to generate. And she knew the reason they should—because the kids would enjoy it, and so would she and Luke.

"Susie seems a little nervous about going to school," Luke continued pensively. "I'm not sure why."

Meg noted the concern in Luke's eyes. "Because it's new?" she asked curiously.

Luke paused. "The child care center at the hospital was new, too," he said finally. "But Susie didn't bat an eye about going there this week."

"Maybe because she knows you're nearby, working in the same building. This time you won't be."

"I hadn't thought of that." Luke watched as Meg began to make the frosting for the brownies. "Is Jeremy worried about school?"

"He seems fine so far, but there's no telling how he'll react when the time actually comes."

"It'll be a hard day for me. It'll mean my little girl is growing up."

"I know what you mean." Meg snapped the beater into place and turned the mixer on. "Jeremy's such a big part of my life now." Sighing, Meg glanced at Luke. "I don't know how I'll cope when he grows up and goes off to college."

"Getting a little ahead of ourselves here, aren't we?" Luke teased.

"I guess. But you know what I mean."

"Yeah, I do know—too well." Luke's eyes gleamed compassionately. He nudged her with his elbow. "Which is why you should hurry up with that frosting so we can start sampling those brownies."

As eager to have him sample her culinary efforts as he had been for her to sample his, Meg frosted a pan of brownies, cut Luke a square, and held it up to his lips. "How is it?" she asked as the gooey confection melted on his tongue.

Luke's I'm-in-heaven grin and the contented gleam in his eyes told the story. "Best I've ever tasted," he declared. "Aren't you going to have any?"

"Can't," Meg sighed. "I'm a chocoholic. If I eat one, I'll eat half a dozen. And then go back for half a dozen more."

Having finished one, Luke reached for another. "I see your point," Luke said as he ate that, too.

"What'd I tell you?" Meg declared on a disgruntled sigh. "They're addictive."

"Mmm." Luke finished the rich, gooey treat, then took a long thirsty drink of water. "Not as addictive as some things I can think of," he taunted boldly.

"Like what?" Meg demanded, ignoring the ardent gleam in his eyes and the equally sexy turn of her thoughts.

Luke's hands caressed her shoulders. "The taste of your lips." He wrapped his hands around her waist and brought her close. "The fragrance of your hair." He kissed her temple. "The softness of your skin."

"Luke." Meg's heart slammed against her ribs, even as she splayed both her hands across his chest.

"One kiss, Meg." Luke tucked a hand beneath her chin and lifted her face to his. Looking deep into her eyes, he vowed, "That's all I want."

Chapter Six

But was it all she wanted? Meg didn't think so.

Meg regarded Luke breathlessly as she extricated herself from the warm, strong cradle of his arms. "That's never all you want when you look at me like that."

"Like how?" Luke drawled as if there were no doubt, in his mind anyway, of what the outcome of this evening was going to be.

Meg slipped to the other side of the kitchen. "Like...you want me in your bed."

Luke's eyes grew thoughtful. Keeping his eyes on her face, he sauntered closer. "What's wrong with that?" he asked bluntly.

A little thrown by his determination to have her, Meg dropped her gaze. And found herself at eye level with the crisp dark-gold hair curling out of the opening of his shirt. Desire rippling through her, she tore her eyes from Luke's golden skin. "The problem is," she snapped archly, "I'm susceptible to that kind of look." *Especially when it comes from you.*

"Aha," his face lit with a mixture of pleasure and bemusement, "you're a secret romantic at heart."

"A secret romantic with a very practical side," Meg corrected. Turning away from him, she gathered up some dirty dishes and slid them into the sink. To her dismay, her hands were shaking as she turned on the hot water and squirted in a generous dollop of dishwashing soap.

Hand on her shoulder, Luke wheeled her around to face him. He hadn't shaved since early that morning, and the hint of evening beard on his face gave him a dark and dangerous look.

"Okay. I'll bite," Luke growled, exasperated, as he eyed her lazily in a very predatory, very male way. "What is your practical side telling you right now?"

Still locked in the battle of wills, Meg stared at Luke. Every inch of her was taut, ready to do combat with him, even looking forward to a fight. Why? So he could kiss her again? So things could get out of hand—again? The passion would flare and they could make love without really having to deal with the consequences? She couldn't afford to lose control here, couldn't afford to let Luke get any closer to her than he already had, until she figured out what to do about Luke and herself and the future they might or might not have.

Her heart hammering her chest, Meg drew a bolstering breath and forced herself to maintain a serene expression. "My practical side says that if I let you talk me into this, we'll both regret it."

"And why would we do that?" Luke countered.

Meg released a breath and turned to face Luke so suddenly her hips grazed the front of his shorts. "Because it would ruin our friendship," she explained impatiently. "Just the way it did before."

"Or enhance it," Luke interrupted. He stepped so close they nudged torsos again.

Tingling all over, Meg shifted away from him. Being that close to him had put all her senses in overdrive. "The difference is this time we can't run from whatever happens between us," Meg continued as if Luke hadn't spoken. She plunged her hands into the soapy water and, grabbing a sponge, began scrubbing the dishes with more than necessary force. "Because we still have to live next door to each other and set good examples for our kids. Having a clandestine love affair would not be doing that." For Jeremy's sake, for Luke's girls, she and Luke had to be responsible about their emotional entanglements.

"I agree with you totally." Luke grabbed a towel and began to dry the dishes she set in the rack. "Lovemaking should not happen unless the two people involved care about each other very much and are committed to having a deep and meaningful relationship with each other."

"Exactly." Meg sighed her relief as their eyes meshed. She felt the warmth of his desire for her mixing with his ever-present need to protect her as a friend, and suddenly all was right with the world.

"Fortunately," Luke continued, dropping the dish towel and taking her into his arms once again, "a deep and lasting relationship is exactly what I want with you, Meg Lockhart."

The dampness from her soapy hands soaked into his shirt. "We can't leap into something like this just because we're friends," she sputtered, wondering if Luke was ever going to give up, if she even wanted him to give up, considering the intensity of her feelings for him. "Or...or...because we made love once and the sex was...was..."

"...extraordinary?" Grinning, Luke guessed at what she was trying to say.

Meg flushed self-consciously. She hated it when he read her mind at moments like this. She tilted her chin and looked at him with all the sternness she could muster. "For all we know, Luke Carrigan, that was a fluke." A single golden memory that she wasn't sure she ever wanted replaced. At this point, she didn't want to risk having her last romantic notion shattered by any heartbreaking reality. Which was, she knew all too well, exactly what could happen if she discovered that that night…and what she'd felt that night…had all been a grief- and need-induced illusion. That night she'd thought—hoped—that Luke had wanted her the way she had always secretly wanted him. To find out now it wasn't true would be devastating.

Luke remained as supremely confident as always. He lifted her hands and touched his lips to her palms, one by one. "The kisses we've shared the past few days say differently."

Once again Meg had that melting sensation in her knees. Feeling far too vulnerable, she hitched in a breath. "I want love, Luke." *The kind that makes a marriage and lasts a lifetime.*

"So do I, Meg, so do I," Luke whispered as he touched the side of her face and tilted her face up to his. "And I wouldn't be here with you like this unless I thought we could give each other what we needed."

Luke caged her with his arms, and their lips met in a firestorm of need. Years of pent-up passion poured into their kiss. The forbidden nature of their desire intensified everything they felt.

Meg surged against him, every inch of her wanting every inch of him. So he hadn't exactly come right out and said he was falling in love with her, or even could be falling in love with her, she thought as she responded to the implacable nature of his embrace. So he still didn't know the truth about the mistakes she'd made. When he kissed her and held her and touched her like this, it felt like love. And love—from Luke—was all she had ever wanted....

Luke had lost his chance with Meg before by holding back, by forcing himself to be content with only friendship when he had wanted so much from her. He wasn't going to do it again, he determined fiercely as he threaded one hand through Meg's hair and splayed the other across her spine, bringing her closer yet.

This time he was going to pursue Meg with every fiber of his being, Luke thought as he kissed her thoroughly, claiming her as his. This time he was going to put everything he had into their embrace until there was no more room for doubt, no room for anything but the incredible passion and heat they were feeling. So what if it was too soon for him to be telling her how much he wanted to marry her and so what if there was only the remotest chance she'd believe it, he thought as their lips melded and their tongues parried and stroked. So what if it was too soon for him to be telling her he wanted to be there for Jeremy, too. If he could make Meg feel for him even one-tenth of what he was feeling for her, they were well on their way to being the family the two of them should have been all along. Would have been, if only they hadn't been afraid to risk it all to be together.

Luke tore his lips from the yielding softness of hers, looked into turbulent blue eyes that were still innocent. Still trusting. Still afraid. Realizing all over again how much was at stake here, how much he stood to win—or lose—Luke pushed his own needs and wants aside and said gruffly, "Tell me this is what you want, Meg." Please tell me this is what you want. "I won't continue unless you do."

As the moment of truth came upon them, Meg hitched in a breath and looked deep into his eyes. "It's what I want," she said quietly. "Maybe more important, it's what I need."

Her throaty whisper was all he needed to hear to propel him to the next stage. His heart pounding, his spirit soaring, Luke swept her into his arms and carried her up the stairs to her bedroom. He tumbled her to the bed and draped his body over hers. "Tell me you care," he demanded fiercely, more determined than ever to make up for all the days and nights that had been stolen from them.

Meg wreathed her arms around his neck and again looked deep into his eyes. "I care," she said softly.

Then that was all they needed, Luke decided, as they came together once again. Kissing. Touching. Caressing.

The rest, the love, the commitment, the truth about the past and the mistakes she'd made and the child she'd borne, would come later. Right now, Luke thought as he pulled off her clothes and tugged off his own, the pleasure of being together was enough. It was more than enough to get them through the initial phases of their relationship. He kissed her again—hard, soft, and every way in between—holding her so close their bodies were almost one. His own body throbbing, he moved down her body, exploring as he went. Wooing and seducing until her whole body seemed to come alive in his arms, until he was sure she wanted him as much as he wanted her. Only then, when she was trembling and arching and surging against him, did he glide upward once again. Wanting her just that way, naked and yearning, beneath him, he spread her knees and slipped between them. The V of her thighs cradled his hardness, and his sex throbbed as he lifted her against him and surged into her surrendering softness. Whimpering her pleasure in a way that drove him wild with desire, she moved to receive him, and he pushed all the way inside. Being inside her was like being held in the grip of a soft, tight glove, and it was all he could do to contain himself. "Oh, Meg," Luke whispered.

Meg surged upward, the soft silky curves of her breasts and her tightly budding nipples pressing against his chest. "Don't hold back," Meg pleaded, her insides closing around him tightly, urging him on to release.

"Not much chance of that," Luke groaned, unable to get enough of her, as she shuddered and writhed beneath him, just as insatiable as he. Touching him. Loving him. Kissing him. Urging him to go deeper, harder still. Until there was no doubting they needed each other, needed this...not just to survive, but to thrive. Until at last he soared higher than he'd ever thought he could and together they catapulted into a cascading pleasure unlike anything either of them had ever known.

THE SHEETS WERE TANGLED around them as Meg lay in Luke's arms, her head on his chest. She knew that making love now, when so much was still unresolved between them, hadn't been the smartest move she'd ever made, given all the problems that could still crop up between them. But at the same time, loving Luke had never felt more right.

Maybe what Luke said was true, she thought, sighing softly, as her body continued to tremble with the aftershocks of their potent lovemaking. Maybe she and Luke did belong together this way. And every other way. Because the truth was, their lovemaking had been even more fulfilling, soothing and passionate than it had been the first—and only—other time they'd been together like this.

"What are you thinking?" Luke asked tenderly as he stroked a hand through her hair.

That I wish I had talked to you before I left Chicago and again immediately after I returned to Texas. That I wish I had turned to you long ago, when I needed you most. But not wanting to get into any of that for fear of where such a discussion could ultimately lead, Meg sighed and shifted away from him. The last thing she wanted to do was hurt him. And until she figured out what was right—for all of them—she couldn't go dredging up the past, jeopardizing the present or complicating their future. Not unless she was sure Luke wanted and needed them in his life as much as she and Jeremy needed him and his girls in theirs.

"I'm wishing I didn't have to get up," she confessed, as she plucked her robe off the end of her bed and shrugged it on. *Because there's nothing I'd like to do more than spend the entire night here, cuddling and making love with you.*

Luke lounged against the pillows. "So don't get up."

Meg only wished their lives were that simple and devoid of responsibilities. "I have to. Tomorrow's the chili cook-off, and I still have to frost those brownies."

Luke got up and tugged on his shorts. "I guess that's what we get for letting ourselves get distracted."

At the companionable note in his voice, Meg shot him a surprised glance. "You're going to help?"

"Of course." Grinning, Luke wrapped an arm affectionately about her waist and accompanied her down to the kitchen. "I wouldn't be much of a gentleman if I let you do this work all by yourself. Besides—" he winked at her playfully "—if I'm down here, I'll be able to taste test a few more."

Understanding that part of his motivation completely, Meg chuckled as she picked up the knife and began frosting the pans of freshly baked brownies. "I can see you're going to be a very handy man to have around."

"The same goes for you." Luke held the stainless steel

mixing bowl while Meg scooped out a generous amount of frosting for each pan. "Considering how well you cook and look and move and love and do just about everything."

Meg studied him, for a moment allowing herself to imagine what it would be like if she and Luke blended their lives this way permanently. Even if they never married, and combined lives, children and households, they could still face life's challenges together as friends, lovers, confidantes. Once again she wished she'd told Luke everything years ago. But she hadn't, and now she had to face the consequences of her mistake. She had to confront the possibility he might see what she'd done as not only foolish, but unforgivably reckless and selfish.

Knowing she was getting ahead of herself again, Meg forced herself to slow down and concentrate only on the moment at hand.

"You look happy," Meg said.

"I am happy." Luke watched as Meg spread frosting with quick, even strokes. "You want to know why?"

Finished, Meg dropped the spatula into the empty bowl and turned to Luke, keeping her eyes on his.

"Because what's happened here tonight changes everything," Luke said huskily as he took her into his arms.

She knew what he was thinking—that they were officially a couple now, and soon everyone would know. Aware he was moving a little too fast for her, once again, especially considering the complicated situation they were in, Meg pressed her hands against his chest. "I'm not sure I'm ready yet to run around announcing we're a couple to everyone in town, never mind our kids and my sisters—who, in case you don't know, can be awfully darn protective of me and each other."

Luke grinned, not minding at all what he was getting

into there. Families were a challenge he could handle. He kissed the inside of her wrist. "Prefer to keep it to ourselves?" he asked gently.

"For a little bit, if you don't mind." Meg sighed her relief, glad he was so quick to understand at least that much. "The kids have had a lot to handle. I think it might be easier if we let them adjust to the idea of us being friends and neighbors first. Boyfriend and girlfriend later."

Luke knew it was more than that, even if Meg wouldn't yet admit it to herself. They were apart because she wouldn't—couldn't—let herself confide in him yet. There would be no real lasting intimacy between them until she allowed herself to turn to him, not just in passion, but when she was troubled or sad, too. He wanted her to realize she could tell him anything and know he would not just listen but understand. He also knew Meg was still suffering from whatever foolish mistakes she had made years ago, and that she was doing her best to protect her son from any grief over any misstep she had taken, then or now. It was just like Meg to put the happiness of literally everyone else ahead of her own. It was one of the things he loved about her, even as he knew he also had to make her understand that it was okay for her to be happy, to take time for herself, too. "I don't mind keeping our romance under wraps for the time being, as long as I know the two of us will be together whenever we have a chance to be together," he stipulated firmly, kissing her once again.

"There's no one whose arms I'd rather be in than yours," Meg confessed.

"Exactly what I wanted to hear." Luke grinned his delight as he swept her up in his arms and carried her back upstairs to bed. He could accept they didn't have much time together, for the present, as long as they didn't waste a single second of it. Just as he could accept her silence on Jeremy's parentage, as long as she eventually trusted him enough to tell him everything and let him help her deal with it.

"Now," he teased, opening her robe and sliding his hands inside to the silky skin beneath, "where were we...?"

TO MEG AND LUKE'S mutual dismay, morning came all too soon. And with it, the need to hide any and all evidence of their tryst, as well as gather up everything they needed before heading out to the county fairgrounds for the chili cook-off. Luke still managed to steal a few kisses and talk her into going in the same vehicle, his Expedition, but as soon as they arrived, they had to go off to their separate stations. Luke with the other chili-cooking contestants, and Meg to the air-conditioned dining hall, where she dropped off her brownies for sale, then went to the ringtoss booth across the fairway where she would be working all morning.

While Meg worked hard with some of the other volunteers to set up her booth, Luke found his assigned place—on the corner, next to John McCabe—and began cooking. He was just putting the finishing touches on the big vat of chili he had prepared when his worst nightmare came true.

"What the heck is he doing here?" Luke announced to John McCabe, as the local high school band marched past to the catchy beat of a drum.

"Who?" John asked, confused.

Luke gave his chili another stir as he glared at the Austin, Texas, attorney. "Kip Brewster," Luke said unhappily. "Meg used to date him." Maybe it was selfish on his part, but the last thing Luke wanted was any more men lining up to be potential husbands for Meg and father figures for her son. He'd been without her too long to patiently suffer any competition now.

"She certainly does seem to remember him," John said dryly. "Although I'm not sure you need to be jealous. Even from here I can see Meg is giving him a polite but cool reception."

"That's not what I'm worried about," Luke murmured, his jealousy deflating as quickly as it had appeared as he added a little more chili powder to his concoction and waited for the rest of the judges to make their way down the lone line of entries to his booth.

"Then what?" John demanded, adding a little more onion to his.

"Kip's the guy I went to see last week. Meg still doesn't know about that, and if he tells her..."

"Trouble in paradise," John concluded.

Luke nodded, guilt washing over him anew. He should have told her. Lord knows if he'd had a lick of sense he would have told her. But he'd known if he had, Meg would've been furious.

John studied Luke with fatherly concern as the marching band made its way along the aisle adjacent to Meg's booth. "If she doesn't know that, then I'd wager she doesn't know you made inquiries on her and Jeremy's behalf, either," John said softly.

"You'd wager right." Luke frowned. "And I'll tell you this. A self-sufficient woman like Meg is not going to appreciate my attempts to look out for her and her son."

"Has she said anything more to you on that subject?" John asked.

"No." Luke sighed his regret. "I was hoping she'd tell me more when we began to get close again, but so far she hasn't divulged anything. Whenever the subject of Jeremy's father comes up, she—well, let's just say I can see the fear on her face."

Abruptly John looked as troubled as Luke felt about that. "Lasting relationships require a solid foundation. No foundation is possible without a lot of straight talk and honesty."

Luke grimaced in frustration. "That's why I want her to tell me the truth about Jeremy's father. I want to know for certain if it is or isn't me."

"Would it make a difference in how you feel about Jeremy if you were his father?"

"No. I can care for and love Jeremy in either case. But it would make a difference in the way I feel about Meg, if I saw her start to open up to me a little more. As it is, I have a feeling she's only going to let me get so close to her before she starts to pull back again."

"It's a two-way street, Luke. You've got to stop holding back, too. The sooner you level with her, the better."

Luke watched Meg continue to talk to Kip. To do that would be to lose every gain he'd made. "I'm not going to push her into something she isn't ready for." He would, however, find out what Kip was up to, Luke decided firmly. His chance to talk to Meg alone came midafternoon. She smiled as they met up on the midway. "I heard you sold all your chili," she said.

Luke pushed aside the guilt he felt for keeping anything from Meg. It was too late to go back now. Too late to pretend he hadn't been foolish or to analyze what made him so all-fired certain this was his business in the first place. All he knew was that he was in a very tricky situation that could potentially go quickly awry. All he knew was that the happiness of his future and Meg's and the kids' hung in the balance. He would tell Meg about his

Play **LUCKY HEARTS** for this...

exciting FREE gift!
This surprise mystery gift could be yours free

when you play **LUCKY HEARTS!**
...then continue your lucky streak with a sweetheart of a deal!

1. Play Lucky Hearts as instructed on the opposite page.

2. Send back this card and you'll receive 2 brand-new Harlequin American Romance® novels. These books have a cover price of $4.25 each in the U.S. and $4.99 each in Canada, but they are yours to keep absolutely free.

3. There's no catch! You're under no obligation to buy anything. We charge nothing—ZERO—for your first shipment. And you don't have to make any minimum number of purchases—not even one!

4. The fact is thousands of readers enjoy receiving their books by mail from the Harlequin Reader Service®. They enjoy the convenience of home delivery...they like getting the best new novels at discount prices, BEFORE they're available in stores...and they love their *Heart to Heart* subscriber newsletter featuring author news, horoscopes, recipes, book reviews and much more!

5. We hope that after receiving your free books you'll want to remain a subscriber. But the choice is yours—to continue or cancel, any time at all! So why not take us up on our invitation, with no risk of any kind. You'll be glad you did!

Visit us online at
www.eHarlequin.com

The Harlequin Reader Service®—Here's how it works:

Accepting your 2 free books and gift places you under no obligation to buy anything. You may keep the books and gift and return the shipping statement marked "cancel." If you do not cancel, about a month later we'll send you 4 additional novels and bill you just $3.57 each in the U.S., or $3.96 each in Canada, plus 25¢ shipping & handling per book and applicable taxes if any.* That's the complete price and — compared to cover prices of $4.25 each in the U.S. and $4.99 each in Canada — it's quite a bargain! You may cancel at any time, but if you choose to continue, every month we'll send you 4 more books, which you may either purchase at the discount price or return to us and cancel your subscription.

*Terms and prices subject to change without notice. Sales tax applicable in N.Y. Canadian residents will be charged applicable provincial taxes and GST.

If offer card is missing write to: Harlequin Reader Service, 3010 Walden Ave., P.O. Box 1867, Buffalo, NY 14240-1867

BUSINESS REPLY MAIL
FIRST-CLASS MAIL   PERMIT NO. 717   BUFFALO, NY

POSTAGE WILL BE PAID BY ADDRESSEE

HARLEQUIN READER SERVICE
3010 WALDEN AVE
PO BOX 1867
BUFFALO NY 14240-9952

NO POSTAGE
NECESSARY
IF MAILED
IN THE
UNITED STATES

visit to Kip and his continued hope that Jeremy was his son, but only when the time was right. Only when he thought it was something Meg needed to hear. Until then he would continue to pursue her, to woo and win her the way he should have from the first.

Aware Meg was still waiting for his reaction to the sale of his chili, he said, "It went a lot faster than I thought it would."

"Good for you." Meg paused and looked at him in a way that made him want to protect her all the more.

"Did you see the kids?"

Luke nodded. Meg's sisters—who were taking all five kids around together—had stopped by to see him several times during the morning, the children looking happy as could be. They'd also apparently had a great time at their sleepover at Alexandra's the previous night. Luke was glad they were having such a good time. Knowing they were well taken care of gave him the freedom and peace of mind to concentrate on his pursuit of Meg.

Luke fell into step beside Meg. She had caught her auburn hair into a bouncy ponytail on the back of her head and put a white tennis visor on to shade her face from the afternoon sun. Like the rest of the volunteers, she had on a white T-shirt with a giant red chili pepper on the front, festival lettering on the back. Pleated red shorts nicely cupped her backside and showed off her long, sexy legs to advantage. White crew socks covered her slender ankles, white running shoes cushioned her feet. She looked pretty and sexy in a very down-to-earth, approachable way.

Wishing he could think of something else besides kissing her and making love to her again whenever he was this close to her, he took over the metal cart she was pulling along behind her. "Where are you headed?"

Instead of letting go of the handle as he'd expected, Meg continued pulling the cart right along with him. "All the game booths are running out of prizes. I'm going out to the rental truck in the parking lot and bring some back."

Now there was an errand that would lend them some privacy, Luke thought. "I'll go with you and give you a hand," Luke volunteered.

"Thanks." Meg flashed him a smile. "I'd appreciate a pair of strong arms."

"Have you seen the kids recently?"

Meg nodded. "Dani and Beau were taking them to the showing of the Disney flick in the fairground auditorium."

Luke nodded as the security guard opened both sides of the gate and waved them through the service exit. "Good idea for the hottest part of the day."

"I have to tell you…" Meg searched her pockets and came up with the truck key. "I don't think they're going to make it much longer. I know they wanted to stay and see the fireworks tonight, but they all looked pretty tired to me."

"It's the heat," Luke sympathized, as Meg led the way down the row of vehicles to where the U-Haul was parked. "Even with all the tents they've got set up and the air-conditioned dining hall and display buildings, it really wears on you."

"I know." Meg unlocked the padlock on the rear door, then waited while Luke pushed it up. "Kelsey offered to take Jeremy home after the movie, and baby-sit until I get home tonight, and I think I'm going to take her up on the offer. If you want to send the girls home with her, I'm sure it would be okay."

Luke waited for all the hot air trapped inside the cargo

area to rush out, then gave Meg a leg up into the bed of the truck. "That's probably a good idea. I'm on a lunch break now, but I'm signed up to work a booth from three to six, the dining hall from seven to ten, and the first-aid tent from ten to midnight."

Meg looked over the stacks of boxes, reading the writing on the sides. "Which booth?"

"The basketball toss."

The corners of Meg's lips lifted wryly as she stopped and slanted him a glance. "Funny, I have the exact same schedule the rest of the day. You know who made up the schedule, don't you?"

Deciding she might need help finding the stuffed animals, Luke climbed up into the back of the truck, too. "Lilah McCabe."

Meg sighed and, finally locating the box she wanted, pointed it out to Luke. Naturally, it was beneath four other boxes. "That was no accident, you know. Lilah's matchmaking."

"I don't mind." Luke lifted off the other boxes one by one. "Do you?"

"I guess not." When they finally reached the box they needed, Meg moved it out. "Although I've always liked to make my own choices in the romance department."

"And every other," Luke said as he carried the box of stuffed animals over to the edge of the cargo area and dropped it down onto the cart, then went back to get the three others Meg had found that also needed to be transported.

"True," Meg admitted with a sassy smile. "I like to be the one giving marching orders, not taking them."

"Same here."

Meg sighed, looking suddenly as hot and tired as she had every right to be. She looked longingly at the snow cone truck on the other side of the fence and sat down on the closest box. "Looks like we're stuck, anyway—since I doubt Lilah McCabe is going to stop matchmaking anytime soon."

Luke figured he'd take all the help he could get in making Meg his permanently. But sensing she didn't want to hear that just yet, he merely grinned and said, "Wait here. I'll be right back." Before she had a chance to question him, he headed off, returning several minutes later with two large, cherry snow cones and a handful of paper napkins.

"You read my mind." Meg accepted hers gratefully and took a long thirst-quenching drink.

"We both need a break. It's been a long morning," he said, sitting beside her.

"After an even longer night," Meg murmured unexpectedly, a teasing light coming into her blue eyes.

Happiness swept through Luke as their eyes met and they both ruminated on the passion they'd discovered the night before. Passion that had only gotten stronger and more vital during the years they'd spent apart. "Guess we didn't get much sleep last night, did we?" he teased back, aware it was suddenly a struggle to keep from reaching for her again. But that wasn't why he'd wanted to talk to her alone, Luke reminded himself sternly. It was about what Meg's ex-boyfriend, Kip, knew that Meg still apparently didn't. As casually as he could, Luke said, "By the way, was that Kip Brewster I saw you talking with earlier?"

Meg licked the excess off the side of her paper cone. "Amazingly enough, it was. He read about the chili cookoff in the Austin paper." Meg frowned and blotted her lips with a napkin. "I'm surprised he didn't come by and see you—I told him you were in one of the cooking booths with a chili entry.''

Luke had an idea why that was, but found he was in the frustrating position of being unable to tell Meg everything here and now. ''Maybe I'll see him later,'' he said.

Meg looked at him, her eyes level and filled with a confused mixture of emotion Luke couldn't begin to decipher.

''I had the distinct impression he wasn't going to stay all that long,'' she said after a moment, and left it at that.

''Was he going to come by and see you again?'' Luke asked carefully, hating this position he'd gotten himself in, yet helpless to do anything about it for fear of ruining the resurgence of their romance.

''No.'' Meg's spine stiffened and she didn't look exactly happy again to be talking about this. ''I think Kip and I said everything we had to say to each other this morning.''

''Which was…?''

Refusing to give ground, Meg arched a brow at him and continued to enjoy her snow cone. ''You're awfully curious.''

''Give me a break.'' Refusing to examine his own emotions, he moved closer. ''I'm dating you.''

''Actually, Doctor,'' Meg corrected playfully **as** she swiveled to face him, her bare knee nudging his in the process, ''you and I haven't had an actual date.''

Liking the warmth of her bare skin pressed against his, even in this innocuous way, Luke grinned and tapped Meg on the end of her nose. ''That's something that can be easily corrected, Nurse.'' Noting she had nearly finished her snow cone, he went back to eating his. ''And stop torturing me and tell me what Kip wanted.''

Meg glanced at the tourists winding their way through

the parking lot, several rows over. Her eyes clouded. She sighed. "He wanted us to start fresh and begin dating all over again."

Somehow Luke wasn't surprised. Meg was one hell of a woman—a guy would have to be out of his mind not to want her. Kip wasn't out of his mind. Luke inclined his head to the side, wondering why Meg wouldn't quite meet his eyes. "You weren't interested?" he asked casually.

"No." Meg shook her head grimly, then turned back to Luke. "Kip lied to me so many times, with me never even for one moment suspecting."

Unfortunately, Kip wasn't the only one who had deceived Meg, Luke thought, as guilt flowed through him, stronger than ever. Aware their impromptu break was almost over, Luke finished his snow cone and crumpled the cup in his hand. "What happened between the two of you, anyway?" he asked, unable to keep his questions to himself. At the time of her breakup, Meg had refused to tell anyone. Luke had let it go, even though he'd thought it might help Meg more than she knew to unburden herself to someone. Now things were different. He wanted to be close to her. He knew he would never understand her the way he wanted to unless she trusted him enough to confide everything in him.

As skittish as ever when pressed, however, Meg stood and stepped away. Thrusting her hands into the pockets of her shorts, she turned her back to him. "It's a long story."

Not about to let it go when Kip was threatening—with his mere presence—to undo every ounce of renewed friendship and passion Luke had worked so hard to achieve, Luke watched her pace restlessly at the back of the truck. "I've got time," he said quietly.

She turned her eyes to his, looking both pleased and a little annoyed by his persistence. "You're beginning to sound jealous," she said.

Luke shrugged, not too proud to admit he was. "I guess I am. After all, you dated the guy for almost a year. For all intents and purposes it looked pretty serious to everyone who knew you."

"It was."

"And...?"

"And yet there was just something missing," Meg said quietly, coming back to sit beside Luke. She clasped her hands in her lap. "Kip kept pressuring me to move in with him. I wasn't ready, even though I knew he wanted to marry me, and I thought at the time that I might someday want to marry him. We fought about it a lot and then finally Kip backed off completely. I thought it was because he understood and respected my feelings about the two of us living together."

"But that wasn't the case," Luke guessed slowly, aware Kip hadn't told him this. Just as Meg wasn't telling him she hadn't slept with Kip.

"No." Meg let out a tremulous breath. A bleak look came into her eyes. "Kip, being the creative thinker he is, decided the perfect solution to our dilemma was to continue to date and eventually marry me, and see another law student, who didn't mind spending her nights with him whenever he was in the mood for overnight company, on the sly."

As stunned by the revelation as Meg had apparently once been, Luke could only stare at Meg.

Meg looked at the toe of her shoe, shook her head and continued ruefully, "I think at first Kip's other girlfriend really got off on all the sneaking around and pulling something over on me. But eventually she wanted more out of her relationship with Kip than she was getting, so she came to see me.'' Meg lifted her head, her eyes glimmering. "I can't tell you how foolish I felt.'' Embarrassed color pinkened Meg's cheeks. She spread her hands helplessly on either side of her. "Here I was,'' she continued in a low, humiliated voice, "ready to take Kip home to meet my folks and probably say yes to his proposal of marriage, and this other girl comes to see me, tells me she's tired of playing second fiddle. She wanted to move in with Kip full-time and she wanted me to know what was going on.''

Meg closed her eyes and continued in a low, devastated voice. "I felt so betrayed. Kip, of course, hinted it was all my fault. He said if I hadn't been such an uptight Southern girl about the whole living-together thing... Anyway, looking back I guess the betrayal left me feeling like I had something to prove on that score. Which is why I went off the deep end there a little bit, after my parents died. I needed to know there wasn't anything wrong with me. I needed to prove to myself that I could feel just as deeply and passionately as everyone else.''

Luke was silent. Was she trying to tell him that their night of passion had been just a morale-building experiment or that there had very briefly been others? He didn't want to think that had been the case, but he could also understand how and why it had happened if there had been.

"Worst of all,'' she continued, looking as thoroughly and understandably devastated at the memory as Luke would've expected her to be, "was how blind I had been to Kip's deception, never once picking up on any of the clues even when they were staring me in the face.''

Regret darkened Meg's blue eyes as she explained in a low, heartfelt voice, "I compared that to my mom and dad and how in tune they were with each other, how they knew what each other was thinking or feeling without ever saying a word.''

Meg reached over and took Luke's hand in hers. "There were no secrets between them. They were so close. And that's what I wanted for myself," she confided earnestly, "that kind of deep and abiding intimacy.''

Regret washed through Luke as he thought about all the things he and Meg still couldn't seem to tell each other.

"Anyway, I decided right then and there that only if I found that kind of intimacy would I ever marry.'' Meg's jaw set stubbornly. "Kip and I didn't have it. Never would.''

The question was…would Meg come to the same conclusion about the two of them if she knew the truth? Luke wondered uncomfortably. Wishing he'd realized what Kip was up to back then, and that he could have somehow intervened or prevented her hurt, Luke studied Meg with a depth of compassion he didn't even know he had. "You don't even want to be friends with Kip now?''

Meg paused uncertainly, her emotions in turmoil. "That is something I am going to have to think about,'' she said eventually, still looking as if she felt a little distressed by what had happened. "On the one hand, I don't see the point in having any ill will between us now, since what happened was a long time ago. On the other hand, I'm not totally sure I could ever trust him to be a really good friend again, either. Not after the way he repeatedly lied to me and I bought it hook, line and sinker. 'Cause I would just be wondering whenever I was with him, if he was pulling something over on me again, going behind my back and me too blind to see. I don't know,'' she ruminated in a low, anguished voice, looking away before turning back to him. "Maybe the solution is for Kip and me to be civil and polite whenever we do run into each other and let it go at that."

The question was, would Kip be content to let it go at that? Just the fact Kip had driven all the way out here to see Meg again showed a level of interest Luke didn't like or trust.

John and Lilah were right, Luke thought uncomfortably. He should have told Meg he had been to see Kip on her and Jeremy's behalf. Because if she found out he had known for days now that Kip could not be Jeremy's father, and had not said a word to her, she might never forgive him.

ALTHOUGH THE ACTUAL JUDGING had been done at noon traditionally, and the various concoctions sold directly from their vats on the midway as well as taken to the dining hall for sampling, the winners of the cook-off weren't announced until 6:00 p.m. that evening.

"Sorry yours didn't win," Meg turned to Luke, who, along with her, had just entered the dining hall on his dinner break.

"That's okay," Luke said confidently as they entered the cafeteria-style line and picked up two plastic trays. "It was only my first year. I made a respectable showing, which, given my lack of experience in this venue, was all I could expect. I've got twelve months to come up with a chili that will knock everybody's socks off."

"Not competitive, are you?" Meg flashed him a teasing grin as she added a salad to her plate, then watched as Luke did the same.

"Not in the least," Luke lied through his teeth.

Meg looked beyond Luke. Her smile faded as fast as it had appeared. "Oh, no."

Luke grew alarmed at the dread on Meg's face. "What?" he demanded.

Meg grabbed Luke's elbow. "Here comes Shane McCabe."

"So?"

"So hide me."

Too late. Shane had spotted her and come over to see her, his new wife, Greta, right behind him. "You can duck but you can't hide," Shane taunted, plucking Meg out from behind Luke. "And don't try fibbing to me, 'cause I know you haven't even had a spoonful of my chili yet."

Meg beamed and extended a hand. "Congratulations for winning the fire-eaters category."

"Thanks," Shane said, looking pleased as punch about his win. "It's definitely six-alarm this year, even if I do say so myself. Only problem is," he confided with a woeful sigh, "people are afraid to even try it."

Meg rolled her eyes and offered no sympathy. "For good reason, given your list of ingredients."

"Since when have you been afraid of a few jalapeño peppers?" Shane demanded with the ease and familiarity of a childhood friend. "Why, I remember when you could down half a dozen of them—whole—at a time, with only a little root beer for a chaser."

"I was sixteen, and I didn't have the sense God gave a goose," Meg said as she continued to move down the line, selecting some corn bread and iced tea, too.

"C'mon, Meg," Shane McCabe pleaded shamelessly, "if you eat it, everyone else will, too. I'm humiliated, seeing everyone else's vats of chili get emptied out, while I'm standing there with nearly a full kettle of it. I even brought some in here and put it over there, in the warmer, and I still can't get rid of it."

"It's actually pretty good," Greta promised.

"And if there's one thing Greta knows, as owner of the best dinner-and-dance hall in Texas, it's food," Shane enthused.

Luke shrugged. "I've always liked hot stuff. I'll give it a try."

"That's the spirit!" Shane clapped Luke on the back. He rushed around behind the counter to ladle up a big bowl of steaming chili. "Meg?" Shane looked at her hopefully.

Meg sighed and gave in, already looking as if she was going to regret it. "I'll take a bowl, too, but make it a small one, Shane. I'm not as adventurous as I used to be."

"HEARTBURN?" Luke guessed at the reason behind the pained expression on Meg's face.

"Like you wouldn't believe," Meg drawled as she plucked one of the festival's complementary rolls of antacids from her pocket and popped a couple of chalky-tasting tablets in her mouth. She shook her head ruefully as the burning in her entire digestive tract began, at last, to ease. "I should have known better than to trust Shane's cooking."

"It was nice of you to eat the whole bowl, though," Luke said, wishing their duties there were over and the day was done so he could pull her into his arms and make love to her all over again.

Oblivious to the sensual nature of his thoughts, Meg slanted Luke a glance as they walked through the warm, food-scented darkness toward the first aid tent where their next—and last—work assignment of the night was located. "You ate yours, too," she pointed out cheerfully, looking a little peeved he didn't have some sort of indigestion.

"Yeah, but I like really spicy food," Luke countered,

deciding this was not the time to tell her he had a cast iron stomach.

"I used to, too." Meg sighed lustily as she pressed a hand to her rib cage, just below her breasts.

"Until you developed heartburn in reaction to it?" Luke guessed, tearing his eyes from the way her T-shirt clung to her sexy curves.

A telltale hint of color added to the sunburn on Meg's cheeks. "Actually, I always had heartburn if I ate too many jalapeños," she confided, easing closer to him as they threaded their way through the throngs of people on the midway. "I was just too stubborn to admit it."

Luke rested his hand on her waist as they went single file through a narrow opening in the crowd, then, liking the way it felt to hold on to her that way, kept his arm around her as they walked side by side again. The more he was with her, the more she revealed. "So you suffered in silence," he guessed, happy to feel them getting closer with every moment that passed.

Meg shrugged, curving contentedly into his side. "Better than listening to my parents and everyone else say, 'I told you so.'"

"They did that a lot, hmm?" Luke tugged playfully at the bouncy ponytail on the back of Meg's head.

"Not really." Meg smiled, recollecting blissfully. "I just remember the times they said it. They always left it up to us to determine what we could or could not handle. That's the way they taught us good judgment, by leaving a lot of the decisions up to us. I can still hear my mom and dad saying to us, 'Yes, it's fine with us. If you think you can handle it....' Because I was the oldest I always wanted to do more than maybe I should have. I was always out to prove how responsible and independent I was."

Luke could imagine that. "So you got into jalapeño-eating contests with Shane McCabe," he guessed dryly.

"Among other things." Meg led the way through another narrow gap in the crowd. "Fortunately, I've grown up and I don't have as much to prove."

Luke wasn't sure he agreed with that. From what he could see, Meg was still independent to a fault and out to prove she hadn't made a mistake, in deciding to bring up Jeremy on her own and not divulge who his father was. Even if she had realized she had made a mistake in choosing that particular path, it was going to be very hard for her to admit that was the case and do otherwise.

As they reached the first aid tent, Meg paused. "I want to call home before I start my shift and check on the kids."

"Good idea." Luke handed over the cell phone he wore clipped to his belt. He watched as Meg studied the function keys on the front of it. "I hope they're not giving Kelsey a hard time."

"Ten-to-one, they're asleep," Meg predicted as she began to dial.

"Well?" Luke said minutes later when Meg had hung up.

Meg's smile flashed, warm and mesmerizing in its intensity. "Kelsey said they've been asleep since eight in their sleeping bags on the living room floor. She's been napping on and off, too, and finally decided to borrow some of my pajamas, sack out on my sofa next to them and stay the night."

Luke relaxed, glad things were under control. "What time did you tell her we'd be home?"

"Twelve-thirty. She said not to worry—we can stay out as late as we want."

Now that sounded like a good idea, Luke thought, as

all sorts of wonderful possibilities sprang to mind. He reached down and brushed a tendril of auburn hair from Meg's cheek and tucked it behind her ear. "Do you want to go out after we're done here?"

Meg shot him a quick, astonished glance. "Do you?"

Chapter Seven

"I can't believe I'm such a party-pooper," Meg said, as Luke pulled into his driveway, shortly after midnight Saturday evening.

"Given how many people are currently trying to match-make us into a couple, there will be plenty more chances for us to kick up our heels and stay out half the night. Right now, we've got to do something about that heart-burn of yours. You definitely need something stronger than the over-the-counter stuff you've been munching on all evening."

Meg climbed out of Luke's Expedition with his assistance. "Unfortunately, I don't have something stronger."

"Luckily for you, I do." Luke took her elbow and steered her inside his house.

As he turned on lights, Meg was struck by two things: the faint smell of new paint and the taupe-colored walls with white trim. The neutral color was fashionable, mas-culine and coordinated nicely with both the oak floors and the eclectic mix of furniture and area rugs he already had.

Meg turned to him admiringly. "Oh, Luke, this looks so much nicer inside having all the walls down here painted the same color." It made the large airy rooms of the century-old house seem to flow into each other.

Luke grinned, pleased by the final result, too. "I'm glad you like it. Because it's the same color on all the walls upstairs, too—except for the girls' rooms and bath, which are painted in pastels."

Luke opened up his medical bag, took out a sample packet of prescription acid-reflux medicine and got her a glass of ice water. "Try this."

"Thanks." Meg opened the packet and gulped the medicine.

Luke threw the paper wrapping away. "Just think of it as one of the side benefits of dating a doctor," he teased, leading her through the living room to the leather sofa in his study.

"Well, I need you now," Meg quipped back as she sank down on the smooth, cool cushions. She rubbed her sternum with her fist, impatiently waiting for the discomfort to ease as she confessed, "This is the worst case of heartburn I've had since I was pregnant with Jeremy."

Luke's eyes darkened with interest as he closed the wooden blinds and put on some soft, relaxing music, and Meg tried not to feel so vulnerable where he was concerned. "What was your pregnancy like?" he asked, coming back to her side.

Meg's mood shifted as she thought back to that very difficult time of her life. Aware she wouldn't have wanted to share any of this with him a few days ago, she admitted, "It was hard, from an emotional standpoint." Appreciating the way he was fussing over her, despite her protests it wasn't necessary, Meg leaned forward, so he could put a pillow behind her back. She smiled as he knelt in front of her and began taking off her running shoes. "It was fairly easy from a physiological one."

Luke sat in the middle of the sofa and shifted Meg around so she was sitting with her back to the arm of the sofa, her feet in his lap. "What kind of physical complaints did you have?" Luke asked as he worked off her socks and began to massage her tired arches.

Meg had known Luke was a man of many talents, but she couldn't believe how good his impromptu massage felt. She uttered a blissful sigh, glad to be with him like this. Happier still to finally be able to share this much of her pregnancy with Luke—even if she hadn't yet worked up the courage to tell him the truth. "I had occasional bouts of really fierce heartburn, swollen ankles and an aching back during the last trimester. That was it."

"No morning sickness?" Luke asked gently, surprised.

Meg shook her head, as the heartburn generated by Shane McCabe's outrageously hot chili finally began to ease. "Nope. Not once, amazingly enough, which is part of the reason it took me so long to realize I was pregnant." Meg relaxed even more as Luke moved from her arches to the balls of her feet.

His expression as tender as his touch, Luke asked quietly, "When did you figure it out?"

Knowing—as a nurse—she should have been more aware of what was going on with her, Meg admitted with no small amount of embarrassment, "Not until I was a good three and a half months along. I thought my lack of periods was due to stress at losing my parents, dropping out of the MSN program in Chicago, moving back to Laramie and trying to be a mother to my three younger sisters, all of whom resented me as much as they needed me." She shook her head ruefully, looking back. "The tornado touched down only in rural areas, sparing the town. But many ranches in the area had been hit. Fences knocked down, trees uprooted, roofs blown off. Our parents were the only fatalities among all the injuries. It wasn't an easy time for any of us," Meg continued, wanting Luke to understand the enormity of the trauma they'd been through. "Kelsey felt very guilty because she wasn't where she was supposed to be and my parents had been out frantically looking for her at the time the tornado hit. Jenna was so traumatized by the loss she tried to elope with Jake, even though they were underage. And I was so clueless as to what was going on there I didn't even know they were eloping! His parents did, however, and promptly put a stop to it, and then Jake married someone else. It was an awful summer for her."

Luke's golden-brown eyes gentled all the more as he asked sympathetically, "What about Dani?"

Meg tensed as she thought back to the way she had, in one way or another, failed all three of her sisters during that awful time in their lives, just as she had failed Luke and Jeremy, too. Meg looked at Luke. "She changed overnight, going from this dreamy kid to a completely cynical adult who didn't believe that anyone would ever live happily again."

"Sounds like you had your hands full."

"Oh, yeah, and then some." Meg blew out a weary breath, trying hard not to focus on how good, how right it felt to be here with him like this. "Plus there were problems with my parents' estate—we had to sell the ranch and rent a much smaller house so Dani and Kelsey could finish high school and Jenna could go to college and study fashion design."

"What about your master's?" Luke moved on to her toes, working the same subtle magic there.

"I finally finished it last May."

"Good for you."

Meg smiled, her insides warming at his praise, her body melting at his touch.

Luke looked at her steadily. "How did your sisters feel about you being pregnant and keeping Jeremy?"

Remembering the awful mess she'd found herself in, not to mention her distress at having to handle it all by herself all the while acting as if it were no big deal, Meg tensed and shook her head. She'd made mistakes there. Big ones. No doubt about it.

Yet, knowing there was no one else on earth she would talk to about this, except Luke, Meg looked at him and confided, "My sisters were shocked to discover I was pregnant and so was practically everyone else in Laramie. I had a rep for being Miss Goody Two-shoes of all time. The wildest thing I'd ever done was try to eat more jalapeño peppers at one sitting than Shane McCabe. They just couldn't picture me having a baby out of wedlock. They were even more infuriated that I wouldn't disclose...to anyone...who the father was." Some of the loneliness and despair she'd felt at the time came back to wrap around her heart. "It was something I had to handle by myself." And she had done so with unflagging courage.

Regret darkened Luke's eyes. "I'm sorry you had to go through it alone. I wish I'd known. I wish I'd been there to help you through Jeremy's birth—even just as a friend."

Meg ducked her head, guilt washing all over her anew, for all Luke still didn't know...might never know...unless she could figure out a way to tell him without hurting anyone else. Especially him. "There isn't anything you could have done for me. You were starting your residency in California, you had a new wife, and a baby of your own on the way. Gwyneth needed you, too. And because she was your wife," Meg continued firmly, sure about this much, "Gwyneth's needs, and the demands of your marriage, took precedence over mine."

AS MUCH AS LUKE WAS LOATH to admit it, Meg was right. There wasn't much he could have done from California except maybe make things worse for Meg. Because Gwyneth would not have made it easy on him, and she would have made it hell on Meg. If Jeremy had turned out to be Luke's child, there would have either been a messy divorce, and a child custody battle over Susie, or a marriage made in hell from that point forward, with Gwyneth punishing him for his "infidelity to her while they were dating" every step of the way. He would have been torn between Susie and Jeremy, unable to live in the same community or geographical proximity to both. At that time Meg hadn't needed any more stress or grief in her life. As far as Meg and he were concerned, Luke thought, Meg had done the only thing she could to survive, which was to handle everything without Luke's help. And if Jeremy hadn't been his, Gwyneth would have resented Luke's involvement in what Gwyneth would have considered to be Meg's problem. It had been a losing situation, either way.

"Don't feel bad for me, Luke." Meg swung her legs off his lap and shifted around so she was sitting beside him, facing him, her legs tucked to the other side. "It was tough but I got though it okay," she said softly, earnestly. "And so did Jeremy."

"I still wish I had made things easier for you after your parents died, instead of more difficult."

Meg took his hands in both of hers. "I'm the one who made love impulsively without a thought to contraception, and then ended up pregnant." She pressed her free hand to her chest. "I'm the one who didn't return your calls and sent your letters back unopened and asked my sisters to ask you never to call me again." Her eyes still holding his with difficulty, Meg released a tremulous sigh and shook her head in regret. "I couldn't have been plainer about what I wanted from you that summer, which was to be left alone. You did what I asked, and there's a part of me that's even grateful that you did, because it was better for all of us then."

Meg's voice dropped a notch and her fingers tightened affectionately on his. "Just as there's a part of me now that's grateful you've come back into my life." Meg gave him a watery smile. Her lower lip trembled, yet her voice remained steady. "Because the truth is I missed you. I missed our talks. I missed the way you were always there for me, to applaud my successes and mourn my failures and to cheer me on no matter what. You were—and are again—a really, really good friend."

Luke wanted to be a hell of a lot more than Meg's friend. He wanted to be her husband and her lover and the father to her son. But he figured they'd get there. Right now it was enough that Meg had trusted him to tell him as much as she had. If they kept getting closer, he knew it wouldn't be long before she told him the rest. And once she had, there'd be no more secrets between them, nothing to keep them apart. He would have the woman he'd always wanted permanently in his life, a son to love, and his daughters would have a mother again, too.

Grinning, Luke hooked his hands around Meg's slender waist and shifted her onto his lap. "I'm glad to hear it," he drawled, tucking his hand beneath her chin and kissing her gently. "Because the truth is, I missed you, too." He looked deep into her eyes. "I've never enjoyed being with anyone as much as I enjoy being with you."

Meg took a deep breath and again seemed to be struggling with something. "All I want is for us to move forward and forget everything that happened in the past that shouldn't have happened." Tentatively she traced the chili-pepper design on his shirt. "Do you think we can do that?"

Luke nodded. Capturing her fingers, he brought them to his lips for a kiss. "I know we can."

For a moment they sat together in comfortable silence. Aware how much he wanted to make love with her, Luke looked over at Meg. "How are you feeling now?" he asked gently.

Meg relaxed against him. "The medicine worked. My heartburn has totally gone away."

"Glad to hear it," Luke said, doing what he'd been thinking about all evening and easing the hem of her T-shirt from the waistband of her shorts. He slid his hands over the silky warmth of her skin, moving them up over her ribs. He pressed his lips to her neck and tasted the salty residue of a day spent working in the Texas sun. "Because talking about the past is not the way I want the evening to end."

Meg shuddered as his hands claimed her breasts. "It isn't."

"No," Luke said, his mood purposeful as he shifted Meg again so she was lying back on the sofa and he was draped over her. He kissed the inside of each wrist. "This is how I want our evening to end."

Meg moaned as she melted against him. "I want to make love, too," she whispered. "But I feel so grimy and sweaty."

So did he. "Fortunately, we can remedy that."

Meg gasped as Luke lifted her off the sofa, stood and then swept her right back into his arms. "What are you doing?"

Feeling every bit as mischievous as he had in his youth, Luke said, "Seeing we both get the nice long hot shower we need."

Anticipation glimmered in her aqua eyes. "Somehow I think that's not all you have in mind," Meg teased as she clung to his shoulders.

"Somehow I think you're right." A very primitive satisfaction rushed through Luke as he swept Meg up the stairs to the master bedroom, past the rumpled covers on his bed to the completely redone master bath.

Meg sucked in her breath as Luke set her down just outside the tile-walled shower. A recent addition to the house, it was big enough for two and even featured dual shower heads, one on each side of the rectangular enclosure. Luke hadn't thought much about that—until now. His mind filled with fantasies of the two of them, showering together each morning, making love there at night. He had definitely bought the right house. When they got married—and he was beginning to believe that might happen even sooner than he hoped—she could move right in.

Luke reached in and turned on both spigots, letting the water come out full force, then adjusted the water to warm. A scant minute later they were standing naked beneath the spray.

He covered a washcloth with soapy lather and washed her from head to toe. He was so aroused he could barely catch his breath as she did the same. And then they were standing beneath the spray, kissing, using cupped handfuls of water and sweet, gentle touches to rinse the bubbles away. They made love against the wall of the shower and again in his bed. Exhausted, they clung together, her head on his chest. "Five minutes," Meg said sleepily, as she cuddled even closer. "Then I'm definitely getting up and going home."

Luke pressed a kiss to the top of her head and dreamed of the day this would be her home. "I'll walk you," he promised. And at 4:00 a.m. he did.

"DON'T TELL ME YOU FORGOT we were all coming over here for brunch today," Jenna said to Meg as she stood in the doorway, a plate of freshly baked blueberry muffins in hand.

Dani strode up the walk after her sister while Jake and Beau struggled to control Buster and Miss Kitty, Alexandra's golden retriever puppy and striped gray kitten, who'd also come for a visit and a romp with the kids on the lawn. Dani took one look at Meg's face and said with sisterly amusement, "She forgot, all right."

Luke came out of his house, saw the commotion and headed over to say hello to his kids. Meg's heart rate kicked up and her spirits soared, just watching him stroll toward her.

"What's going on here?" Dani demanded, staring at Meg as if she'd never seen this side of her before. "You know you host all of us for brunch every weekend. This weekend it happens to be on Sunday instead of Saturday, because of the chili cook-off yesterday."

Kelsey yawned and stretched and came up off the sofa, where she'd been lazing since Meg and the kids had awakened half an hour earlier. "I'll tell you what's happening—our dependable big sister's in love. And it's made every rational thought fly right out of her head."

"I never said that!" Meg asserted as Luke made his way through the hedge to greet his children. He was wearing a plain navy T-shirt, stone-colored cotton shorts and deck shoes. He looked handsome and freshly shaved and showered. Which in turn made her think of all the wild and wicked things they'd done in his shower the night before.

"You didn't say you aren't in love, either," Dani noted, analyzing Meg bluntly. "So what is it?" Dani asked, zeroing in on the telltale blush in Meg's cheeks. "Are you or aren't you?"

Thank heaven Kelsey didn't know how late she had come in last night, or that she'd practically spent the whole night in Luke's bed, Meg thought, or she'd be telling Meg's sisters that, too. Meg brushed her hands through her hair. "I...um...well..."

"Yes?" All three of her sisters leaned closer, hanging on Meg's every word.

"Luke and I haven't discussed that," Meg said finally. They hadn't had time, they'd been so busy discovering the many ways to pleasure each other.

"She's in love," all three sisters decided in unison.

"Who's in love?" Luke asked curiously as he came in the back door, walked straight over to Meg, put his arm around her waist and planted a kiss on her forehead.

Knowing full well what her sisters would make of that, Meg blushed from the soles of her feet to the roots of her hair.

"Well?" Luke said, obviously curious as to what was going on.

Meg's flush deepened. She wanted to tell Luke she loved him, she wanted to ask him to be the father Jeremy needed, but when she did, it wasn't going to be like this, Meg determined firmly, with all her sisters around, watching. When she did tell him all that was in her heart and on her mind, the time would be right. They would be alone. It would be completely private. They would already have worked out every problem and potential area of conflict between them, and she'd know without a doubt in the world that she was doing the right thing for her and for Jeremy inviting Luke to become a permanent part of their lives. She would know for certain Luke could and would forgive her for all the mistakes she'd made in the past. Because if he couldn't...well, Meg knew they'd all suffered way too much hurt in their lives to intentionally inflict any more.

"It's nothing," Meg fibbed, slipping out of Luke's embrace, wishing once again she'd never decided to protect everyone with her silence. "We're having brunch. You and the girls should stay."

The argument—about imposing—that would have happened only days before never came.

"Sounds good," Luke said casually, looking as if there was nowhere else he'd rather be on earth than right there with Meg and all of her sisters and their loved ones. He turned to Kelsey. "I wanted to thank you all for helping watch the kids yesterday while we worked at the festival. It was really nice of you."

"That's what family is for," Jenna said gently.

Dani nodded. "We always help out Meg, and she helps us. If you're going to be part of her life on a continuing basis, of course that will include you, too," she finished, meaning dripping from her every word.

"Geez. Why not just come right out and ask him what his intentions are toward Meg?" Kelsey chided as she plucked a grape off the counter.

"Okay," Jenna said with a shrug, refusing to be called off, now that she was in familial-protection mode. "What are your intentions toward our sister, Luke Carrigan!"

"For heaven's sake!" Meg interrupted the interrogation, incensed. She turned to Luke, feeling embarrassed and uneasy. "You do not have to answer that question."

"Sure I do." Luke grinned and turned back to her sisters. "I like her, I respect her and consider us to be exclusively involved with each other. Is that plain enough for all of you?"

"Yes, but are you going to marry her—that's what they want to know," Kelsey said impatiently as she popped a grape in her mouth. "Since Jenna and Dani got married, all they want to do is marry Meg and me off, too. Only in my case," Kelsey boasted cheerfully, "I can assure you it is not going to happen. When it comes to Meg…before you moved next door, I would have said that was the case, too…but now I don't know."

Meg held up both hands. "Okay, sisters, that's quite enough discussion of my love life."

Luke shot a look at Meg. That quickly, he took charge and regarded them with a serious expression. "I want to answer this, Meg." Bracing his hands on his waist, Luke turned back to Meg's sisters. "If I have my way, marriage may very well be in the cards someday. But you can bet your bottom dollar I won't be proposing to your sister in front of all of you. When and if it happens, it will be in the right place at the right time. Where I can steal a kiss or two or three." Luke grinned mischievously at Meg's protectors. "Got it?"

Dani pretended to wipe sweat from her brow. "Whew, Sis, I think you've met your match."

Jenna nodded. "Me, too."

Kelsey regarded Luke. "Well, I'll say this for you," she eventually drawled, "you've certainly made my big sis blush and smile more in ten minutes than I've ever seen her blush and smile in her life. That's gotta count for something."

"THANKS AGAIN FOR BABY-SITTING," Luke said later as Kelsey prepared to head on home. She had given him and Meg some much-needed time alone.

"No problem." Kelsey grinned, looking as relaxed and carefree as always. "Especially—" she winked mischievously at Luke and Meg "—now that it's your turn to do a favor for me."

Luke figured he owed Kelsey a favor and then some. "Name it."

"Brady Anderson, my business partner, is bringing a half dozen Shetland ponies out to the ranch today. I'm thinking about buying at least two of them for my riding stables. But before I make a commitment like that, I need to try them out, and I need some kids to do the riding so I can see which two I like best. Jake and Jenna already said they'd bring Alexandra—I asked them yesterday. I would really like it if you would bring Jeremy, Susie, Becca and Amy, too. It'd give them a chance to have some pony rides and me to really put the ponies to the test before I make a decision whether to buy them or not."

"Sure. Sounds like fun," Luke responded, before Meg could think of a reason why not.

"How about this evening, say around seven? That'll give us plenty of time to work with them before you get out there."

"We'll see you then."

Luke noted Meg didn't look as happy about the plan as he was. But just then there was a crisis as Jake and Jenna tried somewhat unsuccessfully to round up Buster and Miss Kitty, who had apparently decided they were having too much fun to go home, and he had no chance to ask her about it.

Another crisis—this one at the hospital—had him over at the emergency room most of the afternoon, with him arriving home just in time to load up the kids and head out to the Lockhart Ranch along with Meg.

Meg was unusually quiet on the ride out there, speaking only to give him directions. But whether that was because she was exhausted from the chili festival the day before, their late night and almost no sleep, the morning with her family, plus baby-sitting all four of their kids that afternoon, or because she had some objection to going out to Kelsey's, Luke couldn't tell. He only knew she'd put a wall up between them again, and he didn't like it one bit.

When they arrived, Jake and Jenna were already there with Alexandra—who was already seated on one of the half dozen Shetland ponies. Kelsey introduced her partner, Brady Anderson, to Luke. Dani and Beau had come out, to watch and lend a hand. But instead of being happy to see all three of her sisters, and the three experienced cowboys on hand, never mind the exuberance of all five of the kids, Meg looked even more unhappy and ill at ease.

Her sisters noticed, too.

Luke watched them all exchange worried glances before Kelsey suggested, "Meg, why don't you show Luke around? He hasn't been here before, and I'm sure he'd like to see the place where we all grew up, hear some of the stories. We've got plenty of adults here to supervise the riding."

Meg looked even grimmer. For a moment Luke thought she was going to refuse, then she smiled tightly and said, "Fine." She turned on her heel and stomped off in the direction of the fields, not the ranch house.

"We'll be back," Luke said with a disgruntled exhalation of breath and headed after her. Because they were going to be out on the ranch, they'd all had to change into boots, jeans, long-sleeved shirts and hats, as well as mosquito and tick repellent and sunscreen. Luke tramped through the tall grass after her, ducking sagebrush and mesquite as he went. "Do you want to tell me what's going on or am I just supposed to guess why you're so unhappy?"

Meg scowled at him like he was the one at fault and kept going. "I don't like being manipulated or pushed into something I don't want to do."

Luke lengthened his strides and caught up with her. "Which is to what," he interjected sarcastically, "let Jeremy ride a Shetland pony?"

"Which is to come out here," Meg corrected, just as testily, tugging her hat lower on her brow. Resentment boiled over in her low voice and glittered hotly in her eyes. "Kelsey knows I haven't been back here since we sold the place after Mom and Dad died. She also knows I don't approve of her going in with Brady Anderson to buy it back."

Luke shrugged, still not seeing what the big deal was, despite the full blown temper tantrum Meg was pitching. "Brady seemed like a nice enough guy." As they reached a fence that needed climbing, Luke paused. "He also has a way with horses and kids."

"I know that," Meg retorted as she propped her boot on a rail and propelled herself over the wooden fence and back down onto the ground. "If he weren't a good guy," Meg continued, dusting off her hands, "Travis McCabe—John and Lilah's oldest son—never would have hired him to work on his ranch. The problem is—" Meg paused as Luke vaulted over the fence, too, and landed on the ground beside her "—Kelsey barely knows him. She'd only been acquainted with him for a month before she decided to partner with him."

Luke wanted to gather Meg in his arms and keep her there until she calmed down. Sensing Meg needed to work off her angst, he encouraged her to keep spouting instead. "They seem to be getting along so far," he remarked as they headed off across a field filled with yellow, blue and white wildflowers.

"Only because he's not living out here yet." Ignoring the beauty of their surroundings, Meg stormed along until she came to a small stream and, using the flat rocks lined up for that purpose, walked across it. "He's still working for Travis McCabe and bunking there, and he will be until at least September."

Still kicking water off the bottom of his boots, Luke followed Meg up the bank and into the next pasture. "Why is Brady doing that if he bought this place with Kelsey?"

Meg focused on the first hint of sunset along the horizon. Suspicion lit her eyes. "Brady says it's because he promised Travis he'd stay through the summer, until they can get one of his herds to market, but I think it's a lot more than that." She looked at Luke earnestly. "Travis runs a first-rate spread. He's a fair man, and he pays well. He'd have no problem finding a replacement cowhand. Brady just doesn't want to be out here alone with Kelsey. He's afraid what will happen if they ever do live under one roof."

"And that is...?" Luke asked as they made their way through a small woods.

"One of two things." Meg sighed unhappily, edging closer to him as they picked their way carefully through the trees. "Either their partnership will fall apart, and Kelsey will leave Brady in the dust the way she has every other man she has ever dated. Or they'll become romantically involved, which Brady wouldn't want, either, because he's reportedly every bit as hard to tie down as Kelsey."

"Yet he bought this ranch," Luke pointed out.

"A fact he could already be regretting," Meg predicted glumly.

Luke studied Meg. He'd never seen her this moody or pessimistic. It worried him. "You don't seem to have a lot of faith in your little sister." Luke tried not to sound as critical as he felt.

Meg sighed and rubbed the back of her neck. "It's not that so much as I'm worried about her. Since Mom and Dad died, she's had a dozen careers and two or three times as many boyfriends, none of whom have ever lasted for long."

Luke caught Meg's arm and stopped her headlong flight. "Maybe she's trying to turn over a new leaf. Settle down. Make some kind of stable life for herself."

"But here—of all places," Meg protested, as Luke decided enough was enough and backed her up against a tree.

"It was her home, too," Luke pointed out quietly.

The bleak, unhappy look was back in Meg's eyes. "It's also the place where we lost everything."

"And you're still angry about that," Luke guessed. *And hurt.*

"Yes." Tears in her eyes, Meg swung away from him and pushed on. "And you know why?" she said in a low voice, thick with long-pent-up emotion. "Because this was a tragedy that could have been prevented so easily if my parents had just paid more attention to the weather reports and made Kelsey stay close to the house that afternoon, whether she wanted to or not."

"But they didn't."

"No, they didn't. And that's why I don't like to be out here, and why I didn't approve of her buying this place, either. Because being out here makes me think of all this, and I don't want to think about it. I just want to put it behind me and forget it ever happened."

"But it did happen," Luke said gently, closing the distance between them and taking her resisting body into his arms. "And the sooner you face up to it and deal with it the better."

"I have faced up to it," she defended herself, turning away from him. "I know, maybe better than anyone, that the only person I can count on to take care of me, my son and my sisters is me."

Which was yet another reason why, Luke thought, she hadn't turned to Jeremy's father, because she was afraid to count on him, afraid to count on anyone, ever again, after the way life had let her down. Hating to see her continue to push people away to shield herself from hurt, Luke took her by the shoulders and forced her to face him. "Listen to me, Meg, I know what it is to lose a parent. My mom died when I was a baby and my dad was diagnosed with Lou Gehrig's disease when I was sixteen. He struggled with the disease for ten years before he died. You don't think there were times when I was angry, when I railed at the injustice of it all, too?"

Knowing it would help her to hear everything he'd kept locked inside over the years, Luke pushed on bitterly, "They couldn't figure out what was wrong with my dad when he first got sick. He missed so much work he lost his job at the oil refinery and soon couldn't get any other kind of work, either. He lost his pride as well as our income, and I had to put my own life on hold while I cared for my dad, finished high school and worked full-time."

Luke shook his head, remembering the fatigue, and worse than that, the helplessness. "It took me eight years to get an undergraduate degree that should have taken four, and unable to leave him during the last few months of his life, I had to put my plans to enter medical school on hold, then wait almost another year to start with another class. Believe me, I had plenty of angst inside me. There were a couple years when I was constantly—and privately—cursing the unfairness of it all and struggling with a nearly overwhelming sense of anger and disillusionment. I'd lost my entire family. I was alone. No one my age seemed to have a clue what I'd been through and I didn't think I would ever love anyone else.''

He caught the compassion in her eyes, pushed on, ''Yeah, I had friends, lots of them, but as for making that kind of deep, abiding investment you make in family, well, I just wasn't going to do it. I wasn't going to let myself be in a position to hurt like that again.''

Meg wiped the tears from her face with her fingertips. ''And yet, even feeling all that, suffering all that, you still seem to have come to terms with your loss better than I've come to terms with mine,'' she said self-effacingly.

Luke could feel Meg leaning on him, needing, asking, for help. And he was glad to give it. His heart soaring at the vulnerability she had allowed herself, he reached over and took her hands in his and gripped them tightly. ''That's probably because I had ten years to deal with my dad's illness and knew his death was coming,'' he said softly. ''I had time to work through my feelings, little by little. You were hit out of the blue. You didn't have time to say goodbye or prepare for it. You didn't even have time to deal with your own feelings, you were so busy taking care of your younger sisters.'' *Not to mention what happened between us.*

Meg nodded slowly, as if accepting that much was true. ''So how do you get yourself out of the rut?'' she asked on a beleaguered sigh.

Wanting to give her as much comfort as he could, Luke

held her close and continued gently, "Time helps. So does allowing yourself to feel whatever it is you're feeling without beating yourself up about it. The grieving process is different for every person, of course, but for me the key thing was realizing that there are always gonna be some things in life that are out of our control."

Meg studied him cautiously.

Sensing how foreign it was for Meg to allow herself to lean on anyone, even for a moment, Luke nodded. "You can call it whatever you want. Fate. God's will. Destiny. But there's no changing it. No willing it away or turning back the clock to change events and get a different outcome."

Silence fell between them, more comfortable now, laced with more acceptance than grief.

Luke gently stroked her back as Meg's tears continued to flow. "I decided it's how we react to those things—knowing we did what was right, what was needed when it was needed—that counts." Luke tucked a hand under her chin and lifted her face to his. He could see, although she was struggling not to let him, that Meg was still beating herself up inside for having harbored any resentment toward her parents. Given how long she had been struggling with her guilt, it would take time to fade. In the meantime he would be here for her, ready to hold her and to help. "You have to admit we both did pretty well, putting our own needs aside and coming through for our families," Luke continued gently. "I only had to see you with your sisters once to know how much they all love you. Not to mention how protective they are of you."

At the low note of humor in his voice, Meg dashed away the rest of her tears. Her lips took on a wry curve as she admitted, "They sure didn't hesitate to give you the third degree."

"No, they sure didn't," Luke said. "In fact, I got the feeling if they ever decide my intentions are not 100 percent honorable I'll be dead meat."

"You got that right." Meg chuckled softly. "They'd probably come after you with a posse and a rope."

"Well, just in case there's any question..." Luke wrapped her in his arms and gave her a kiss that telegraphed everything he needed, everything he wanted, everything he felt. "My intentions are honorable as can be. I'm here to help you, Meg, and stand by you, in whatever way you need." He waited, hoping she'd break down and tell him what he wanted—needed—to know. But once again the moment passed and she did not.

Chapter Eight

"Luke, I need a favor from you," Kate Marten said Monday morning at the hospital. "I wanted to get Sam McCabe's boys in for some kind of grief counseling—at the very least an assessment meeting—and Sam McCabe isn't returning any of my calls."

Luke put down the stack of lab reports he'd been reading. "Did you try talking to him while he was at the hospital last week?"

"Yes." Cup of coffee in hand, her day planner and pen in the other, Kate came into his private office. "And he turned me down flat."

Luke sat back in his swivel chair and propped his feet on the edge of his desk. "Have you tried talking to John and Lilah about this?"

"Sam resents me enough already." With a glance at the patients beginning to file into the reception area, Kate shut the door behind her. "If I go over his head, to family, about his lack of cooperation he'll resent me even more."

Luke glanced at his watch—his first appointment for the day was in ten minutes. "So instead you come to me," Luke observed, looking back at Kate.

Kate shrugged unapologetically and smoothed a manicured hand over the trim-fitting jacket of her sleek blue suit. "You are their family doctor. And Kevin's due in to have his stitches removed when?"

Luke didn't even have to look at his appointment calendar to know that, since a special before-office-hours appointment had been made with him directly. Sam had wanted to be there for that himself, and doing it that way was the only way the CEO's busy schedule would accommodate it. "Tomorrow morning," Luke replied. "Seven-thirty."

Kate set her coffee on Luke's desk and sat down. "And how long will it take to remove Kevin's stitches?"

"Five, ten minutes, tops."

Kate opened her day planner and turned to the appropriate page. "Suppose I just happen to come by about that time, to talk to you about someone else. I could catch Sam on his way out, mention it again, and you could back me up on it being a good idea."

"You don't think Sam will see through that and resent us both?" Luke asked, beginning to understand how Sam McCabe could be a little irked with Kate.

Kate's pen remained poised over the page as she regarded Luke steadily. "Sam already resents me for bringing it up the first time. Bottom line, his boys need some help dealing with their mother's death. I want to make sure they get it before something worse happens than Kevin falling off the porch roof into some bushes."

"Okay, come by, and I'll back you up, but if Sam resists, I want you to back off immediately. Give me some time to build a rapport with Sam and his kids. Maybe if Sam and his boys all think of me as a family friend as well as their doctor they'll tell me what's been going on there. In the meantime Sam's taken steps to make sure something like this doesn't happen again. He hired a housekeeper to ride herd on his boys and keep any more wild behavior from happening. I checked. Her name is Mrs. Grunwald, she's a former lady marine and fraternity housemother, and she started last week, the day after Kevin was in the E.R.''

As far as Kate was concerned, Luke noted, that changed nothing.

She sighed worriedly and closed her day planner. ''If Sam would just listen to me, he'd realize he and his boys need help right now.''

Luke focused on the fact Kate was no longer talking about counseling just the boys, but Sam, too. More to the point, she seemed to be taking Sam's rejection very personally. Granted, he hadn't been at the hospital long, but he'd been there long enough to have several dealings with Kate. She was capable and efficient, cheerful and outgoing, and she hadn't been as worked up about anyone else as she was about Sam McCabe and his boys. ''Is there a history between the two of you I should know about?'' Luke asked.

''No,'' Kate said, shutting down abruptly and turning away.

''You sure?'' Luke pressed.

''Positive. We both grew up in this town, and were both close to John and Lilah and their four sons, as well as the Lockharts, but Sam's never given me the time of day, then or now,'' Kate said flatly.

Which maybe was the point, Luke thought, Sam's lack of attention and respect where Kate was concerned.

''I'll see you tomorrow,'' Kate said.

Meg came in just as Kate was leaving. Briefly the two women talked about a seminar Kate was going to give for the community wellness program held at the hospital, then Kate continued on out.

"Everything okay with her?" Meg asked. "She looked upset."

Briefly Luke explained what had been going on. None of which seemed to be any surprise to Meg. "Does she have an unrequited crush on Sam McCabe?" Luke asked.

Meg shrugged off the possibility as she handed him a list of the community health classes she and the other nurses were going to be giving over the next six weeks. "We all had crushes on Sam at one time or another growing up. He was a lot older than us and the high school football star, but it didn't do us any good. Sam only had eyes for Ellie."

Thinking how good it was to see Meg again, even for a moment, Luke stepped close enough to inhale the scent of shampoo clinging to her hair. "I meant now."

"I don't think so." Meg perched on the edge of Luke's desk. "I mean, for heaven's sake, Kate's getting married soon to Craig Farrell, who by the way is every bit the local hero, too."

"Which maybe is another problem," Luke said cryptically, as he set the flyers Meg had handed him on his desk.

Meg's brows knit together quizzically. "What's that supposed to mean?"

"I had the feeling Kate isn't as excited about getting married to this hotshot pilot of hers as she should be."

Meg looked at Luke.

Luke covered her hand with his own. "Having been there myself, I know the signs," he explained gently. "I know what it's like to have committed to something and then be unwilling, unable, to let everyone down."

An abrupt silence fell between them. Meg's shoulders tensed. She shot him a carefully controlled glance. "You're talking about Gwyneth now?"

Luke nodded and tightened his fingers over Meg's. "I shouldn't have married her. In fact, I almost didn't. We broke up for a while that summer."

Meg's face paled. She studied him intently. "Then why did you?" she asked eventually, stunned, struggling to understand.

Luke shrugged, not sure even he could comprehend all he'd done that spring, summer and fall, he'd been so depressed about the end of his close friendship with Meg. "There were a lot of reasons," Luke said gruffly. None of which made sense now. "Gwyneth wasn't recovering from our breakup and moving on with her life the way she should have." Remembering, Luke pressed his lips together, admitting grimly, "I felt responsible for that—I'd made a commitment and in the end I hadn't honored it. For a while I hoped you and I might...but then that didn't happen and clearly wasn't going to. In the end honoring my promise to Gwyneth seemed like the right thing to do." Luke paused and tightened his fingers over Meg's. "I didn't love her, Meg, not the way I should, but we had been talking marriage for a while. She needed me. In the end the promise I'd initially made to her was all that mattered. I have a feeling it's the same way for Kate."

MEG WANTED TO ASK LUKE more about that. She wanted to make sure he wasn't pursuing her simply because he felt she and Jeremy needed someone, too. But as luck would have it, he got paged, and the discussion had to be tabled for later. The rest of the day passed quickly, and before they knew it, they were home, rushing through supper and trying to get ready to go to the elementary school for late-registration night.

Jeremy was no problem. He had been excited about entering kindergarten in the fall for weeks. He got his bath, changed into clean clothes and was back downstairs half an hour before they had to leave.

Glad for the extra time, Meg showered, too, slipped into a pretty sundress, put on makeup, swept her hair up into a loose knot on the back of her head. She was just spritzing herself with her favorite perfume when the phone rang. "Jeremy, honey, can you get that?" She shouted down the stairs.

Seconds later Jeremy appeared at her side with the portable phone. "It's Luke, Mom," Jeremy announced loudly as he hopped from one foot to the other. "He says he's got a problem."

"Oh, dear." Meg hoped it was nothing serious—like a call from the hospital that would make Luke miss his daughter's first visit to Laramie Elementary School. Meg took the phone from Jeremy and sat down on the edge of the bed. "Hi, Luke," she said cheerfully, already anticipating the thrill of hearing his voice. "What's up?"

Luke sounded bewildered and a little exasperated. "Susie doesn't want to go."

Meg frowned. From what she'd seen, when it was time to go somewhere, Susie was the first one out the door. "Did she say why?"

"No, and she won't give me a clue as to what's going on," Luke reported in a low, frustrated voice. "I was wondering if you could try talking to her and get some enthusiasm going, since you attended school there as a kid."

"Sure," Meg said, eager to help. "Jeremy and I will be right over."

Luke was waiting for them as they crossed the yard. Like Meg, he looked fresh out of the shower and as spiffed-up as if he were about to go out on a date. Her heart did a somersault in her chest as their eyes met.

Amy and Becca were wearing colorful cotton smocks and white patent-leather shoes. Their just-shampooed hair curled damply around their heads. They looked every bit as darling and huggable as their daddy.

"Hi, Jeremy." Luke high-fived Jeremy. Turning to Meg, Luke's eyes said another kind of hello altogether— the kind that promised unlimited kisses the next time they were alone.

Unfortunately, Meg wasn't sure when that would be, due to their unending familial responsibilities and busy schedules.

Luke turned his attention back to Jeremy. "Mind having a seat on the sofa with Becca and Amy while your mom and I go upstairs and help Susie finish getting ready?"

"Okay, but you better hurry up," Jeremy advised excitedly, still hopping from foot to foot. "We don't want to be late!"

As they mounted the stairs, Luke squeezed Meg's hand. He shot her a desperate, grateful look. "Thanks for coming over. If ever we needed a mom on the premises it's now."

He wasn't kidding, Meg noted, as she entered the bedroom where all three girls slept. Susie had put her pajamas on, instead of the pretty cotton smock Luke had laid out for her, and was sitting in the middle of her bed, playing with her toys.

Knowing this was going to take very careful handling, Meg sat down next to her. "Not going with us tonight, huh?"

Susie shook her head and continued playing.

"Don't you want to see where you're going to go to school this fall?"

Susie pouted. "I don't want to go to school."

"You go to day care," Meg pointed out.

Susie turned her head to look at Meg. "That's different," she said stubbornly.

"Not so different," Meg soothed, picking up some plastic blocks and fitting them together. "You will still get to play games and sing songs, play outside, read stories, do arts and crafts."

"But Becca and Amy won't be there!" Susie stormed unhappily.

"Is that what the problem is?" Luke asked, stunned. He sat down on the other side of Meg, so Susie was facing them both. "You want your sisters to go to school with you, too?"

Susie nodded. Abruptly, tears glistened in her eyes.

Knowing this was no time to skimp on the sympathy, Meg wrapped her arms around Susie's shoulders. "Well, no wonder you're scared. I felt exactly the same way when I first went to school there," Meg said.

Susie stopped what she was doing and rubbed her eyes with her fists. "You did?"

"Oh, yes." Meg smoothed Susie's hair from her forehead. "I was the oldest, too, you know, and I had to do everything first—before the rest of my sisters did—and I had to do it all by myself." Meg sighed, just remembering. "Every time something new came up I was really scared and nervous about it."

Susie's glance narrowed suspiciously. "So what'd you do?"

"Well, I talked to my mom and my dad about how I was feeling and they told me not to worry, that they'd be there for me whenever I needed them." *And they had been,* Meg amended silently, *until they died.*

Susie thought about that for a moment. She leaned against Meg. "Was it scary at school?"

"That's the good part. It actually wasn't," Meg said gently. "It was just different. And different can be good. Like this house is different from my house, but you like them both, don't you?"

"Yeah," Susie allowed.

"Well, it's kind of like that," Meg explained, catching Luke's exceedingly grateful look out of the corner of her eye. "The school we are going to visit tonight is going to be different from the day care center at the hospital. But it's a pretty fun place, too. I know, because I went there as a kid."

Susie perked up. "You did?"

"Yep. All my sisters did, too, just like all your sisters will when they are old enough. And the teachers there are all very nice—you'll even get to meet some of them tonight. And your friends, like Jeremy and Alexandra are going to be there, as well as some of your friends from the day care center at the hospital. And you know what the best part of it is?" Meg continued enthusiastically as Susie shook her head. "When Becca and Amy get ready to go to school there, you will be able to tell them all about it, so they won't be scared. Now," Meg said, glancing at her watch, "do you want me to help you get dressed?"

Susie nodded and looked over at Luke importantly. "Daddy, you can wait downstairs."

"Okay, honey." Luke smiled gently. "You feeling better now?"

Susie nodded. Luke gave his daughter a heartfelt hug, then reluctantly departed.

Meg could tell by the look in his eyes that Luke felt he had failed his daughter in some respect. She'd have to let him know later that it wasn't true. There was just some times when only a mother—or a father—would do.

"DADDY, PLEASE CAN WE GO to Meg's and watch a video and have cookies and milk?"

"Would that be okay?" Luke asked Meg as they parked in the driveway between their two homes and piled out of his Expedition. "It's awfully late."

Meg knew it was already eight-thirty. "They're not going to go to sleep anytime soon. They're too wound up." This would give her some extra time to spend with Luke she wouldn't otherwise have. She wanted to talk to him alone about what had happened earlier with Susie, get his impressions on the school and see if he could figure out what was going on with Jeremy—who had seemed to get quieter and less outgoing as the evening progressed. "In fact," Meg continued, "you can go ahead and put them in their pajamas now if you want. That way if they fall asleep during the video..."

"All I'll have to do is carry them home and tuck them in," Luke said with a grin, reading Meg's mind as easily as ever. While Luke went home to put the girls in their pajamas, Meg took Jeremy upstairs to help him change into his. She'd barely gotten his cowboy boots off when he began telling her what was on his mind. "I don't think I want to go to kinda-garden after all," Jeremy said.

"Why not?" Meg asked as she helped him out of his khaki pants.

"Because. Everybody there had a daddy and I don't have a daddy, so I don't wanta go there," Jeremy said.

Back to this again, Meg thought with a troubled sigh. She'd thought her son's intense interest in who his biological daddy was had begun to abate. "Not everyone there had a daddy," Meg reminded her son gently as she helped Jeremy unbutton his oxford cloth shirt. "And not everyone had a mommy, either. Susie didn't have a mommy. She just had her daddy." A fact that hadn't seemed to bother Susie at all, luckily for Luke.

"Yeah, but most of the kids had both a mommy and a daddy." Jeremy held his arms akimbo after Meg helped him off with his shirt, and into his pajamas. "And I don't see why I can't have both, too."

Meg found Jeremy's slippers. Downstairs she heard Luke and the girls come back in. "We're back!" Luke shouted up the stairs. "And we brought our *Tarzan, Lion King* and *Prince of Egypt* videos!"

"Did you hear that? Luke and the girls brought three Disney videos over."

"I don't care. I'm not even sure I want to watch a Disney video at all." Jeremy contentiously plopped down onto his bed.

Meg stepped out into the hall. She went to the top of the stairs. Luke caught sight of the expression on her face. "Problem?" he asked softly.

Meg let him know that was the case with a look, then turned and smiled at the three little pajama-clad girls standing right beside Luke. "Jeremy's still getting his pajamas on. Why don't you pick one of the videos and start it for the girls."

"*Tarzan!*" all three little girls shouted at once. "We want to watch the *Tarzan* cartoon, Daddy!"

Meg smiled and went back to Jeremy's room. He was sitting, just as she'd left him, looking as vulnerable and upset as he had the night he'd run away. "Honey, I know you're upset. But can't we talk about this tomorrow?"

"No," Jeremy said obstinately, staring straight ahead. Downstairs, the music started.

Seconds later Luke appeared in the doorway. "Anything I can do to help?"

Before Meg could formulate a reply, Jeremy blurted out

the problem. Luke listened intently, then hunkered down in front of him. "I understand why you want a daddy."

Jeremy looked simultaneously thrilled and relieved. "You do?"

"Sure." Luke patted Jeremy's knee affectionately. "I grew up without a mama, and that was all I ever wanted." Luke sat down beside Jeremy and confided man-to-man, "I used to miss having a mom around so bad."

Jeremy scooted closer to Luke. "So what'd you do?"

"Some of my mom's friends sort of filled in and did the things a mom does, like bake me cookies and read me stories. And that usually made me feel better. Maybe you could find someone to do the sort of things a dad would do with you. And then you'll feel better, too," Luke said gently.

"Like my uncle Beau and my uncle Jake."

"Right," Luke smiled, obviously remembering that had been Meg's plan, she just hadn't had time to implement it yet.

"What about you?" Jeremy demanded pensively. "Can you do guy stuff with me, too?"

For a second Luke seemed taken aback by the swiftness and seriousness of Jeremy's request. He looked at Meg, ready and willing to help. Not wanting to interfere.

"Can he, Mom?" Jeremy persisted eagerly.

Meg hesitated, knowing full well all the complicated reasons she should have her son continue to rely only on her and her sisters and their husbands. And yet when she looked at the wistfulness on her son's face, the willingness on Luke's, she couldn't do it.

"It doesn't have to be anything elaborate," Luke continued casually.

That was just it, Meg thought. Even the most low-key event wouldn't be that big a deal to Luke. It would mean the world to her son. And Meg didn't want her son hurt. She looked from Jeremy's wistful expression to Luke's steady pragmatic gaze.

"Can you and me do something tomorrow?" Jeremy continued to insist.

Luke thought a moment and shrugged, again as if it were no big deal. "I have to get a haircut after work." He looked at Meg. "Jeremy can go with me, too, if he wants."

Jeremy bobbed up and down excitedly. "Can I, Mom? Can I get a haircut with Luke?"

Meg nodded reluctantly.

Jeremy looked at Luke, his expression as troubled as ever. "I still don't know who my daddy is. What am I going to do when the kids at school ask me? What am I going to say?"

Meg and Luke exchanged brief glances. Then Meg looked back at her son, her heart heavy with the secret she was continuing to keep.

"That's a tough one, buddy." Luke regarded Jeremy with concern. "I think you should trust that your mom has your best interests at heart and will tell you everything there is to tell about your father when you are old enough and ready to hear it. But in the meantime you're right, Jeremy. You really need more of a plan to handle this very tricky situation. So, how about this? While you're watching the video with Susie, Becca and Amy, your mom and I'll go bake the cookies and talk about it and try to figure out what you should say to the other kids."

"Okay."

Jeremy went downstairs and settled on the sofa with Luke's girls. Promising the milk and cookies would be ready in twenty minutes, Meg and Luke went into the kitchen.

Meg switched the oven to 350 degrees. She didn't know whether to resent Luke for his offer to take Jeremy for a haircut or be grateful to him for trying to ease Jeremy's pain, but she knew what politeness demanded. "Thanks for offering to help us out like this," she said.

"What are friends and neighbors and 'the man in your life' for?" Luke quipped lightly.

Meg slanted Luke a glance, wondering just how serious his intentions were here. It was one thing to want to be her lover and her friend—quite another to be making himself a permanent part of her and Jeremy's lives. If this evening had shown one thing, it was that they were both swamped with parental responsibilities. If they were to take on each other's as well, it would double their load. Meg regarded Luke steadily. "It's a little more than that. You just made yourself an unofficial father figure to my son."

Luke smiled as if he'd just gotten the best present of his life. "Given the fact that I've always wanted a son and Jeremy's always wanted a dad and we both adore you and will be spending time together, anyway, it just makes sense for us to be there for each other. Unless, of course—" Luke paused, studying her face, disappointment coming back into his eyes "—there's some reason you don't want me spending time with your son."

His question felt like a test. Her spine prickling, Meg turned away from him and got the roll of premade cookie dough out of the refrigerator. "Of course I don't mind you spending time with Jeremy, Luke."

"Then…?" Deliberately Luke moved where he could see her face.

Meg didn't want to get into any of this, but Luke's actions had left her no choice. "He's starting to love you, Luke."

A shadow of disappointment crossed Luke's face. "And this bothers you?" he asked gruffly.

Meg spread her hands wide on either side of her. "If you become such a big part of his life and then our relationship doesn't work out, or we decide we're uncomfortable seeing so much of each other— Luke, he'd be so devastated."

Luke lounged against the kitchen counter, a determined expression on his handsome face. "That's not going to happen," Luke said, as confident as always that he would get what he wanted in the end.

"But if it does," Meg persisted, more troubled than ever, knowing their relationship had ended badly once and hence, could again. Especially if she were to tell Luke the truth…and he couldn't forgive her the mistakes she'd made.

"It's not going to happen, Meg," Luke reiterated firmly, folding his arms in front of him. And the way he said it, with such heartfelt conviction, Meg could almost…almost…believe him. "I'm not walking out of your life again."

Chapter Nine

"You don't believe me, do you?" Luke asked with a sigh of regret, wondering if they would be back to being "just friends" before they knew it.

"We can't see into the future, Luke." With studied concentration Meg put the ready-to-bake cookie dough onto the cutting board and sliced it according to the marks on the packaging. "If we could, I would have seen this situation with Jeremy coming years ago."

Luke watched her peel the strips of plastic off each round slice and lay it onto a baking sheet. Was that his imagination or were her hands shaking just a tad? He edged closer, wishing he could identify her feelings as easily as he could see her face. "You think you made a mistake—not telling Jeremy's father you were pregnant?"

"In retrospect I know I did." Meg's spine stiffened as she slid the cookies into the oven to bake. Straightening, she grabbed a dishcloth and wiped her hands. "But...he was unavailable at the time...."

"And now?" Luke prompted when she didn't go on, wishing Meg would confide everything in him. Here. Now. But she didn't. Instead, she looked away, her expression strained as she continued to avoid his gaze. She opened the refrigerator, got out a quart of milk and set it on the table, all without looking at him.

"I don't know what the situation is now, exactly."

"How about approximately, then?" Luke looked into her eyes, willing her to tell him the truth, knowing it would change everything for the better if she did. Because it was her silence...her lack of faith in him, more than anything, that was keeping them apart.

But to his mounting disappointment, as their gazes met and held, all she did was seem to get further away from him. Finally she swallowed and took a deep breath. As remote, as self-sufficient as ever, she reiterated calmly, "The bottom line is, I've painted myself into a corner with all this, Luke. What is Jeremy going to tell the other kids at school?"

"How about the truth?" Luke suggested pointedly.

Meg shoved her hands through the loose auburn waves of her hair as she turned away. She looked more emotionally inaccessible to Luke than ever. "I'm serious."

"So am I." Luke grabbed her by the arms and turned her to face him. His patience with her, with the whole situation, fading fast, he demanded in a voice the kids could not possibly overhear, "Is there some reason you can't give Jeremy some basic facts about his dad, or at least something to hang on to?" Was it possible Jeremy's father was someone other than him? Luke wondered, upset.

Backed into a corner, Meg became angry. "How about the fact his dad would never forgive me for keeping a secret like this from him all these years?" she asked bitterly, resentment glittering in her eyes.

"You don't know that would be the case, Meg," Luke argued.

Meg gave him a soul-weary look that seemed to say,

Don't I? She regarded Luke steadily. "Would you forgive someone who'd denied you the first five years of your child's life?"

All too aware how much was riding on his answer, Luke dropped his hold on her and formulated his answer with care. "I'd be upset and hurt initially—who wouldn't be after being deliberately shut out that way? But if…this person's reasons were as valid as yours were at the time, I'd do what was best for us and for the child, and I'd forgive her."

"Just like that?" Meg looked skeptical that anything this complicated and emotional could be that easy. But Luke knew, with determination and considerable self-restraint, it would be possible.

"Yes," Luke replied passionately. "I'd forgive her. Just like that. Providing, of course," Luke amended, "that she promised never to keep anything like that from me again." Luke paused. He was beginning to get through to her—he could tell. "You ought to give the guy a chance to come through for Jeremy, Meg." *Especially if it's me, because I could be everything Jeremy wants and needs in a father and more.*

Meg bit her lower lip. Luke knew she was this close to telling him everything. And then, as luck would have it, the kids came barreling in, en masse. "Where are our cookies?" they demanded boisterously, climbing all over him and Meg.

"Yeah, we're hungry."

"The movie's at the sad part."

"Tarzan loses his mommy and his daddy."

"The gorillas in the forest take care of him."

Jeremy tugged on Luke's sleeve. "If we lost our mommy and our daddy, would the gorillas in the forest take care of us?" he wanted to know.

Luke looked at Meg. She didn't seem to know where to draw the line between fact and fantasy, either. All Luke knew for sure was that the kids needed reassurance to feel safe. And maybe, just maybe, Meg did, too.

"If you get shipwrecked and then lost in the forest, someone will find you and take care of you," he said firmly.

Amy held on to Luke, burying her face in his leg. "I don't want to lose you, Daddy." She wrapped her other arm around Meg's knee. "You either, Meg."

"You're not going to lose either of us," Luke said, still looking at Meg. "And that's a promise."

One way or another he was going to find a way to make this work. Not just for now, but for all time, whether Meg ever came right out and told him the truth or not.

"WE WANT ANOTHER SLEEPOVER tonight, and we want it at our house this time," Becca told Luke the next morning as they hurriedly packed their lunches, with each of his three daughters getting the sandwich of her choice.

"Yeah," Susie chimed in authoritatively, "it's not fair that only Jeremy gets to have sleepovers at his house."

"We want Meg and Jeremy to sleep here, with us," Amy pouted.

So do I. And not just tonight—every night, Luke thought, with a wistfulness that was new to him.

"I'll ask Meg."

"Make her say yes, Daddy." Becca jumped up and down enthusiastically.

"I'll try."

"Can you do it right now?" Susie insisted, just as excitedly.

Luke hadn't seen his girls this happy and excited in a

very long time. He reached over and tickled their noses. "You little munchkins don't ask for much, do you?"

They giggled so hard they collapsed, then stood up and started begging all over again. "Puhleeeze, Daddy? We really like having Meg and Jeremy around."

"All right." Aware how pressed they were for time this and every morning, Luke checked the lunch sacks, then shepherded the children toward the door. It was like herding cats. "I've got five minutes before we have to leave for the hospital," he said as they danced their way out the door.

"Can we play on our swing set while you talk to Meg?"

"Sure."

Luke spied Meg, who was just coming out of her house. Damned if she didn't look pretty in a nurse's uniform, her hair swept up on top of her head. He waved at her. "Got a minute?"

Meg nodded. As Jeremy dashed off to play with the girls while they talked, Meg turned to Luke. "What's up?"

"The girls asked me to invite you and Jeremy to a sleepover tonight."

Meg's quick smile said her first thoughts were every bit as sexy and romantic as his. *At least I'm winning one battle,* Luke thought. *Now if I could just win her trust the way I've won her heart.* A hint of color flooding her cheeks, she said, "I don't know, Luke." She looked at him uncertainly, her desire to give in plainly evident, as was her need to proceed with a bit more caution for all their sakes. She bit her lower lip. "We've been together an awful lot."

Luke knew it was true. And he still hadn't seen her nearly enough. Every second he was away from her was a second he wanted to be spending time with her. "They've slept over at your place twice, and you've never slept over at our place. They think that's unfair."

Luke could see her starting to weaken. He leaned over and, wrapping an arm about her waist, whispered in her ear. "I missed you last night."

Her blush arrived, delightfully pinkening her cheeks. "We were together until almost midnight," Meg protested softly.

But they'd been chaperoned by four little ones, who— even long after they'd fallen asleep on Meg's sofa—had kept Meg and Luke behaving themselves. If they were married, it'd be no big deal. The two could retire to their bedroom after the kids were asleep and have plenty of time to make love and be alone without wondering what kind of precedents they were setting. But as it was they had examples to set, and it had been all he could do to steal a kiss or two or three from her in the kitchen as the evening progressed. Any romantic entanglement, not to mention the kind of intimate adult relationship he wanted, with Meg required time alone—lots of it.

That was something that, to Luke's chagrin, had been nonexistent since he'd made love to Meg Saturday night. "You know what I mean," he said, holding her gaze.

"Yeah," she admitted self-consciously, finally seeming to realize the futility of pretending otherwise, "I do know. And for the record," she whispered back, "I missed you, too."

"So, is it a date?" Luke asked. He was aware he was pressuring her. Taking unfair advantage. He couldn't help himself. They'd been apart for so many years. There had been so many wasted days. So many wasted nights. He didn't want there to be any more.

And still she hesitated.

"Say yes," Luke repeated, a little impatiently.

"Just so long as you and the kids realize we can't do this every night," Meg finally relented.

Wanna bet? Luke thought.

All he had to do was convince her they were meant to be together for the rest of their lives. Once that was done, the rest would be a snap.

"YOU GET A GOLD STAR TODAY, Kevin McCabe, for being such a good patient," Luke told Sam McCabe's youngest son as he finished taking the stitches out of his scalp wound.

Kevin reacted by grasping his father's hand even tighter.

"Would you like to pick out a sticker?" Luke asked. He handed Kevin a sheet of stickers. Kevin looked up at Luke questioningly. "You can pick out any one you want," Luke said gently. "Take your time."

To Sam McCabe Luke said, "His wrist is healing nicely, too. You still want to keep it wrapped in an elastic bandage, though, and keep him from putting a lot of weight on it for the next week."

"Will do." Sam smiled his relief. "And thanks for seeing Kev before office hours officially begin today," he said.

Luke nodded. While Kevin continued to study the stickers, Luke rewrapped his wrist. "How are things going with the new housekeeper?" Luke asked Sam, and, out of the corner of his eye, saw Kevin frown, almost imperceptibly.

"I think it's going to work out fine. If anyone can get my home life back in shipshape, it'll be Mrs. Grunwald. She was a lady marine, you know."

"The boys like her then?" Luke asked.

A look of sadness and grief moved across Sam Mc-Cabe's face. "They're not going to like anyone who takes Ellie's place. But she'll at least be able to keep them warm and safe while I'm at work."

Aware Sam was anxious to get going, Luke cut to the chase. "Kate Marten stopped by the other day."

Frowning, Sam gave Luke a man-to-man glance. "I know she means well, but I'd appreciate it if you could get her off my back."

Sam's request was blunt and matter-of-fact. Unfortunately, because he was their physician and responsible for the health of the family, Luke couldn't honor it. "She wants to help and she thinks she can, if you and the boys will just give her a chance."

Sam's eyes narrowed. His lips clamped together as he regarded Luke with resentment. "The best thing Kate Marten can do is leave me and my boys alone," Sam returned gruffly. "Kev, hurry up and pick a sticker and then we'll go."

Quickly Kevin peeled off a sticker of a cartoon figure and pasted it on his shirt. He handed the sheet of stickers back to Luke. Gently Sam lifted his youngest son down from the examining table, then turned to Luke and offered his hand. "Thanks again."

Luke nodded. Sam McCabe was clearly a man still locked in the throes of grief. Building a rapport with Sam McCabe was going to take time. Luke knew he would have to start by backing off, and try to get Kate Marten to do the same, at least for the time being. "I'll talk to Kate for you," he promised.

"Thanks." Sam sighed his relief.

Luke scribbled his home phone number down. He handed it to Sam, looking him straight in the eye all the while. "In the meantime if you ever feel the need to talk, day or night, you can call me. I'm a pretty decent listener and I've been where you are now, Sam. I know what it's like to lose your wife and try to comfort your kids through the loss. It gets better, but it takes awhile.''

Even as Sam nodded his understanding of what had been said, Luke knew Sam wouldn't call. Not now. Not unless things got really desperate.

LUKE SPENT the rest of the morning seeing patients. He had just finished the last of six school physicals and was headed for the hospital employees' child care center when he caught sight of Meg in the hallway, coming out of the child care center. Much to his chagrin, Kip Brewster was beside her. Luke had once thought Kip was a pretty decent guy. But that was before he'd learned why Meg had broken up with Kip. Kip had made a fool of Meg once, by sleeping around on her. Luke didn't want him hurting her again.

''Okay, I'll call you with the details,'' Kip was saying as Luke stepped back, out of sight.

''I'll look forward to it,'' Meg replied cheerfully. ''See you later.'' A stack of papers in her hand, she headed off in the opposite direction without ever seeing Luke.

Kip headed toward the main exit.

Figuring these were questions best put to Kip without Meg present, Luke cut Meg's ex-boyfriend off at the pass. After their initial greeting, Luke asked casually, his protective instincts on full alert, ''What brings you back to Laramie again so soon?''

Kip headed for the beverage machine in the snack room, just off the reception area. ''I'm organizing a reunion of the Homesick Texans Club. I asked Meg to help me contact people.''

It was a solid reason for being there. Luke didn't buy

it for a moment. He watched Kip put some change into the machine. "Why the sudden interest in bringing together the old gang?"

"I think it'll be fun. So does Meg." Kip fished his soda can out of the machine and turned it upright. "She suggested I ask you to help, too, but I don't know, I think three might be a crowd."

For what Kip seemed to have on his mind, Luke was pretty sure it would be. Luke put some change in the machine, also. "Meg's taken."

"She said pretty much the same thing." Kip regarded Luke steadily as he popped the top of his soda and lifted the can to his lips. "Of course, she also didn't seem to know you had been to Austin to visit me not too long ago."

His heart thudding heavily in his chest, Luke slid some change into the machine, too. "Did you tell her?" he asked casually.

"No," Kip said pleasantly. He narrowed his glance at Luke consideringly. "And it made me wonder why you didn't tell her, either, if the two of you are so close now."

Because then I would have had to admit that I had gone behind her back to see you, Luke thought.

"Unless, of course, you're hiding something from Meg," Kip continued, protecting Meg now the way he had failed to do in the past. "Something you don't want her to know about." Kip took another sip of his soda and continued to look at Luke steadily.

Cursing his decision to bring the Austin attorney in on this—even though it was Kip's disclaimer that made Luke think there was still a damn good chance, if not a dead certainty, he was Jeremy's father—Luke demanded gruffly, "Why are you here?"

Kip sighed, sincere regret in his eyes. "The worst mistake I ever made was letting Meg go."

"Actually, that's not quite the way it happened. She dumped you because she found out you were cheating on her."

Realizing Luke could only have heard that from Meg, Kip looked at Luke with new respect. "I've changed," he said flatly. "I'm older, wiser now. I know what's important in a relationship and I wouldn't run around on her again. If I can convince her of that, then I just might be able to get her to give me another chance."

Luke shook his head, wanting nothing more at that moment than to get Kip Brewster out of his and Meg's lives forever. "You're wasting your time," Luke warned impatiently. "It's not going to happen. You're all wrong for each other. You always have been."

"Given your interest in her, you would say that. But the way I see it—" Kip gave Luke a smart-aleck grin "—it's still a wide open field. And that son of hers is pretty cute, too. Meg ought to marry and give him a dad."

Luke didn't have to ask if Kip had anyone particular in mind. That was as clear as the wistful look in his eyes. Luke couldn't blame Kip for regretting his mistakes and wanting Meg back, but that didn't mean he was prepared to let Kip elbow his way into their lives, either, not after the way he'd hurt and humiliated Meg the first time around.

Meg came back around the corner. She no longer had the papers in her hand. Luke could tell she noted the tension between him and her ex-boyfriend from college as she came up to them and was just as determined to ignore it. "Did Kip tell you about the reunion?" she asked Luke enthusiastically.

Luke nodded, knowing there was no way on this earth

he was letting Kip make time with Meg. "Sounds like fun," Luke said cheerfully. "I'd like to help."

"Great!" Meg said.

Kip shot a piqued look at Luke and then glanced at his watch. "Listen, I've got to run if I'm going to make that appointment. But I'll call you?" He looked at Meg.

Meg nodded. "The sooner, the better. Once school starts in the fall, it will be a lot harder to get people together."

"I thought you weren't ever going to forgive him or trust him again, for what he did," Luke said when Kip had gone.

Luke bought Meg a can of fruit juice from one of the machines and handed it to her. "And I won't—romantically," Meg said with a soft contentment that rankled Luke even more than her air of happiness. "But this is something altogether different."

His every muscle tensing, Luke said, "He doesn't seem to think so."

Meg opened her juice and took a sip, studying Luke curiously all the while. "The two of us won't be alone. You'll be there, helping organize the reunion of the club, right along with Kip and me." Meg paused, knowing it wasn't like Luke to react jealously, under any circumstances. "Luke, Kip can't hurt me anymore."

Yes, Luke thought unhappily, Kip could. All it would take was one revelation.

Like it or not, Luke had a secret now, too. For the first time Luke had sympathy for Meg's predicament. For the first time he understood, on a gut level, why she didn't want to delve into the past or anything else that was liable to cause tension or dissension between them. She didn't want to rock the boat, either. Maybe Meg was right.

Maybe what happened in the past wasn't important. Maybe what mattered was going on now. "You're right," Luke said after a moment. "I'm being a little overprotective."

"A little?" Meg looked amused.

But then, Luke thought, she didn't know what was at stake. Just everything he'd ever wanted. Everything he'd ever hoped or dreamed about.

As she continued to study him, Meg's happiness faded. Beneath her surface cheer, she looked a little uneasy. Wary.

Easing gracefully onto another subject, she asked softly, "Are you still taking Jeremy for a haircut after work?"

Luke nodded, glad to be able to concentrate on something else. "Think he could be ready to go around five?"

Meg's blue eyes brightened. "He's really looking forward to it."

So was Luke.

"BYE, MOM."

"Bye, honey." Meg knelt to give Jeremy a hug.

"Any special instructions?" Luke looked at Meg.

Meg shook her head. "Just tell Clyde, down at the barbershop, the usual little-boy's haircut. He'll know what to do."

His hand tucked securely in Luke's, the two headed for Luke's SUV. The sight of the two of them, walking together, hand in hand, was almost more poignant than Meg could bear. Jeremy looked so happy. All this time she had thought she was protecting Jeremy by not uniting him with his father. Now she saw the opposite was true. Jeremy was thriving in the glow of Luke's attention. And

Luke seemed really happy, too. Finally things were working out. For the first time since her parents died, her world was as it should be once again.

"Can we watch you cook supper now?"

"Absolutely." Meg led Becca, Amy and Susie back inside her cottage. "And while you do that, we can talk about our day."

By the time Luke and Jeremy returned, looking handsome as could be with their newly shorn hair, Meg and the girls had dinner ready and the table set. The six of them sat down to dinner together, then the kids went out to play in the backyard while Luke and Meg did the dishes together.

"I could get used to this," Meg smiled.

"Having six for dinner every night?" Luke murmured in a voice that sent frissons of desire racing down her spine.

"As well as being with you, day and night," Meg said, not sure she trusted this blissful feeling of contentment.

Her heart skipped a beat as Luke took her in his arms and lowered his mouth to hers. Before she could do more than draw a breath, he took her lips with a rush of passion, kissing her long and hard and deep. Meg clung to him, reveling in the euphoric sensations rushing through her. Only Luke had ever made her feel this loved and desired. Only Luke had made her feel that as long as they were together, everything was going to be all right.

"Life feels pretty perfect about now, doesn't it?" Luke teased, when he finally lifted his head.

Extremely perfect, Meg thought, as she buried her face against his shoulder. Which was what scared her and made it so hard, continuing to keep this secret from him. She knew she was going to have to tell him about Jeremy.

She wanted to tell him. She just wanted a little more time...a few more days. Then, when she'd worked up her nerve...

"Mom!" Jeremy raced back inside, followed swiftly by Susie, Becca and Amy. "Are we still having a sleep-over at Luke's house tonight?"

Meg nodded, glad for the respite, as she and Luke drew apart. She didn't want to think about what problems might come. For the first time in a long time, she just wanted to completely and thoroughly enjoy the moment. She just wanted to be with Luke and celebrate the happiness they'd found. The problems would still be there later, when she felt more able, more ready, to deal with them....

As they began making preparations for the sleepover at Luke's, all four kids were deliriously happy, too. And the merriment continued until bedtime was actually upon them. Almost as soon as Luke and Meg had everybody tucked in and had settled themselves on the living room sofa for some quiet time, pandemonium broke out up-stairs. Luke groaned and made a comical face. "I should have known it was too good to be true."

Meg chuckled at his antics. "I'll check on them."

"No, I'll go." He pulled her back into her seat. "It sounds like it's mostly my girls, anyway."

He went up.

He returned, concern mingled with pique on his face. "Becca's crying. She says she can't go to sleep until she talks to you."

Surprised by the request, Meg stood. "Did she say what it was about?"

"No." Luke looked more than a little exasperated about that. Perhaps with good reason, Meg thought, since it was the second time in two days he'd had trouble communicating with his girls. "She won't tell me a thing. She says she can only talk to you, because only you will understand."

"Maybe it's a girl thing," Meg suggested, remembering times in her own life where only her mother would do.

Luke looked skeptical about that and didn't reply. Meg could tell he was hurt, suddenly being excluded that way from whatever was going on with Becca, just as he'd been hurt by Susie's refusal to confide in him the day before.

"She's probably just overtired," Meg soothed. "It's been a busy few days. I'll see what I can do." She headed up the stairs. Susie and Amy were in their beds. Jeremy was on the cot they'd set up for him. They all looked drowsy and a little irritated by the commotion. Only Becca was sitting up in her bed, tears streaming down her face.

Meg sat down beside her. "What's wrong, honey?"

Becca spread her hands in frustration. "Daddy won't understand."

"What won't he understand, sweetheart?" Meg lifted Becca onto her lap.

"Why I need a light in my room," Becca sniffled miserably.

Meg looked at the ballerina light next to Becca's bed. It was on and it seemed to be working just fine. "You have a lamp in your room."

"No," Becca protested with a heartfelt pout. She gestured with her thumb and index finger. "A little tiny one. The kind Jeremy has, so you can see where you are even when it's dark."

Finally, Meg got it. "A night-light."

Still sniffling, Becca nodded vigorously.

"Did you ask your daddy for one?" Meg said. It didn't sound like the kind of thing Luke would refuse.

Becca shook her head and continued in a voice full of self-pity. "Daddy doesn't know about things like that. He always leaves the bathroom light on. He doesn't leave lights on in our rooms. And I'm scared, Meg, when I don't have a light on at night…this house is so big."

So Luke's little troupers were having trouble with the move from California after all, Meg thought. Noting that Jeremy, Susie and Amy had already fallen asleep, Meg smoothed Becca's hair from her face. "You want me to go and get a night-light for you?" she asked.

Again Becca nodded vigorously.

"First you have to tell daddy it's okay for me to have one, though," Becca said, as if permission just might not be granted.

Luke was stunned when Meg went down to tell him what the problem was. "She could have asked me that! I would have gotten her one. I just didn't know she wanted or needed one."

"I know." Meg touched Luke's arm gently, wishing he wouldn't feel so bad about such a silly miscommunication. "It's okay. I'll run next door and get one and then be right back."

Concern etching his face, Luke nodded his thanks and said, "I'll go up and talk to her, too."

Twenty minutes later, with Becca soothed and almost asleep, with the borrowed night-light on and a promise to purchase another one the next day, Meg and Luke went back downstairs and settled on the living room sofa. Luke suggested they watch some TV. Meg agreed. But it was quickly clear he wasn't the least bit interested in the riotously funny comedy program. Meg studied Luke. "You're still upset, aren't you?"

Luke nodded. "She was scared, Meg," he said grimly, zapping off the television.

Taking Meg's hand, he led her to the kitchen, where it would be easier to talk with some privacy. He rummaged around in the refrigerator and finally brought out a pitcher of ice water and a lemon meringue pie from Isabel Buchanon's bakery. "I don't know what's worse," Luke said, looking increasingly restless and dissatisfied as he got out the pie server and two plates. "The fact I had no idea Becca felt that way. Or the fact she didn't feel she could come to me with her problems any more than Susie felt she could come to me with her fears about kindergarten."

Meg watched Luke cut two wedges of pie and slide them onto the plates. She felt he was being unnecessarily hard on himself. "Susie was just trying to shield you from seeing she was scared. She didn't want to disappoint you. As for Becca...she probably just knew you were swamped, moving in, getting settled in at work and here at home and trying to do everything at once. And didn't want to add to that."

Luke sighed as he put the pie back in the refrigerator and carried the plates over to the table. "That would be a lot easier to believe if it were the first time someone close to me felt they couldn't come to me with a problem, Meg, but it's not." Pain and frustration laced his low voice. As he turned back to her, guilt sharpened the handsome features of his face. "In fact, I'm beginning to think it's a pattern with all the women in my life."

"What are you talking about?" Meg asked cautiously as alarm welled like a tidal wave inside her.

Oblivious to the panicked nature of Meg's thoughts,

Luke confided harshly, "Gwyneth couldn't come to me with her problems, either. If she had—" Luke paused, his eyes darkening with the depth of his regret "—she might be alive today."

Chapter Ten

Meg's heart began to pound as the two of them sat down
at the kitchen table. "You can't mean that," she whispered, aghast.

Self-recrimination flashed in his eyes. "She didn't just
die in a car accident, Meg. She ran her car off the road,
into a tree."

Meg stared at him, barely able to comprehend the
trauma he and the girls had obviously been through. She
willed herself to be as strong as he needed her to be. "You
think she committed suicide."

Luke swallowed and to her frustration looked all the
more tortured and remote as he poured them each a glass
of ice water. "Officially, her death was ruled accidental,
but I know better." Clenching his jaw, he continued in a
low, unforgiving voice, "Gwyneth was depressed at the
time she died. To the point where she'd begun considering
going to a doctor for help. And I didn't have a clue until
I found her journal a couple months after she died. Oh, I
knew she was tired, stressed out. Having three babies in
three years is a lot for anyone to handle, especially when
your husband is never home, but she told me she was
doing fine, and I believed her." Luke shook his head
grimly. "If she had just come to me, told me how over-

whelmed she was feeling, I could have helped her, but she obviously didn't think she could.''

Struggling for an air of normalcy, she picked up her fork and began to eat. "Why not?"

Luke swallowed and toyed with a bite of pie. "Probably because we had argued over whether we should start a family right away or not. I knew I was going to be working around the clock and I didn't want us to start having kids until I had finished my residency, settled into private practice and had more normal hours. And I really didn't want her to have that many kids so quickly. But Gwyneth was desperate to have the kind of happy family she'd been denied as a kid, and she kept getting pregnant, first with Susie, then Becca. By the time Amy came along, there was no getting around it. I knew Gwyneth was sabotaging our birth control and getting pregnant deliberately. I confronted her and we argued about it. She admitted what she had done and promised it wouldn't happen again. We agreed she needed more help on the home front than I could give her, and I figured out a way to stretch our budget to include both a part-time baby-sitter and a once-a-week cleaning service. She seemed grateful for the extra help, and her mood lifted to the point she was almost ebullient. A couple of weeks later she was dead.''

Meg could only imagine the shock, the devastation, Luke had felt when he learned what his wife had done. Meg looked into Luke's dark, brooding eyes. "Did she write about all this in her diary?"

Luke nodded, set his fork down and pushed his plate aside. "She knew that although I'd never leave her or the kids, I didn't love her the way I should. Never had, never would. But she liked being pregnant…liked the attention she got when she was expecting…the way she was filled with hope and a sense of a miracle during the entire nine months. And she had hoped to tie me to her with kids. With that avenue no longer open to her—I'd taken charge of the birth control to make certain she didn't get pregnant again—it was clear from her ramblings that she was in a lot of emotional distress and had been for some time." Luke sighed, suddenly looking older than his years. A faraway look crept into his golden-brown eyes as he continued sadly, "Through it all she managed to take good care of the kids and present a happy—if extremely tired—facade to me, but inside, she was falling apart, bit by bit."

"To the point she just drove off the road rather than continue," Meg guessed sorrowfully.

"Yes," Luke's eyes glimmered with hurt as he stood and began to pace. He stared out the window at the backyard. "She killed herself rather than come to me and tell me what she needed."

Meg got up and crossed to his side. "That's why you were so upset about Becca not confiding in you tonight."

Luke turned to face her. "I would have gotten Becca a night-light. All she had to do was ask. But she didn't come to me. She went to you instead."

"Yes, she did, but not because she couldn't go to you," Meg replied, taking his hand in hers and doing her best to ease his hurt. "Those girls know you're there for them, Luke," she continued firmly.

Luke wanted to believe her—Meg could tell—he just wasn't sure he should. "Then why did Becca summon you tonight?" Luke asked.

Meg smiled gently, sure about this much. "A couple of reasons," she said, drawing on her own expertise as a parent. "One, Susie got to confide in me last night, about her fears about going to kindergarten. And two, Jeremy has been having special talks with you, too, and even went to get a haircut with you. Becca probably figured it was her turn for some special attention, and because everyone else had a crisis that immediately got our sole attention, she had a crisis, too. The crisis being the need for a night-light.''

Luke's shoulders sagged with relief. ''You think that's all it is?'' He did not take his eyes from her face.

''I have three sisters.'' Meg grinned and went into his arms. She laced both her arms about his waist. ''With four girls, there was constant drama. Still is.'' She shook her head, remembering. ''There must have been times when our parents wanted to pull out their hair. You'd know that, too, if you hadn't been an only child.''

The worry lines around his eyes softened. ''I guess you're right.'' He anchored her against him tightly with one arm, smoothed the hair from her face with his other hand. ''Promise me something,'' he murmured softly, searching her eyes.

''Anything,'' Meg whispered back, holding him tightly, too.

''If you need me…if you ever need anything again…you'll come to me.''

Meg's body softened against the hard, unyielding musculature of his. She was beginning to see she could rely on Luke in ways she had always wanted to and had never dreamed possible. ''I promise,'' she said softly. Standing on tiptoe, she kissed him deeply as another torrent of need swept through her. He kissed her back, fervently, thoroughly. Then, looking at her adoringly all the while, urged hoarsely, ''Promise me you'll never be afraid to tell me anything again. Because I love you, Meg. I love you with all my heart and soul.''

''YOU'RE WALKING ON AIR,'' Kelsey observed, when the two met for lunch at the hospital the following day.

Meg had every reason to feel that way. Luke had said he loved her! And she'd finally opened up and told him she loved him, too. But not wanting to discuss that with anyone else just yet, Meg merely smiled and looked down at her feet as they moved through the cafeteria line.

"Looks like terra firma to me," Meg quipped.

Kelsey rolled her eyes and, following Meg's lead, selected a grilled chicken salad and a bottle of water and put them on her tray. "Ha, ha. I'm serious. What's going on with you and Luke?"

Meg selected a table near the back, where they could talk privately. "Luke and I have a date tonight. A real one. Two grown-ups. No kids. I know it's short notice, but I was hoping I could talk you into baby-sitting for all four of our kids."

Kelsey grinned, looking almost as happy for Meg as Meg was. "I'll do better than that," Kelsey volunteered enthusiastically. "I'll spend the night."

Meg blew out a sigh of relief. "You are such a life-saver."

"Yeah, that's me, all right." Kelsey mugged comically, then angled a thumb at her chest. "Just don't expect me to cook dinner. You know what a lousy cook I am."

"I'll supply the pizza and salad. What time do you think you can be there?"

Kelsey contemplated a moment. "Six o'clock okay?"

"It's more than okay. I owe you for this one, little sis."

KELSEY WAS AS GOOD AS HER WORD, showing up in time to have supper with all four kids in Meg's kitchen, while Meg and Luke got ready for their date.

"Wow," Kelsey said when Meg floated down the stairs.

"Think Luke will like it?" Meg asked, twirling around

so Kelsey and the kids could get the full view of her pale-yellow sundress.

"Luke would have to be an idiot not to like it," Luke said, grinning as he let himself in the door. His glance warmed as he took her in from head to toe, noting every detail of the figure-hugging dress that left most of her back and shoulders bare and fell to just above her knee. "Luke is no idiot."

"You look really pretty!" Becca, Susie and Amy chimed in unison.

Not to be outdone, Jeremy nodded. "I think so, too, Mommy."

"Luke, there, doesn't look so bad himself," Kelsey grinned, giving him a teasing once-over. "Appears to me he's even shaved again!"

He did look good, Meg thought, in the tan summer-weight suit, ecru shirt and matching tie. In fact, she couldn't remember ever seeing him look that handsome.

"You know what they say—you can't do too much in the grooming department when you're taking your woman out on the town," Luke winked.

Kelsey's brow lifted at the possessiveness in Luke's voice. "This sounds serious," she said approvingly.

Luke merely smiled. He kissed all the kids in turn, admonished them all to be good and mind Kelsey, and watched as Meg did the same. Luke took Meg's hand and clasped it firmly in his. "Ready?"

Aware she was practically trembling with excitement, Meg drew a bolstering breath. "As I'll ever be," she said.

"I'VE NEVER HAD such a lovely evening," Meg said hours later as they parked in the driveway that ran between their two houses. Luke had taken her to a country inn for a quiet, intimate dinner, and they'd stopped by Greta

McCabe's country-and-western dance hall for dancing after that. It had been an incredibly romantic date, the kind she had always wanted to have with Luke, and Meg hated for it to end.

Luke cut the motor on his SUV. He glanced toward Meg's house. It looked like all was quiet, with the kids and Kelsey asleep. Glad everything was okay on the domestic front, Meg breathed a sigh of relief as Luke climbed out of the truck and came around to help her out. Both hands circling her waist, he lowered her slowly to the ground and smiled down at her sexily. Looking at her as if she were the most beautiful woman in the world, he promised softly, "It's not over yet."

"It isn't," Meg drawled happily, reluctant to admit how much she had been hoping the evening would end with even more intimate contact between the two of them. Luke had only been back in her life a matter of days, but in that time he had become a very major part of her life, hopes and dreams. She was beginning to resent the time— especially the nights—they had to spend apart. She was beginning to want to feel him next to her—so warm and solid and strong—not just for stolen moments here and there during the day, but all night long. She was beginning to want to make love to him every night and wake up in his arms every morning. And that had never happened to her before.

His eyes never leaving hers, Luke shook his head. "As far as I'm concerned, sweetheart, the evening's just beginning." He took her in his arms and kissed her until she was tingling from head to toe with the promise of what they both wanted to happen next. When they drew apart, Meg was shaking. Holding her face between his hands, he tilted her head up to his and rubbed his thumb across her cheek. He looked deep into her eyes, and in that instant, was more vulnerable than Meg had ever seen him. "Come inside with me," he whispered.

Meg could no more have refused him than she could have stopped breathing. Luke took her inside and led her to the sofa. "Sit here. I'll be right back."

Meg was trembling with anticipation as Luke returned with a bucket of champagne on ice and two long-stemmed glasses. "You're really going all out tonight."

Luke shrugged off his sport coat, loosened his tie and unbuttoned the first two buttons on his shirt. Grinning, he sat down beside her and poured them each some champagne. "I want you to know there's more to me than an ability to stitch a cut and make peanut butter sandwiches," he said as he handed her a glass and picked one up for himself.

Deciding it was a great idea to get comfortable, Meg kicked off her heels, stretched her legs out in front of her and joyfully wiggled her toes. She slanted him a playful glance—if ever there was a Renaissance man, it was Luke. "I think I knew that," she said dryly.

"Good." Luke curved an arm around her bare shoulder and brought her close. "'Cause there's more to you, too," he said confidently as they both sipped their champagne. "And it's time we spent some energy on something other than our jobs and our kids. It's time we paid attention to what we want and need ourselves."

Meg smiled, liking the sound of that. "And that would be?" she prodded teasingly, content to let him take the lead.

Luke set their glasses aside. "Kisses," he said, as he shifted her onto his lap and ran a playful hand down her spine. "I need kisses," he confessed softly, easing the ribbon-thin straps of her dress off her shoulders. "Do you?"

Meg's back arched as he kissed his way from her collarbone to her shoulder and back again. "Oh yes."

"Soft kisses?" One hand playing down her spine, Luke gave her other shoulder the same tender treatment.

Her eyes half-closed, her head thrown back in abandonment, Meg wreathed her arms about his shoulders and reveled in the sensuality of his warm breath ghosting over her skin. She sighed as his lips touched and caressed the uppermost curves of her breasts, spilling out of the pale yellow cotton, then tensed with disappointment when he went no farther.

"I...like those," she said eventually.

Luke's hands palmed the weight of her breasts through her dress, easily working the nipples to aching peaks. "How about wet kisses..." he murmured, lifting her hair away from her neck and kissing the delicate skin behind her ear.

Able to feel his growing hardness beneath her, Meg shifted restlessly on his lap. A shallow breath soughed between her lips as he kissed her cheek, her chin, then hovered maddeningly just above her lips. "Mmm." Meg encouraged him by lifting her lips to his.

"...like this?" Luke murmured, ably demonstrating a very potent lip lock that involved a lot of delicious heat and pressure. And left Meg pulsing and straining for more than the small taste of Luke he had offered.

Luke grinned as his hands slid down her hips, and he pulled her even tighter against him. Meg's heart fluttered in her chest as she felt his arousal pressing against her. "Then there is the more passionate variety," Luke explained with mock solemnity. He swept his tongue into her mouth and kissed her so hotly and rapaciously she moaned low in her throat and, wreathing her arms about his neck, dragged him even closer, so her breasts were pressed against the unyielding hardness of his chest. Longing swept through her and she boldly met him, kiss for kiss, as they experimented and tested and learned all about each other's wants and needs and desires, until he was rock hard and she was filled with a need unlike anything she had ever felt before.

Grinning with thorough male satisfaction, Luke slowly ended the kiss, drew his head back and waited for the verdict. Not sure whether she wanted to kiss him senseless or rip all his clothes off then and there, Meg admitted breathlessly, "I like those, too." And, judging by the gleam in his eyes, he did, as well.

Luke shifted Meg from his lap, stood. Before she could do more than take a shocked breath, he had tugged her to her feet and swept her up into his arms. "And let's not forget the kind of kisses that can only be conducted in bed." Holding her masterfully in his arms, Luke strode out of the room and carried Meg up the stairs. He didn't stop until he had reached his bedroom, where a single lamp was burning.

To Meg's shock the room was filled with flowers and candles. His sleigh-style bed had been made up neatly with crisp clean sheets that were already neatly turned down.

Luke set her down gently beside the bed, then went to light the candles, one by one. When they were all burning, he turned off the single light. The room was infused with a soft, ultraromantic glow.

Her mouth dry, Meg watched him take off his tie, shrug out of his shirt and drop them both on the overstuffed reading chair in the corner. "When did you do all this?" she asked, amazed.

Luke unbuckled his belt and unzipped his fly. Swiftly, methodically, the rest of his clothes joined the ones on the chair. "On my lunch hour," he admitted, striding toward her, naked and unashamed. "I wanted everything to be perfect tonight," he said as he took her into his arms.

"It was," Meg replied, as Luke drew down the zipper of her dress and slipped that off. "Is."

Luke reached behind her to unfasten her bra. "I'm glad you think so," he murmured, as her breasts fell free and he palmed them with his hands. "Because it's the very least you deserve, Meg."

Meg put her arms around his neck. "You're full of surprises, aren't you?"

Luke tucked his thumbs into her panties and drew them down, too. "Wouldn't want you to get bored."

"Little chance of that," Meg murmured as he aligned her against him firmly. And she reacted with everything that was feminine and feisty within her.

"Now, where were we?" he teased.

Meg surged against him, throbbing all over, and they were only just getting started, she knew. "You were going to give me the kind of kiss you can only give me in bed." The kind of nothing-held-back kiss she had been wanting all evening.

"Oh, yeah," he recalled with playful abandon, anchoring her against him firmly with one arm. With his free hand he sifted his fingers through her hair and tilted her head back so as to offer him maximum access and control. His eyes swept her face. Then his head dropped and his lips met hers and all was lost in the wild, sweet wonder of the kiss. His mouth moved on hers effortlessly, demandingly, taking complete control of the kiss with ease. Meg dragged him closer still, burying both her hands in his hair, opening her mouth to his, every ardent sense in her aroused by his unswerving determination to make her his. As he continued to kiss her, lazily now, seductively, he cupped her breasts in his hands, with infinite slowness brushed his thumbs across the tips…again and again, until her nipples budded tightly and need swept through her middle, pooling low.

Meg's knees weakened treacherously. She wanted them on the bed. Luke, she discovered, had other ideas, as he backed her to the wall and positioned her against it. Not content just to touch her, he bent his head and moistened the delicate aureole of her breast with his tongue. Blew it dry. Then suckled her tenderly. When she thought she could stand it no more, he turned his attention to her other breast and did the same.

Just when she thought she could stand it no more, he dropped to his knees. "Luke," Meg whispered, already writhing impatiently against him. She didn't know how much more of this slow, thorough loving she could take.

"Let me worship you, Meg, the way you were meant to be worshiped." Kneeling in front of her, he swept his hands down her body and gently parted her legs. Meg moaned as his fingers found her, then his lips. Meg gasped in delight, already trembling on the edge of release. Trembling, she rested her hands on his shoulders, moaned as he stroked and licked and sucked and then his lips were on her again in the most intimate of caresses and she was catapulting head over heels into bliss.

She'd barely stopped shuddering before he led her back to the bed, placed her on the sheets and covered her body with his own. Luke looked down at her with such intensity she caught her breath. Parting her knees with his, he braced a hand on either side of her and situated himself between her thighs. "This is just the beginning for us, Meg," he promised.

"I know," Meg whispered back, finding him with her hands, filling her fingers with his hard, hot flesh. She wanted to touch and caress him. To make this a mutual giving of pleasure, but Luke was insistent he be the one in control as he took one of her wrists in each hand and then anchored them together above her head. They locked eyes, and she offered herself to him completely, giving him the kind of access to her heart and soul she'd yearned to be able to give him in the past.

There for her in a way he never had been before, too, Luke lowered his mouth to hers once again, lifted her against him and surged into her, slowly and deliberately making them one. Over and over he kissed her, entering and withdrawing in slow shallow strokes that soon had her moaning and shuddering with an urgency unlike anything she'd felt before. Trembling with her need for him, she took up the rhythm he'd started, until their hearts thundered in unison and he too was straining against her, rocking with her, into her, aware only of the heat and pleasure and the urgent need for release. And then they were clinging together, with nothing…save one secret…standing between them, their passion so strong and so right and so total it didn't feel quite real. *But it is,* Meg thought, as the two of them soared, shuddering and unrestrained into bliss, and then slowly, slowly floated back down. *It is.*

For long moments after, both were silent, the only sound in the room the uneven rhythm of their mingled breaths. Eventually, realizing his weight was too much for Meg to bear, Luke rolled onto his back and took her with him. Reveling in the feel of his warm strong arms against her, Meg collapsed against Luke's chest. She smiled as he pressed a kiss into her hair, another on her temple, then frowned minutes later as Luke unexpectedly rose from the bed. Feeling cold and lonely already, Meg rose on her elbow. "Where are you going?" She hadn't had near her fill of cuddling!

"Downstairs—" Luke sent her a grin that let her know he'd be right back "—to get the champagne."

He returned with the tray, set it on the table next to the bed, then offered her a glass, still nearly brimming with champagne. "What shall we drink to?" Meg asked happily as they faced each other, cross-legged, on the bed.

"Your acceptance to my proposal." Luke looked deep into her eyes. "Marry me, Meg."

THEY WERE THE WORDS Meg had longed to hear for so long, and yet they filled her with dread for one simple reason—she hadn't been honest with him. And she couldn't marry him with a secret like that between them. Meg put her glass of champagne aside. "I can't."

She wrapped a sheet around her, toga-style, and moved away from the bed. Aware her knees were suddenly trembling so hard they would barely support her, Meg backed into the reading chair in the corner and sat down.

Looking both hurt and stunned, Luke stared at her. "Why not?" he said finally.

Meg swallowed, knowing she was risking it all, but knowing she couldn't say yes, the way she wanted to say yes, to Luke's proposal without disclosing the truth. Gathering her courage, she stood and crossed to his side. Sat down next to him, touched his arm and plunged on in the steadiest voice she could manage. "Because there's something I haven't told you," Meg said miserably.

"About Jeremy," Luke guessed quietly, suddenly looking every bit as tense and wary and uneasy as she felt.

Relying on her love for Luke and her faith in the future, Meg struggled against the fear welling up inside her. "You need to find out what happened now...before this goes any further...because once you know the truth you might not feel the same way about me that you do now."

He grasped her shoulders warmly. "Nothing is going to change the way I feel about you, Meg," Luke reassured her gruffly.

Worry pinched her face as their gazes collided, held. "You say that now," Meg said as she gave herself up to the raw jumble of feeling deep inside her heart.

"And I mean it," Luke said firmly. "I've had plenty of time to think about this. The only thing that matters is that I love you and I want to be with you."

Meg trembled as her heart roared in her ears. "But Jeremy—"

"—will be my son in every way that counts from this moment on. Our DNA doesn't have to be the same for me to love Jeremy and Jeremy to love me, Meg. Being father and son is something that's done here—" Luke touched his chest "—in our hearts."

Tears of happiness and relief slid down Meg's face. "Oh, Luke, I should have told you the truth when you first came to see me and asked those questions. But I was scared you'd be angry with me. Scared you'd try to take him away from me, so I made it sound like there were other possibilities when that was never the case at all."

"What are you saying?" His expression as tense and unyielding as the rest of him, Luke waited.

"That there is...was...never anyone else," Meg whispered around the ache in her throat. "He's your son, Luke. Jeremy is your son."

"I knew he was mine," Luke said with a quiet contentment that seemed to radiate from deep inside his heart and soul. He hugged her fiercely. "I knew it all along."

Completely thrown by his reaction, Meg blinked. She had expected him to be shocked, disbelieving, maybe even argue dates, at which point she would have to explain what few people aside from her sisters and John and Lilah McCabe knew, that Jeremy had been born prematurely. "What do you mean, you knew it all along?" How was it possible Luke had figured all this out—some time ago, it seemed—and come to grips with the situation. And all the while she hadn't had a clue he was grappling with such weighty issues, had thought he'd accepted her denials.

Luke sighed and clasped her hand tightly in his. "To tell you the truth, I think I knew in my heart Jeremy was my son from the first moment I heard you had a little boy."

"When did you learn I had a son, precisely?" Meg asked cautiously, her every instinct telling her to be very clear on all the details, before she came to any conclusions about why Luke had done everything he had to put himself back in her—and his son's—life. Because if he was only here, making love to her, proposing marriage, out of a sense of obligation...

"When I met John McCabe at that medical conference last spring," Luke said seriously. "He was looking for his replacement and trying to sell me on the job in Laramie. John McCabe was going down the list of pluses for Laramie Community Hospital. You taking the nurse supervisor job was one of them."

What should have made her happy made her all the more wary. Especially since it was beginning to seem that a life with her was the least of what Luke wanted here. "John realized we knew each other?" Meg asked cautiously.

Luke nodded, not at all chagrined. "I mentioned to John right off the bat that I knew you from our year in Chicago. I wondered if you were still in Laramie. He told me you were, that you had never married but had a five-year-old boy that was cute as the dickens. I did the math, remembered we had not used any contraception the night we were together and just assumed Jeremy was mine."

Beginning to feel like one of the biggest fools ever, for having dared to think that Luke wanted anything more than friendship, sex and a complete family for their children here, Meg extricated her hand from his. She stood and, looking into his eyes, said as calmly as she could, "And you took the job in Laramie, having already made the assumption that Jeremy was your child."

"Right. Although I would have taken it in any case, once I visited. I admired what John and Lilah did, starting the hospital and building it from the ground up. I had been looking for a quieter place to bring up the girls, and I wanted to return to my Texas roots. Knowing you had just moved back here, too, well it seemed meant to be."

Barely able to believe how stupid and gullible she'd been, thinking Luke wanted her and not just his son, Meg gritted her teeth. "And buying the house next door to mine?"

Luke shrugged his broad shoulders carelessly. Finally he had the grace to look a little bit chagrined as he admitted, "I knew you'd bought the cottage on the property. There were a couple others I could have taken, but this one was the largest and seemed right. Knowing you'd be next door…well, it didn't actually seal the deal, but it did nothing to deter me, either," he finished honestly.

Meg's head was reeling at the calculated way Luke had gone about inserting himself in his son's life that would allow maximum contact on a daily, sometimes hourly, basis, even before any official paternal claim was made. "So you purchased the house already thinking you were Jeremy's father and then you came and confronted me and asked me point-blank when Jeremy's birth date was. When you realized it was eight months, not nine, after the night we were together, Luke, you concluded you weren't his father." And in her efforts to protect Jeremy from any future custody battle, she had done nothing to correct Luke.

Luke frowned unhappily. Clearly this was something he didn't want to hash out at all. Restlessly he moved to his feet and squared off with her. "The only thing I accepted that night was that Jeremy needed a father desperately and you had so much pride you weren't willing to discuss the situation with me or anyone else. So, for your sake, for Jeremy's, I took matters into my own hands." Luke drew a deep breath and folded his arms across his bare chest. "I went to see Kip Brewster. I told him you had a son and suggested rather firmly that he do right by you and Jeremy."

Hot, embarrassed color swept into Meg's face as she imagined that scene. "And Kip said..." she prodded hoarsely.

Luke grimaced at the memory and continued to look at Meg steadily. "That he couldn't possibly be the father because the two of you had never slept together. At which point I went back to Laramie and asked John and Lilah McCabe if Jeremy had been born a month or so prematurely."

"You talked to them about this, too?"

Luke nodded. "I felt I had to know. Don't you see, Meg? If he was my son, I had to be responsible. And if I hadn't come to that conclusion on my own, I certainly would have done so after talking to Jeremy and realizing how desperately he needed and wanted a father in his life."

"What did John and Lilah tell you?"

"They said I'd have to get the information from you. I knew you weren't going to confide in me, at least not then. Which only gave me a few options. Hire an attorney and demand a DNA test, or find out some other way if Jeremy was mine either by talking to people who knew you and asking questions or simply looking it up in the hospital computers. But I didn't want to do that, Meg. I wanted you to tell me."

"Which is when you began pursuing me, trying to spend a lot of time with me."

Luke nodded. "I knew you would have to trust me and feel close to me before you confided in me."

Meg laughed at the bitter irony of it all, realizing that not only had she been hiding the truth from Luke, but that Luke had lied to her, not just once, but over and over. She threw up her hands in disgust, not sure who she was unhappier with, Luke or herself. "No wonder you were so alarmed when you saw Kip here!" She speared him with an accusing gaze. "You were afraid Kip was going to tell me you'd been to see him in Austin. You were afraid I'd figure out that you knew about Jeremy before you'd finished enacting your scheme to gain custody of your son."

Luke's lips thinned in frustration. "I admit I should have told you about going to see Kip and Lilah and John a lot sooner," he allowed curtly.

"Then why didn't you?" Meg demanded.

"The same reason you didn't tell me I had a son, even after we started to become close." He advanced on her slowly, deliberately. "Because I knew it would make you angry. And I didn't want you to be angry with me."

Or realize you were just doing the noble thing in pursuing me, Meg thought angrily. Because if there was one thing Luke had in excess, it was compassion and empathy.

That was part of the reason he was such a good physician. No doubt Luke figured if he married her now and provided Jeremy with a father, he would be making up for his mistake in sleeping with her and then walking away from her, six years ago. But she didn't want his pity, never had.

Meg glared at Luke. "If you knew all this days ago, why didn't you confront me with the truth then? Why all the games? Why did you pretend to accept my decision not to divulge Jeremy's paternity when you really hadn't done so at all? Darn it all, Luke, why did you continue to pursue me like I was the love of your life, instead of just the mother of your son?"

His patience exhausted, Luke gave Meg a withering look. "Believe me, I wanted to read you the riot act for the way you'd shut me out of the first five years of Jeremy's life," Luke said, his own temper beginning to flare. "But when I got back home that night, after talking with Kip and John and Lilah, your sisters were at your place and I was busy taking care of my girls. It had to wait. When I calmed down and really had time to think about it, I realized that whatever you'd done, you probably hadn't felt you had any choice." Luke sighed, regret sharpening his handsome features. "I knew I'd had a part in your feeling abandoned, and I figured the best thing for me to do was to get close to you again and get to know Jeremy. And hope one day you would be able to trust me enough, and love me enough, to come to me with your problems and tell me the truth about your son. In the meantime I could watch over Jeremy and you and be a part of your lives in a way I wasn't able to do before."

"So you did all this—you romanced me, you asked me to marry you, because of Jeremy?" Meg asked, tears flooding her eyes as her hurt and disillusionment increased by leaps and bounds. "Because you thought he might be yours, after all, and you were trying to make up for the mistakes you'd made in the past?"

Luke took her hands in his. "I did all this because I want you in my life."

An overwhelming sadness swept through Meg as she pulled away from him. "I wish I could believe that."

"Why can't you?" he demanded angrily.

"Because I know how responsible you are, Luke." Meg regarded him with mounting impatience as she began gathering up her clothes. "I know how seriously you take your obligations and how determined you are to always do the right thing. You told me yourself that you never loved Gwyneth the way you should. But you married her because you felt you owed her, and you stayed with her and would have remained married to her for the rest of your life because the two of you had kids. I know how hard it was for you, growing up without a mother. I know how strongly you feel that whenever possible, kids need both a mother and a father, and that you were ready and willing to do whatever necessary to make that happen for your kids."

Luke watched as Meg slipped into her bra and panties. "I don't deny any of that."

"But...?" Meg stepped into her dress.

His eyes holding hers, Luke continued bluntly, "I love you in a way I have never loved anyone."

Meg knew he thought he did. She also knew guilt and compassion and wanting to do right by someone were no basis for the kind of marriage they both deserved. "Are you sure, Luke?" Meg demanded, her own frustration mounting. "Or are you just trying to lessen the guilt you feel about making love to me that night in Chicago and leaving me to bear my pregnancy alone?"

Luke closed the distance between them and took her by the arms. "I know what I feel, Meg."

"And I know you've always wanted a son." Meg flattened her hands on his chest and pushed him away from her. "I know that you want to get married again. That you want a mother for your girls. I know we get along. That we could make a good team and be good for all our children. But don't you see," she cried, upset, "that's not enough for the kind of fulfilling, lifelong marriage we both deserve?"

Sighing, Luke grabbed his slacks and tugged them on. "Then what would be?" he asked, exasperated.

"I want the kind of marriage my parents had," Meg insisted stubbornly. "The kind John and Lilah have. I want to know you would have come after me and made me yours no matter what. And that didn't happen. If not for a chance meeting with John McCabe at a medical seminar...if not for Jeremy...you never would have seen me again, never mind come after me. If not for the fact we share a son, our romance would have begun and ended that night in Chicago when I was reeling with grief and confusion. And that is all there ever would have been to it."

"So that's what this is about?" he said, abruptly looking every bit as betrayed and upset as she felt. "You're angry because I didn't come after you that summer."

"Hurt and disillusioned," Meg corrected archly, forcing herself to face the truth, painful as it was. "And yes, I guess I was disappointed initially, but I'm past that now."

Luke gave her a look that said, Are you? He didn't believe it. Not for a second. "Let me get this straight. For months after you went back to Texas, you returned my letters unopened and refused my phone calls and told me in every way possible that you regretted our making love and because of that, had no interest whatsoever in continuing our friendship, on any level. Then, when I finally did reach you by phone, you curtly asked me to leave you alone, to never call you or speak to you or get in touch with you again. And, out of deference to the terrible tragedy you and your sisters were dealing with, *I did what you asked.*"

Yes, and that devastation on top of the loss of her parents had left her feeling even more abandoned and bereft. "Exactly," Meg said, feeling like her heart was breaking all over again, just talking about it. Only it hurt worse this time than it had the first. She regarded him steadily. "If you had really loved me, the way people who vow to spend the rest of their lives together do, it wouldn't have ended like that, Luke, no matter how hurt or angry or frustrated we both were. Don't you see? If you had really loved me, Luke, you wouldn't have eventually gone on to marry Gwyneth, just as you had planned. You would have known what I didn't at the time—which was that I wasn't thinking clearly, because of all I'd been through—and you would have waited for me. Or come after me. Or found a way to change my mind. You would have done something besides marry someone else!"

"I agree I made a huge mistake letting you go," Luke said gruffly, grabbing his shirt as he followed her down the stairs, taking them two at a time. "But I did that out of respect for your feelings, because I felt so badly for what I had done in making love to you that night, when all I should have done was hold you."

Meg sighed sadly as she rummaged around in her purse for her hairbrush. Half an hour ago she'd felt like the most wanted woman in the world. Now she felt like an unwanted liability—like the part of a package deal that you buy to get what you really want—and whether Luke could or would admit it to himself, what he really wanted here was his son. The trick now would be to act like adults and not let themselves be misled by their mutual affection for Jeremy.

"That wasn't all your fault, Luke," Meg told him gently. She forced herself to be brutally honest, for all their sakes, especially the children's. "I wanted you that night. I had always wanted you, even though I knew from the way you acted toward me that a romance between us wasn't in the cards." Tears blurred her eyes. Not wanting him to see the love in her eyes, she had to turn away. "I just let myself take what I wanted that night, because I didn't care about anything or anyone, I just wanted to stop hurting. And being with you that way was the only thing that made me stop hurting, for just a little while." Had reality not intruded…but it had then, just as it had now.

"Damn it, Meg, if it felt that good…" Luke watched her restore order to her hair. "Then why can't you let yourself be with me again—for the rest of your life this time?" he asked gruffly.

Meg tried one last time to make him see reason. "Because it takes more than a friendship and a physical attraction between two people to make a marriage. We have to face it, Luke. The night we made Jeremy, we slept together for all the wrong reasons. You were trying to help me—just as you are now, and I needed someone to lean on. I was reeling with grief and hurt and fear. But as soon as the morning dawned and we came to our senses, we both knew it was wrong, that we didn't belong together. And we went our separate ways."

Meg drew a deep breath and steeled herself, refusing to let herself go all weak and needy again. She looked at Luke sternly, wanting him to know. "That day I promised myself I would never get involved with someone for all the wrong reasons again. I knew I could have called you and told you I was pregnant and you would have done right by me. But I didn't want you marrying me because I couldn't handle things alone or my son needed a father. I didn't want to hand you the kind of overwhelming responsibility I was left with when I became my sisters' guardian, because it just wasn't fair, especially when the fact we made love at all that night was all my fault." If she hadn't thrown herself at him he never would have made love to her.

Luke gave her a long look, his expression stony. "Fairness is not what this is about, and we both know it," he confided grimly.

"Then what is it about?" Meg asked tersely, bracing herself for the blistering appraisal she knew had to be coming. It wasn't like Luke to get hit without hitting back.

"It's about your inability to trust in the future or depend upon anyone but yourself," Luke said softly, just that quickly getting her where it really hurt. He looked her up and down consideringly, as always seeing—and understanding—more of her than she wanted anyone to see. "You were always independent to a fault, Meg," he told her, "but your parents' death and the responsibility of single motherhood have made you take it a hundred steps further."

The way he said it, it wasn't a compliment. Stung, Meg smiled at him. "Am I paying for this professional assessment, Doctor, or is it free?"

Ignoring her sarcasm, he stepped closer still. Caressing her face gently with his hand, he continued, even more softly, accurately. "Loving me would involve taking the biggest emotional risk you've ever taken in your life. And you're not willing to do that. Why?" Not waiting for her to respond, he pushed on authoritatively. "Because you're afraid if you love me you could lose me. So it'd be better for you just not to love me at all than risk the kind of emotional devastation you felt when your parents died."

Meg stiffened. Worse than the truth was the bitter censure in his low voice. "I admit I don't want to be hurt again," she said thickly, turning away from his fiercely dissecting gaze. "And I don't want you or Jeremy or the girls hurt, either."

Luke grabbed her shoulders and swung her around to face him. "You don't think they'll be hurt by our breakup?"

Her bare skin burning hotly beneath his touch, Meg forced herself to stand completely still as her heart slammed against her ribs. "We can still be friends, Luke."

Luke's gaze darkened contemptuously. "Friendship is not what I want from you, Meg. If you want the truth, it never has been."

Knowing if they talked much more she really would burst into tears, Meg shrugged her shoulders with as much indifference as she could muster and tugged free of him. Chin high, determined to cut their losses while she could, she said, "Under the circumstances, it's all I can reasonably offer."

Luke stepped back, away from her, resentment oozing from every pore. "Is it?" He regarded her furiously.

Meg reached for her purse. It had been a mistake to fall in love with him all over again. "Of course you can see Jeremy whenever you want," she promised, as she searched for her house key. She had no intention of separating father and son again. Bad enough it had taken them this long to get to know each other.

"How very generous of you," Luke snapped, as every

ounce of intimacy they'd won for themselves faded. He watched her close the clasp on her purse and, key in hand, head for the front hall. "But that's not what I want, either." He paused in the portal, a shoulder braced against the frame.

"That's too bad." Meg reached past him to open the door. "Because after everything that's happened, it's all I can—or will—offer." Without a backward glance, Meg walked across the lawn.

Chapter Eleven

John McCabe stopped by to see Luke the following evening after supper, just as Luke was getting out his lawn mower. John said hi to the girls—who were playing with dolls on the back porch—then walked over to speak to Luke. "My nephew Sam told me you were still trying to get him and the boys to Kate Marten for counseling."

Luke nodded as he rolled the mower over to the driveway, well out of earshot of the porch. "Sam's pretty resistant to the idea, but I plan to keep trying."

John nodded his approval as Luke knelt to take the cap off the gasoline reservoir. "Good. Lilah and I have been doing our best to help Sam and the boys, but we're family and they don't always listen to us. Kate has enough distance and perspective to help Sam and the boys get over Ellie's death."

"I agree." Sam checked the fuel level, then added another half gallon or so of fuel. Finished, he replaced the cap tightly, stood and continued talking to John, doctor to doctor. "The problem is getting Sam to realize the grieving process will go a lot faster and easier if they get professional counseling. Kate can't do anything without their cooperation."

Next door the back door slammed. Meg came out, Jeremy right beside her. They waved and got in Meg's car. Luke turned away from the sight of Meg, so lovely and capable and unconsciously sexy. It wouldn't do him any good to admire her from afar or near, now that their love affair was over. He had done everything he could to make her his. And it still hadn't worked, not in the long haul. And the long haul was the only thing he was interested in.

John continued to watch Meg and Jeremy as they drove off. When they were gone he turned back to Luke with almost paternal concern. "Speaking of help, I heard your romance with Meg could use some fixing," he said gently.

Luke steeled himself for the small-town meddling to come. "There is no romance," he said evenly.

"Sure there is. It's just stalled."

Luke stalked over to the garden hose to wash the gasoline off his hands. "You mean dead on arrival, don't you?"

John ambled after him casually. "Lilah and I love Meg and her sisters like our own kids, you know."

Luke knew, which was what made it all the worse. Wordlessly he dried his hands on the clean rag he had tucked inside his belt and waited for John to continue.

"We haven't seen Meg this devastated since her parents died."

Luke met John's concerned glance head-on. "Then you also know she turned down my marriage proposal."

John nodded, seemingly not at all surprised about that. "She's upset you didn't tell her you suspected the truth about Jeremy."

Grimly, Luke shook his head. "That's not why she refused to marry me."

Curious, John asked, "Then why?"

Luke blew out a frustrated breath. "She's afraid to depend on anyone but herself—she has been since her parents died. That's why she insists on doing everything by herself."

"Lilah and I totally agree."

"Then why are you here talking to me?" Luke asked impatiently, not about to kid either John or himself about what was feasible and what wasn't, where his love for Meg was concerned.

"Because you have the power to turn things around for Meg."

"You're wrong, John. I already tried. I failed." Luke was tired of pursuing something that just wasn't going to happen, no matter how gung ho his attitude or how concerted his efforts. Difficult as it was, Luke knew he had to face facts. "Meg doesn't want to marry me. She doesn't want to marry anyone."

Again John was not in the least surprised by Luke's revelation about Meg's aversion to marriage.

"Lilah used to think she'd never get married, either," John confided seriously. "And she continued to feel that way about joining lives with someone else even after she and I first met."

Luke did a double take. "What?"

John nodded, chagrined. "Not very many people know this—for obvious reasons I've kept it to myself—but Lilah didn't say yes the first time I asked her to marry me."

Luke gaped in disbelief. "You're kidding."

"She turned me down the first four times," John continued bluntly.

"Why?" Luke asked. If ever there had seemed a couple totally perfect for each other, it was John and Lilah McCabe!

John shrugged and continued ruefully, "Initially she

thought I only wanted her to be my wife because I needed a nurse in Laramie to help me get my medical practice up and running. I told her that wasn't true, of course, but she didn't buy it."

"But she eventually agreed to be your nurse, anyway."

"Oh, yes, within a week, but she even put a condition on that."

And Luke thought Meg had given him a hard time! "Which was…?"

"She refused to date me as long as she was working for me, and if she wasn't working for me, she wasn't staying in Laramie County, as there would be no point."

This was a side of the happily married John and Lilah Luke hadn't guessed at. Intrigued, he asked, "So what'd you do?"

"I spent every spare second I had letting Lilah know that I adored her. And I kept telling her I loved her and no one else and kept asking her to marry me until she finally said yes, all without going on a single date."

Luke thought about the persistence that had taken. He was no stranger to hard work and dedication. But kicking a dead horse was something else. Regretfully Luke admitted, "I could ask Meg to marry me again every day for the next ten years and she still wouldn't say yes."

Not the least discouraged, John regarded Luke steadily. "Then you've got your work cut out for you, son. Don't you?"

WHILE JEREMY RODE a horse with Shane McCabe, Lilah and Meg sat together in the kitchen of the McCabe ranch house, with Lilah pouring the iced tea and listening to Meg, much as Meg's mother would have done. "You think I was wrong to break it off with Luke, don't you?"

Meg asked Lilah after she had finished unburdening herself.

And like Meg's mother, Lilah did not hesitate to speak straight from the heart. "Love comes along so seldom," she said, obviously disappointed her matchmaking hopes were not going to be realized. "I think it's criminal to throw it all away, if there is any chance at all the relationship can be saved."

Meg pushed back the tears gathering in her eyes. "The only reason he wants to marry me is because of Jeremy."

"Please." Lilah made a pooh-poohing gesture. "Luke could sue you for custody of his son in the blink of an eye if all he wanted was his son."

"True," Meg returned, "but that wouldn't get him a wife and a mother for his girls."

"No, it wouldn't," Lilah agreed practically. "But he doesn't need you for that either, Meg. You're not the only single woman around. There are dozens of attractive, personable women right here in Laramie County who would love to have Luke for a husband, as well as adore being mother to his three charming little girls. I have no doubt he could have any one of them."

Meg hadn't thought about what it would be like watching Luke date and marry someone else. Just the idea of him being with another woman was enough to break her heart. "Okay, you've made your point. He could easily find someone else to warm his bed and mother his children."

"You're darn right he could, but he wants you."

"Only because it's easier and he still feels obligated because he got me pregnant and didn't come after me and marry me years ago."

"Guilt does not make a man look at a woman the way

Luke looks at you, Meg. I've seen the two of you together. That man is head over heels in love with you."

And I am head over heels in love with him, Meg thought. But that didn't mean they could make their relationship work the way it should. And if they couldn't do that, they had no business getting married. "I want the kind of marriage you and John have, the kind my parents had, the kind your boys and my sisters Jenna and Dani have!" Meg said stubbornly.

"So what's stopping you?" Lilah asked.

"Luke and I are not as in tune with each other as we should be, Lilah. As much as I hate to admit it, there is something fundamentally wrong with the two of us in terms of our ability to communicate with each other, and there always has been. Otherwise I certainly would have suspected that he had figured out that Jeremy might be his son and was trying to confirm it—and I didn't have a clue."

Lilah arched a brow. "Maybe you didn't want a clue."

That was certainly true, Meg conceded reluctantly. She had been so happy to be with Luke again, to have him pursue her like there was no tomorrow, that she hadn't wanted anything to interfere with that. Even so, she had to be practical. "My father never could have pulled anything like that over on my mother. John couldn't have done it to you! You and my mother—you knew what your husbands were thinking and doing, almost before they did. You had the same ability to read your children. And I've got it, too, when it comes to my sisters and my son. Instinctively I know what's going on with them in their hearts and their heads."

"Whereas Luke is a tremendous mystery to you," Lilah guessed quietly.

"Yes," Meg admitted miserably.

Lilah's lips curved in a compassionate smile. Gently she touched Meg's hand. "Well, join the club, honey."

Meg blinked. "What do you mean?"

"Husbands and wives are not born knowing how to talk to each other. It takes years of constant communication and concerted effort to develop the kind of shorthand that John and I have with each other. The same goes for you and your sisters. And your son. Maybe it seems like it now, but that didn't happen overnight, either. It took years to develop the kind of closeness you have. And your job isn't over yet. To stay close, you have to work at it."

"But it should be easier with me and Luke," Meg argued, "if we were really meant to be with each other the way I want us to be with each other."

"Oh, honey." Lilah leaned over and gave her a motherly hug. "The fact you and Luke were meant to be together—and John and I both firmly believe that you are, otherwise all this wouldn't have happened—well, that only makes it all the harder. Why? Because there's so much more at stake for you and Luke. The rest of your lives."

As Meg clung to the shred of hope, her spirits began to lift. "You really think we were meant to be together?"

"Think about it, Meg. What are the chances that Luke would run into John at a medical conference in New Mexico at the exact moment Luke was ready to move on with his life and begin again somewhere else? What are the chances that Luke would even attend the particular seminar John was giving at that conference or come up to talk to John afterward and learn you and he had a son? Something is at work here. Something stronger, greater than you or I is pulling you together. You can call it fate or destiny or whatever you want, but there's a force that wants you and Luke together. The question is," Lilah asked softly, "are you going to answer that force? Or run from it?"

LUKE HAD JUST PICKED UP his baby-sitter and was upstairs getting ready to go out when the phone rang Saturday night. "Luke, John McCabe. There's an emergency at the Lockhart Ranch and they need a physician to make a house call out there, stat."

Luke tensed at the thought of anything happening to Meg's sister Kelsey or her business partner, Brady Anderson. The last thing they needed on that ranch was any more tragedy, especially now that the property had just come back into the Lockhart family. "What happened?" Luke bypassed the khaki slacks, shirt and tie he'd been going to wear and grabbed a pair of jeans and a white chambray work shirt.

"I'm not clear on that. All I know is an ambulance is not needed, only a physician. Can you go? Or is it going to be too uncomfortable for you under the circumstances?"

"I can go," Luke said, already reaching for his boots. He just hoped whatever had happened out there didn't involve Meg or Jeremy. He hadn't seen either of them since early this morning. It was very possible they'd spent the day at the ranch, if for no other reason than to help Meg avoid running into Luke on her weekend off.

Luke dashed downstairs, brought the sitter and his girls up-to-date on the abrupt change in his plans, then grabbed his medical bag and headed out. Thirty minutes later he was turning his SUV onto the gravel drive that led to the ranch house.

Kelsey and her partner, Brady Anderson, were both on the porch, pacing restlessly as he drove up. Luke noted they looked very relieved to see him.

"Glad you could get out here so quick, Doc," Brady said.

"What happened?" Luke asked as he took the steps two at a time and joined them on the porch.

Kelsey's eyes darkened and the worry on her face increased tenfold. "You better just go inside," Kelsey said.

Solemnly Brady opened the door and held it.

His fears escalating with every step, Luke took off his hat and strode in. He wasn't sure what he expected to see when he crossed the threshold. Someone hurt or sick, certainly. Not a living room that had been set for seduction. Not Meg, looking lovelier and more vulnerable than he'd ever seen her.

Slowly he set his bag down on the table, all the while taking in the way her aqua-blue dress clung to her slender curves. Her thick auburn hair had been swept up off her neck in tousled curls that begged to be taken down, one pin at a time. Her cheeks glowed with apricot color against the ivory perfection of her skin. But it was her aqua-blue eyes, so determined and calm and yet full of hope, that sent his heart rate soaring. He wasn't sure what to make of any of this. He only knew he didn't want to think Meg was his, and his alone, only to be disappointed again.

He studied her. "You were behind this?" His voice sounded flat, emotionless, even to him.

Meg glided toward him, her cinnamon perfume tantalizing his senses. She clasped her hands in front of her, and he saw her hands tremble slightly. "I wanted to see you alone, without interruption of any kind."

Tired of the half-truths and deceptions and veiled feelings that had marked their relationship from the start, Luke stared into Meg's eyes and thought, but couldn't be sure, he saw a telltale sheen of moisture there despite the laudable coolness of her voice. "You could have just asked me to meet with you, instead of leading me out here on false pretenses," he told her gruffly.

Meg swallowed, still gauging his reaction carefully. Her tongue darted out to moisten her lips. "I was afraid you wouldn't come, after everything I said to you."

"Meaning what?" Luke pressed, secretly welcoming the opportunity to be alone with her, however it had come about. He didn't care how many people were involved in the effort to get him and Meg back together—permanently this time—as long as they ended up in each other's arms in the end.

Meg drifted closer. She took his hand in hers, squeezed it warmly and continued in a low voice brimming with emotion, "Meaning, I'm sorry, Luke, for ever doubting you. Sorry for running, for not trusting you to love me for me and not just the son I could give you."

She led him to the sofa. Luke sat where she directed, then, loath to let go of her, used the grip she had on his hand to pull her down onto his lap. "I hired a sitter tonight, you know." He shifted her, so her bottom was nestled warmly against him.

Meg nodded and, settling even more intimately against him, wreathed her arms about his neck. "I heard you were planning to take whoever you asked out to Greta McCabe's dinner and dance hall," she reported solemnly.

Starting to feel better than he had in years, Luke quirked a brow. He had been trying to keep his plans for the evening a secret, lest Meg get wind of them and foil them. "Word gets around fast," he said.

Meg conceded this as she ran her fingers absently over the front of his shirt. "Laramie is a small town." She paused, looked deep into his eyes. "There are a huge number of people who want to see us together, not the least of whom includes me.''

At the feel of her nestled so contentedly against him, it was all Luke could do not to groan. He had never wanted her more in his life. But he also knew there were things they had to get straight before this reconciliation went any further. His gut twisted into a knot of apprehension. ''So are you doing this because you really want to be with me or because you don't want me to date anyone else?''

Meg's eyes glimmered, and this time he was sure there were tears in them. ''Because I really want to be with you,'' she said in a low, fierce voice.

Remembering how much they had hurt each other in the past, Luke forced himself to go on. ''What makes this different from the other two times you wanted to be with me and then swiftly changed your mind?'' he asked, still holding her close.

Meg drew back to look into his face. ''Because I've changed.''

''Keep talking,'' Luke instructed grimly.

Restless now, Meg eased off his lap. Arms folded tightly in front of her, she swallowed hard and began to pace. ''My whole life I've always been not just the oldest Lockhart sister, but the Lockhart sister everyone relied upon. People were always depending on me, coming to me, not the other way around. It was like that even before I met you, Luke. That's why I dated Kip, instead of you. He didn't want me depending on him. He didn't expect me to need him. Our relationship was all about what I could give him, and even though I didn't love him, I was comfortable with that. You were the first person that didn't want me to do things for you, the way Kip did, or protect and advise them, the way my sisters did, or be the responsible one and watch out for all my younger sisters, the way my parents did. You just wanted me to be me, whoever that might be. You just wanted to be with me. And that scared me—a lot."

Luke stood, crossed to her side and took her in his arms again. "Why?"

Meg tilted her head back to look into his face. "Because I knew I had the capacity to love you like I had never loved anyone else," she confessed, her low voice shimmering with emotion, even as she splayed her hands across his chest. "And I knew that if I was with you, I would change. That I'd no longer be this person I'd been assigned to be, who was always a lot more interested in everyone else's problems than her own. I knew if I were with you, I'd have to give up my total self-reliance and let you in, and I wasn't ready to do that."

"But you are now?" Luke asked quietly.

Meg nodded. "It's time I had a life of my own. Oh, I will always love my baby sisters and take care of them, just like I'll always be Jeremy's mom, and there for you and your daughters, however they need me or want me in their lives, too. But it's time I opened up my heart and let myself want and need and feel and love the way I was meant to love, too."

Luke grinned as all the hopes and dreams he'd ever had for the two of them began to flourish once again. "Got anyone in mind to help you do that?" he drawled happily.

"Only one person," Meg confided, as she went up on tiptoe and put her arms about his neck. "You."

Aware that was all he had wanted—needed—to hear, Luke wrapped her in his arms, bent his head and kissed her thoroughly, letting all he felt pour into the heated caress. When at last they drew apart, he took her by the hand and led her back to the sofa. This time she sat where he directed while he remained standing. "You want to know who I was going to take out on a date tonight—before I got this emergency call?"

Meg stiffened slightly and began to look a little irritated he'd even brought the subject up. "Not really."

Deciding it was time to enjoy the champagne Meg had provided for them, he poured two glasses and, unable to resist, continued teasing her with mock solemnity. "I think you should, sweetheart. I wouldn't want gossip coming back to cause trouble between us later."

Meg released an exasperated breath and rolled her eyes. Luke could tell this was something she would really prefer not to know. "Okay, tell me," she consented reluctantly, seeming to realize he wasn't about to stop until he had confessed all.

Working to keep his expression implacable, Luke handed her a glass brimming with bubbly golden liquid, then sank down beside her and stretched his long legs out in front of him. "You."

Meg blinked in surprise. "But you didn't ask me for a date."

Luke hadn't wanted to give her too much time to think about it, for fear she would have refused. "I was getting around to it. Problem is, you left the house early today and never returned."

"I had stuff to do here…to get ready for what I hoped was an oh-so-romantic evening alone with you."

"Which was, coincidentally, exactly what I had planned for us, too. I even got a sitter for all four kids. She's with my girls now."

"Jeremy's with his cousin Alexandra for the night."

"Good thinking."

Silence fell as they sipped champagne and cuddled together contentedly. "Then it's official, we're back together?" Meg asked as she linked hands with him.

Luke lifted their hands to his face and pressed a kiss onto the back of her hand. "Not quite."

Meg paused. Luke put their champagne aside and, hands on her waist, lifted Meg back onto his lap. He looked into her face solemnly. "I need to confess a few things, too. You aren't the only one to blame for what happened to us. I should have come after you the first time, but I didn't because I was afraid you didn't love me the way I loved you, and that hurt enough, without hearing it from you face-to-face. But the truth is," Luke corrected softly, "I never forgot you. Never got over feeling that everything might have been different if only I had pursued you the way I wanted to pursue you—as a lover instead of a friend—from the very first."

Meg traced aimless patterns on his chest. "Why didn't you?"

"Same reason." Reveling in the knowledge they were together again, Luke held Meg close. "Because I was afraid you weren't attracted to me in the same way I was attracted to you. And I figured it'd be better to have you in my life as a friend than not to have you in my life at all."

Meg's lips curved in a soft, self-deprecating smile. "When what we really wanted, deep down, was to be both friends and lovers."

"As well as man and wife," Luke reminded with a smile.

"Are you saying...?" Meg asked in the soft, serious voice Luke had come to love.

"You bet I still want to marry you," Luke vowed with a grin. "Which is why I've been carrying this around." Luke withdrew a small velvet box from his pocket.

Meg's eyes lit with happiness as she saw the engagement ring. She laid a finger against his lips before he could continue. "You don't have to ask again. The answer is yes." She sealed her promise with a long, heartfelt kiss, then drew back reluctantly. "But we've got to make it as soon as possible," Meg insisted.

Luke kissed his wife-to-be even more thoroughly. "You won't get an argument from me there."

They kissed again, sweetly, lingeringly. "We have just one more thing to work out," Meg said in a low, serious voice as she looked deeply into his eyes. "We've got to stop the secrets, Luke. Keeping secrets have hurt Jeremy and almost destroyed our chance to ever be together the way we were meant to be. We've got to eradicate them from our lives and tell Jeremy and everyone else the truth about who his father is, and we have to do that immediately."

Luke paused, his heart pounding in his chest. "I agree I want to stop the secrets now. But are you sure about this?"

Meg nodded, all the love she felt for him in her eyes. "I'm very sure. I was wrong to keep Jeremy's parentage a secret all these years." Her expression softened contentedly. "Jeremy deserves to know who his real father is. The truth is, he should have known all along. The sooner we tell him and everyone else the better, because the older he gets, the harder it will be to explain."

"A revelation like this is bound to cause some gossip," Luke warned. As much as he wanted to shout out Jeremy's parentage to the world, the last thing he wanted was to see Meg or Jeremy hurt.

"I know, and I've thought about that, too," Meg said seriously. "Here's how I'd like to handle it...."

BIRTH ANNOUNCEMENTS, proclaiming Jeremy the son of Meg Lockhart and Luke Carrigan, were sent out the first of the week. A more complete article, detailing Luke and Meg's love story, appeared in the *Laramie News*. By Wednesday Luke and Meg were being married in an outdoor ceremony on the lawn between their two houses. Meg wore a gauzy white silk-and-chiffon wedding gown designed by her sister Jenna. Amy, Becca and Susie carried baskets of flowers and wore pastel chiffon smocks and pinafores. Luke and Jeremy wore matching dove-gray suits. Jeremy was entrusted with a velvet pillow that bore their wedding rings.

Together, the six of them walked down the aisle and stood in front of the minister. And there, in front of dozens of their friends, all four of their children and the entire Lockhart family, Meg and Luke spoke what was in their hearts.

"I, Meg, take thee Luke..."

"...to have and to hold, from this day forward..."

"...as long as we both shall live."

When the minister pronounced them man and wife and said Luke could kiss his bride, a jubilant cheer went up that could be heard throughout the town.

"Best day of my life," Luke murmured as he kissed Meg once and then again.

"Best day of mine, too," Meg said, hugging and kissing Luke back. "And it's only the beginning." They had fused their hearts and lives with a completeness that would last forever. And for the first time in her life, Meg was sure she could face whatever came next. All she had ever wanted, all she had ever needed, was Luke...and their children...by her side.

"Does this mean we're a family now?" Susie asked, as the backyard reception got in full swing.

"Yep," Jeremy answered before Luke and Meg could reply. He turned to his new sister. "It means I got a daddy and all you girls have a mommy and all four of us kids are brother and sister.''

"Yeah," Becca said, "and we got two houses, the same color, too!"

Amy grinned. "And two swing sets!" she chimed in.

"Sounds like we have everything we need," Luke said as hugs and kisses were exchanged all around.

"Everything we ever wanted and more," Meg agreed, as hope for their future flared inside her heart.

Luke wrapped his arms about her waist and brought her against him. "I love you, Mrs. Carrigan."

Meg snuggled against Luke's warmth and strength, aware nothing had ever felt so right as the two of them together. "And I love you, too," she whispered as she tilted her head back and looked into his eyes.

Luke kissed her thoroughly, deeply and with a dangerous lack of restraint, until joy exploded inside Meg like fireworks in a Texas sky.

John and Lilah McCabe walked up to join them. "Well, Lilah, I think we're on a roll here," John said, elbowing his pretty wife.

Still delighting in her success marrying off all four of her sons and three of the Lockhart women, Lilah grinned. "You bet we are!"

*Next month Harlequin American Romance
brings you a very special story
in the McCabe-Lockhart series
by Cathy Gillen Thacker.*

TEXAS VOWS

*A McCabe Family Saga
Available wherever Harlequin books are sold.
Here's a look from the first chapter...*

Chapter One

It was a bad day and it was getting worse, Sam McCabe thought, as he called all five of his sons to his study for an immediate accounting of what was just the latest event in a whole string of family catastrophes.

"Don't look at me. I don't know what happened." Will, the oldest, shrugged his broad shoulders and regarded Sam indifferently. "I was out running. I wasn't even here."

No surprise there, Sam thought wearily. At seventeen, the only thing Will cared about was getting in shape for the upcoming football season. He was never around to help out or hold down the fort.

Sam looked at sixteen-year-old Brad, who was busy combing his immaculately tended brown hair and checking out his reflection in the glass-fronted bookcase in Sam's study. At Sam's look, Brad pocketed his comb and offered his version. "Actually, Dad, I think it was hormonal. You know, one of those 'women things,' that made Mrs. Grunwald pack up her bags and walk out of here on such short notice."

"Hormonal," Sam repeated disbelievingly. And *no* notice had been more like it. Sam had been called out of an important business meeting and told she'd already left and wasn't coming back—not now, not ever. When he'd tried to get an explanation from her, the irate woman had just said he needed to do something about his home situation, and hung up on him.

Sam turned his attention to Riley, who at fourteen was definitely the most mischievous of his brood. And, unless Sam missed his guess, had probably been instrumental in pushing the retired lady-marine-just-turned-housekeeper to quit.

"I just don't think she's cut out to take care of growing boys," Riley explained with a remarkably sober expression. "You know. Given the fact that she never had any kids herself."

"Face it, Dad." Sensitive as always to what was going on behind the scenes, Lewis stepped forward, suddenly looking much older than his eleven years. "We were never gonna be happy with her here, anyway. Mrs. Grunwald just wasn't Mom."

And no one ever would be, Sam McCabe thought gloomily. Their beloved Ellie had been one of a kind. But that didn't excuse what his boys had done here, chasing away their tenth housekeeper in six months. Not that they would ever come right out and admit that was what they had done. No, they would continue giving excuses and shifting the blame.

Sam turned to Kevin, his youngest, and the only one of his five boys who hadn't yet put in his two cents about the latest episode in their lives. "What do you have to say about all this?" he demanded.

Kevin shrugged and smeared the peanut butter on his mouth to the rest of his face. Sam wasn't surprised his six-year-old had nothing to say about their housekeeper quitting. Kev hadn't talked much to anyone about anything since Ellie had died. In a way Sam could hardly blame him. Since Ellie had passed, the light had gone out of all of their lives, and with it the need to even *pretend* their world would ever be normal again.

Sam looked up to see John and Lilah McCabe in the doorway of his study. His aunt and uncle were not just a gifted nurse and doctor and founders of Laramie Community Hospital, they had been his lifelines to sanity during the past year. They'd provided moral support and guidance when Ellie was ill, as well as help during the dark days after her death.

Sam had moved back to Laramie in order to be closer to them, thinking that more of a sense of family might help his boys adjust to the loss of their mother. And it had helped, but only to a point. The kids still didn't want a housekeeper, and indeed seemed to be doing everything they could to chase away whoever Sam hired.

After the ninth one had walked out on them, Sam had let his sons talk him into being responsible for themselves—only to have Kevin end up in the hospital E.R. with a sprained wrist, numerous abrasions and a cut that needed stitches after a still-unexplained fall off the porch roof. So Sam had given up on that and hired housekeeper number ten. Unfortunately, Mrs. Grunwald's take-charge style had not worked well on the boys. And now here Sam was again, relying on his favorite aunt and uncle to come in and save the day, when what they really should be doing was savoring the first heady days of their long-awaited retirement.

Gently Lilah interrupted. "Guys, we need to speak to your dad alone. So why don't you all see what you can do about cleaning up that kitchen?"

Sam waited until the boys had left, then shut the door to his study, before he turned back to John and Lilah.

"Thanks for coming over. I don't know what I would have done if you hadn't been here."

Sam shook his head grimly, wondering what it would take to get a housekeeper who was reliable and responsible enough to handle all five of his boys even half as well as Ellie. "You'd think Mrs. Grunwald could have waited to quit until I got back from California." Instead, Sam'd gotten a phone message from her after she'd already packed up and left, letting him know he and his boys were on their own—again. He'd had to cut short his business trip in the Silicon Valley and grab the first flight back to Dallas, then drive back to Laramie, where John and Lilah had been holding down the fort, awaiting his return.

"We're glad to help you with the children anytime, you know that," John said, every bit as gently as Lilah.

"But this is out of even our scope," Lilah added, concerned.

Sam didn't like the sound of that. It seemed like John and Lilah were planning to quit on him, too. "What do you mean?" he asked tensely.

John clapped a comforting hand on Sam's shoulder and led him over to the leather sofa. "Your aunt Lilah and I both grew up in large families and reared our own. So we know firsthand how chaotic households with a lot of children can be, from both perspectives, even under the best of circumstances. But what's happening here, Sam, in the aftermath of Ellie's death, is not routine."

"Which is why we've arranged for Kate Marten to talk to you tonight." Lilah sat down on the other side of Sam. "She'll be over as soon as she finishes with her grief group at the hospital."

Sam grimaced. "You know how I feel about that little busybody." He and the boys had barely moved back to

Laramie a month ago, when she'd started bombarding him with literature—none of which he'd read. Then followed that with phone calls—none of which he'd bothered to return—about her professional counseling services.

Lilah and John exchanged a pointed glance. "We know you haven't given her a chance," John said eventually.

What would have been the point in that? Sam wondered, even more exasperated. "She's just a kid."

"No, Sam, she's not," Lilah reiterated firmly as she patted his hand. "And if you took a good look at her, gave her just a few minutes of your time, you'd realize that."

Sam shook his head and pushed to his feet. "Even if I wanted to meet with Kate—" which he didn't, he amended silently "—I don't have time to do so. I've got my hands full with the boys tonight."

"No. You don't," John corrected firmly. "Lilah and I are taking the boys to the ranch for the night."

Lilah added helpfully, "That'll give you time to talk to Kate alone."

Sam knew his aunt and uncle meant well. It didn't mean they were right. He regarded them impatiently. "All I'm going to do is tell her I don't need her." Or her damnable interference.

Lilah paused. "If that's really what you think, then tell her that face-to-face. But at least hear her out, and listen to what she thinks you and the boys need to get your lives back on track."

Sam knew what they needed—they needed for the damn cancer to never have taken hold in his wife's body. They needed their family intact, with everything just as it was. But none of that was possible. Much as he and the boys wanted to, they couldn't turn back the clock. They couldn't make anything happen any differently than it had. They couldn't bring Ellie back.

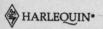
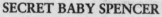
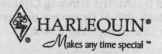

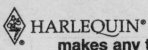

HARLEQUIN®
makes any time special—online...

eHARLEQUIN.com

shop eHarlequin

- Find all the new Harlequin releases at everyday great discounts.
- Try before you buy! Read an excerpt from the latest Harlequin novels.
- Write an online review and share your thoughts with others.

reading room

- Read our Internet exclusive daily and weekly online serials, or vote in our interactive novel.
- Talk to other readers about your favorite novels in our Reading Groups.
- Take our Choose-a-Book quiz to find the series that matches you!

authors' alcove

- Find out interesting tidbits and details about your favorite authors' lives, interests and writing habits.
- Ever dreamed of being an author? Enter our Writing Round Robin. The Winning Chapter will be published online! Or review our writing guidelines for submitting your novel.

If you enjoyed what you just read,
then we've got an offer you can't resist!

Take 2 bestselling
love stories FREE!
Plus get a FREE surprise gift!

Harlequin invites you to walk down the aisle...

To honor our year long celebration of weddings, we are offering an exciting opportunity for you to own the Harlequin Bride Doll. Handcrafted in fine bisque porcelain, the wedding doll is dressed for her wedding day in a cream satin gown accented by lace trim. She carries an exquisite traditional bridal bouquet and wears a cathedral-length dotted Swiss veil. Embroidered flowers cascade down her lace overskirt to the scalloped hemline; underneath all is a multi-layered crinoline.

Join us in our celebration of weddings by sending away for your own Harlequin Bride Doll. This doll regularly retails for $74.95 U.S./approx. $108.68 CDN. One doll per household. Requests must be received no later than June 30, 2001. Offer good while quantities of gifts last. Please allow 6-8 weeks for delivery. Offer good in the U.S. and Canada only. Become part of this exciting offer!

Simply complete the order form and mail to:
"A Walk Down the Aisle"

IN U.S.A
P.O. Box 9057
3010 Walden Ave.
Buffalo, NY 14240-9057

IN CANADA
P.O. Box 622
Fort Erie, Ontario
L2A 5X3

Enclosed are eight (8) proofs of purchase found on the last page of every specially marked Harlequin series book and $3.75 check or money order (for postage and handling). Please send my Harlequin Bride Doll to:

Name (PLEASE PRINT)

Address   Apt. #

City   State/Prov.   Zip/Postal Code

Account # (if applicable)   098 KIK DAEW

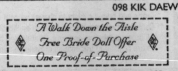

HARLEQUIN®
Makes any time special®

Visit us at www.eHarlequin.com

A Walk Down the Aisle
Free Bride Doll Offer
One Proof-of-Purchase

PHWDAPOP